Settling Up

No Ordinary Love Series, Book One

Michelle D. Rayford

Barrington Drive Publishing Company

Book Cover by CoversinColor.com

Editing: The Writer's Suite

First Edition: April 2025

ISNB: 978-0-9997303-4-8 (ebook), 978-0-9997303-3-1 (paperback)

Contents

Sometimes love does not have the
most honorable beginnings. - Ann Patchett

Chapter One

Carmen

The glass ceiling will shatter today. I imagine glittering shards of glass on the floor-the janitor sweeping eight years of bias and bullshit into the trash.

Sunlight beams through the plate-glass window of my small office and reflects off the gold International Vision Trend award on the credenza. A tangible reward for all the hours and hard work I've put into proving I deserve to be in this position. Not to mention I've been serving in an acting capacity as the Vice President of Marketing for the past five months. The position should have been mine last year when Larry Gilmore left for another opportunity with the company.

Parker & Kramer is a global manufacturing company with offices on both coasts and in other countries. We make thousands of everyday products used in households everywhere. I'm in the Marketing & Brand Managementdepartment in the LA offices, where I've worked my way up from Marketing Researcher to my current role as Marketing Brand Manager. Now it's time to take the next step in my career.

"Are you ready to go upstairs? Your presentation has been uploaded, and the conference room is set." Ruth Roberts' blue eyes twinkle as she hands me a jump drive. She's the Executive Assistant for the marketing area and a surprising cheerleader. Ruth has been here for over thirty years and has seen everything. What she hasn't seen is a woman leading this department.

"Let's do this," I reply and stand, adjusting my ash gray Alexander Wang suit.

Ruth nods in agreement with my look for today. She knows when I pull this skirt and blazer together; I mean business. This promotion is as good as mine.

I turn to follow Ruth out the door when my cell phone vibrates in my hand. My mom is over two thousand miles away in my hometown of Columbia, South Carolina, but my back stiffens when her picture smiles from the screen. I mouth for Ruth to go ahead and answer the call.

"Hey, Mom. What's up? I'm about to go into a meeting..."

"Why are you too busy to cook dinner for your husband?" Mom isn't one for small talk. She launches into every conversation without a greeting. But cutting me off mid-sentence and the full brunt of her Jamaican accent tell me her mood isn't good.

I glance at my watch. It's almost nine in the morning here, which means with the three-hour time difference she should be on her lunch break at work. "What are you talking about?"

"Melvin called to tell me my daughter is neglecting her duties. I know me taught you better than that. How you going to keep a husband if you don't take care of him needs?"

On the list of things I don't have time for, this is tops. "Maybe I don't want to keep him," I mumble and massage the tension throbbing in my neck.

Mom clucks her tongue. "Speak up, girl. What you saying?"

Time is ticking, and I need to get upstairs. "Nothing, Mom. Can we talk about this later? I have a meeting."

"Your head hard," Mom continues her rant. "Didn't I teach you how to take care of your husband? You know I made things work with your stepfather for you and your sister. Lil' Olivia needs her father in the house, and it's your job to keep him happy."

A heavy sigh escapes. Mom believes in her core that children must have a man in the house. Ten years of single motherhood formed a trauma bond and inform her perfect family dynamic.

"Okay, Mom," I concede. "I'll do better. Now I really have to go."

Ending the call, I march toward the elevators, passing empty cubicles on the left and right. Everyone has already made it upstairs to the conference room on the fifth floor. Stabbing the up button doesn't make the door open any faster but helps soothe some of the irritation causing heat to flush through my body.

He did this on purpose. He knew it would upset me, and he did it anyway.

Without fully processing my actions, I dial Melvin'snumber. He answers on the first ring as if he's been anticipating my call.

"Why did you call my mother with this foolishness this morning?" I ask over his greeting.

"Whoa, hold on a moment," he says. "Let me pull over."

Melvin is a package delivery driver. APD, All Packages Delivered,is a global shipping and logistics company.

"Why did you call my mother?"

"What 'cha mean? You talk to my mother all the time. I can call my mother-in-law," he says. The pitch of his bass voice tells me he's smiling and fully enjoying this conversation.

The elevator doors snake open with a ding, and I stab the number five once inside. "You knew if you called her, she would call me.And I don't have time for this when I have a meeting."

Melvin snorts. "I can't help you have mommy and daddy issues. It was a simple call to check in with Katherine. She asked about you,and I told her how busy you've been. That's all."

The doors open, and I pause outside the elevator. Traffic noises blare over the phone as I process Melvin's new tactic to gaslight me into believing he made an innocent phone call. He knew this would ruin my big moment.And I'm letting my anger help him waste my time.

"I may have issues, but what I don't have is a supportive spouse," I whisper through clenched teeth as I approach the conference room.

"Hey, I'm supportive," Melvin says. "I'm the only man who didn't leave you."

The verbal slap hits me in the core and causes my breath to catch. Melvin knows my most sensitive places and picks at the scars of a never-healing wound.

If I allow myself to spiral down the path of rejection from my father, I won't get through this meeting. Words fail me, so there's only one thing to do. I end the call.

I rush into the conference room right on time, hoping the frustrating calls aren't evident on my face. The corporate heads are expecting my usual cool and professional aura.

"There she is," Doug Woo, my immediate supervisor, who is the VP of Regional Communications, announces to the room and gestures to a seat beside him. "You've missed introductions, but you know almost everyone here."

Nodding, I place my tablet and phone on the table and take a deep breath. Surveying the room, it seems as if something is off, but I dismiss the queasiness in my stomach as residue from the rush to get up here.

Seated at the head of the large rectangle wooden table is Gary Moeller, Vice Chairman of Operations. His gelled black hair projects a classic sense of confidence to match the immaculately tailored suit he wears. To his left is a woman I've never seen before, but it's not unusual for people from other departments to sit in on marketing presentations. Other individuals around the table are my counterparts representing various household brands. These are the people who would report to me when I'm the new VP of Marketing. Filling in chairs aligned around the wall are the junior associates.

Each manager is typically assigned one or two employees every couple of years to mentor. This year I have been given the only two Black employees. Kayla Pearson, a textbook millennial, sits with her legs crossed and scrolls through her phone, oblivious to the seriousness of the meeting. I've had to counsel her twice on the appropriate way to dress for work, and today she at least kept it simple with a navy wrap dress and heels.

Her total opposite is my other mentee, Braxton Frazier. He has proven to be a trusted asset on the team with the perfect blend of ambition and willingness to learn. In fact, he volunteered to help me prepare for this presentation and offered valuable insight to ensure the 20-30 demographic is represented. We work well together.

"Are you ready to begin?" Doug asks. He takes a swig from his morning can of soda and glances at Gary. The jolt of caffeine must cause his leg to bounce underneath the table, and I smile to calm his nerves and my own.

"Of course," I begin and nod to Ruth, who hovers in the back of the room near a table that houses coffee, water and pastries. She pushes a button to lower the screen from the ceiling and cues up the PowerPointpresentation. "Apologies for my tardiness, but I had to finish up a call. If everything is keyed up, we can jump right into the presentation."

Now I'm in my element. I've become a pro at giving presentations, and today we're discussing media for a new brand of a home care item. After giving a brief summary to introduce myself and my credentials, I launch into the core of the meeting.

"As everyone at this table knows, the current climate for marketing involves an integrated marketing role. We must include social media and influencers in any successful strategy." I use a laser pointer to highlight key points on the slide. "Fabric & Home Care items make up over30% of net sales for the company. It is imperative that all phases of this new rollout be vetted early, and any negative feedback be handled appropriately."

Gary leans over to share something with the woman beside him. She whispers a response I can't decipher. I turn to glance at Doug, but he avoids eye contact by rearing back in his chair.

Who is this woman?

Braxton draws my attention by removing his suit jacket.He gives me a thumbs-up as encouragement to keep going.

Regaining focus, I click through the next few slides outlining past successes and how they align with our new plan.

"Let me jump in here and ask a quick question," the woman raises a manicured finger. "Aren't influencers the preferred marketing strategy? They seem to be a quick return on investment and have the biggest impact."

She looks to Gary for approval, and he nods as if she just solved world hunger.

"Excuse me," I say and pause to soften my tone. I've been accused of being aggressive when addressing a white woman in the past when I was only being direct. "I don't think we've been properly introduced. You are?"

"I'm Susan," she says.

When she doesn't elaborate further, I assume she's one of the many brand managers gathered here. It's not like I know each of them individually, but I should have seen her around the office. Ignoring a nagging feeling, I answer her question. "Well, that depends more on the product than anything else. Our statistics show that a more integrated marketing strategy to include social media, channels we own, as well as influencers makes for a more positive outcome."

Susan challenges a few more slides. I'm able to answer her questions and demonstrate my knowledge and expertise to the entire room. This woman is helping to prove why the promotion should be forthcoming.

"In conclusion, we've done the necessary cost analysis, and the return on investment is favorable."

I relax in my seat after taking a few questions from the group. The meeting is officially over. Small side conversations take place as people pick up their phones or tablets to leave. Doug taps my shoulder. "Good job as always, Miller."

The kudos from Doug are appreciated, but I'm interested in what Gary thinks. All final decisions are signed off by him, and if I've earned his praise, the promotion should be forthcoming.

"Didn't I tell you Carmen would be an asset to your team, Susan?" Gary walks around the table to refill his coffee cup.

At first my mind registers the positive comment about being an asset and is slow to process the word 'team'. As in, I'm part of this woman's team.

"Am I missing something?" I say after swallowing a bit of dread. The uneasiness returns, causing me to rub my hands together under the table. "What team are you talking about?"

Gary takes a sip of his drink before adding more sugar and returning to his seat. "Oh, that's right. While we were waiting for you, I had a sidebar with Doug to introduce Susan McCall."

The ding on my arrival at the meeting stings, but it's warranted. Company culture dictates you get to meetings at least ten minutes early. I allowed family drama to derail me, and I curse myself for falling into my husband's trap. Again.

"It's nice to meet you, Carmen." Susan tosses long blond strands over one shoulder. "I've heard a lot of good things about you, and I was impressed to see you in action. I'm looking forward to our working together."

"Thank you," I reply, standing to extend my hand to shake hers. "I'm sorry, I must have missed the announcement. Are you part of Gary's section?"

The silence is suddenly loud as the remaining stragglers pause at the door. Susan turns to Gary, who points at Doug. "You didn't tell her? The Board has approved her as our new VP of Marketing."

Doug looks sheepish as he mouths "Sorry" before clearing his throat. I brace myself for the news and concentrate on maintaining a blank expression. A heaviness presses down on my limbs, and I lean against the table to remain standing. I will not give them the satisfaction of seeing my disappointment.

"Congratulations, Susan," I hear myself say to the woman who's waltzed in from nowhere and gotten the job which should be mine. "I look forward to working with you too."

This latest career setback has me glued to my desk, the Vision Trend award now an anchor of mockery. *You're still not worthy. You'll never be enough.* The mantra seems to broadcast from the dimming reflection of the setting sun outside the window.

No reason to rush home. Melvin texted he was picking up our daughter from the after-school program, and I'm in no mood to face his judgment or his delight at my failure.

I sit in this leather chair in this office I've worked so hard for and replay the day. Analyze every conversation over the past month. Trying to see what clues I missed. What interaction could have gone another way? How could I make them see they should've chosen me?

I'm fully spiraling, on the verge of an anxiety attack when there's a knock on the door.

"Are you okay?"

Braxton stands at the threshold with his suit jacket draped over his arm and a look of concern etched on his face.

Before I can respond, he crosses the room in four long strides and pulls me from the chair. His warm embrace cocoons me with his fresh scent, and I relax before pushing him away.

"Don't worry," he says, bringing me back into his chest. "Everyone is gone."

I allow myself another minute and step away again. "Why are you still here?"

Braxton runs his hands down my shoulders, easing the tension from them. "My mentor taught me to never leave before the boss. Got to show them you're a hard worker willing to over deliver on projects, right?"

My laugh has no amusement in it as I turn to gaze out the window. "You might want to disregard everything your mentor told you. Obviously, I don't know what I'm talking about."

"Nonsense." Braxton steps closer, his energy pulsing between us, causing my heartbeat to speed up. He leans close and whispers into my ear. "You're the smartest person on this team. Corporate politics can't dim your shine. They must have on blinders if they can't see you."

I turn and gaze into his hooded brown eyes, and I'm transported back to Monte Carlo. The night I won this useless award was the best and worst night of my life.

The cloudless night sky illuminated the surrounding beach, and the waves played a symphony in tune with my heartbeat. Braxton and I stood on the breezeway after disembarking from the agency yacht cruise, a perk of the annual event held by P & K. The celebratory occasion included heavy hors d'oeuvres and plenty of champagne. Everyone else caught the shuttle to the Casino de Monte Carlo, but we lagged behind.

"Congratulations again," Braxton said. *"And thanks for including me on this trip."*

"You deserved it," I replied, *waving the* award between *us. "You helped make this possible too."*

Braxton had only been working at the agency for six months when we were thrown together on the Seduction campaign. All the long nights and brainstorming sessions revealed an intelligent man with irresistible charm. What began as a working relationship developed into close friends. The result was a campaign that had been more successful than any of the others to date.

"Everything okay at home?"

He'd walked in on the latest argument with Melvin-a tantrum before I left for this trip. Too many strained conversations ended while Braxton stood at my door.

And then, *Braxton shrugging out of his jacket. The warmth of it seeps into my body as he places it around my shoulders.*

A whisper against my ear. *"Can't have the boss lady getting cold."*

His hand on the small of my back, the tingle at the base of my spine from his touch. *"I'm here if you want to talk."*

The scent of his cologne, mixing with the sea air...sandalwood.

Me saying, *"We can't cross the line."* When I already knew we had.

Now here I am in this current moment, broken and discouraged, and this man is here for me. Again.

Braxton gives me a slow, sensual smile that showcases a dimple piercing his left cheek, and hunger causes me to lick my lips.

"Tell me what you need."

Words aren't sufficient for my need, so I put one hand behind his head and pull him in. One touch of his lips and the sensation sends a jolt through my body, causing me to gasp. Braxton wraps his arms around my waist,dropping his jacket to the floor. We explore each other further, and I taste the hint of mint on his tongue.

All sound fades away, and I'm lost in the pleasure of knowing this young man wants me in a way that feels foreign. This is something I don't get at home. Unconditional acceptance and appreciation.

A bang at the door makes us jump apart. Someone is a witness, and I see my entire career implode.

Chapter Two

Carmen

The air conditioner clicks on with a hum and chills my sweat-soaked skin. As I reach for the covers, my hand connects with something warm and solid. My eyes open and focus on the handsome face of a man wearing nothing but a cocky smile. I allow myself the gift of trailing a heated stare across Braxton's underwear model features. He has the body of an Olympic athlete sculpted into smooth umber skin.

"I can't believe this happened again," I mumble and sit up. So much for vowing to stop after almost getting caught at work last week. That night, the poor janitor was startled more than we were. Braxton was able to convince the man nothing was going on.

"What? That you slipped away to meet me today?" An unrepentant grin curves his full lips. "Enjoyed yourself?"

I pull the covers over my exposed breasts. "I'm serious. We can't keep doing this." The words slide past my lips as my body still throbs from the sex.

"Why not?" Braxton uses one finger to lower the bright white material and nibbles a path down my neck.

A slight shudder claims my body as his lips brush my skin. "You know why."

Braxton leans against the wooden headboard with a groan. "How many times are we going to discuss this?" Braxton rotates his shoulders. "Let me run them down so we can address it for the last time. You're thinking I'm too young."

"You are." I've celebrated my thirty-seventh year around the sun while he is ten years my junior.

"Really?" Braxton raises one eyebrow, which is adorable, then counts each point on his long, tapered fingers. "You're worried about us working together. I told you I spoke to Miquel. He's focused on cleaning the offices and not reporting what he may or may not have seen in them."

Our company doesn't outright forbid work relationships, but we should disclose them to prevent workplace issues. My getting caught in the office with a subordinate would be disastrous for what's left of my career.

"You're bougie and I'm not." Another finger goes up. "You graduated from UCLA. I graduated from USC. You're a Libra, I'm a Taurus." Braxton pauses until I make eye contact. "None of that matters to me."

"You left out the biggest obstacle." My naked ring finger shows the fading evidence of a tan line. "I'm married."

Braxton shrugs. "Mistakes were made before me."

I swing a pillow, which he dodges with a laugh. "You think this is funny? This is my life."

"No, this is serious, and it's *our* life." He stuffs the pillow behind his head. "Think of how good we could be together. It may have started with a kiss, but this isn't a fling to me anymore. And I'm not the type of man to walk away from a good thing."

Someone pushes a squeaky wheeled cart outside the hotel room. A warning that our amazing afternoon would soon end. Clothes are strewn across a floral-patterned chair and the floor. The pungent scent of chlorine wafts in from the bathroom. Thick beige drapes are drawn, but a sliver of afternoon sunlight breaks through to illuminate the bed and Braxton's hopeful expression.

He is the type of man any woman would want next to her. Getting to know him over the past year and a half at work made my mundane married life bearable. But it also made me question everything I thought I knew about myself, and the choices made in the past.

"Your brow crinkles when you worry." Braxton strokes the side of my face. I lean into his touch until doubt causes me to move away.

"Maybe we're getting into this too fast. Aren't you worried?" My mind bounces with scenarios of the many ways this can all go wrong. A tingle in my limbs causes me to flex my hands and rub them down my legs.

Braxton captures my hand and intertwines our fingers. "Let's start by going on an actual date."

"You know we can't do that." A reminder spoken all too often.

"Come on, Carmen," he protests, shifting to face me full on. "Stop agonizing over every little detail and let me show you a good time."

Extracting my hand from his is no simple task. "Let's not do this right now, okay?"

Braxton swings his long legs over the side of the bed and growls over his shoulder. "You should have waited."

"Waited for what?"

He turns and locks me with eyes that hypnotize every time. "For me. You should have waited for me."

My lips part as my pulse races. Breaking eye contact helps to center my thoughts. *This can't happen.* The heat between us has been obvious for months, and I already feel guilty for giving in to temptation. My marriage is broken, and I feel like a failure. I was supposed to make my marriage work. Giving the extra effort got me through grad school and should have secured my promotion. Neither of those things has worked out. It stands to reason this thing with Braxton will end horribly too.

I believe in checking the boxes for a traditional life. You get married, have a child, and live happily ever after. No one prepared me for choosing the wrong partner. Definitely no one had prepared me for my failing marriage leading to another man.

"Maybe we need to slow things down. I'll admit *this* was something we needed to get out of our system ..."

Braxton jumps up to pace the suite, breathing hard. "Don't do that. Don't reduce what we're building between us to something basic and casual."

"I thought we could keep things simple." The sheets crumble in my hands, a lifeline to lessen this uncomfortable conversation.

"This is more than just sex. I can get sex from anybody." His dark brown gaze is intense and unwavering. "I'm here with *you*. I've always been there for you, even in your darkest moments."

This is true. Braxton has become more than a colleague; he's my confidant. While my marriage dissolved into careening from one argument to the next, Braxton has allowed me to be vulnerable without judgement. During that trip to Monte Carlo, I shared my personal journey with Braxton.

"He may think he's broken you," Braxton said that night under a starless sky. "But I see the strong, intelligent and amazing woman you are. It's his loss if he carelessly throws someone like you away."

The confidence, power, and grace Braxton exudes is intoxicating, and I'm an addict craving the next high.

Time to get back to reality. Melvin fought dirty, and I don't want Braxton to get caught up in the mess. I have to protect him from the storm sure to come.

"You can take your fantasy somewhere else." My dismissive wave causes him to flinch. "You're dealing with a grown woman who has too much to lose. A woman with a child and a mortgage."

Braxton crosses the room in two strides. "I know all about choices and responsibility. Don't you see a grown man standing here?"

The answer to that question was clear from day one. Braxton is a full-grown man. With perfect abs, broad shoulders, a narrow waist, and big feet. He glowers at me, and I can't help but get turned on. He senses the effect he's having and crosses his arms as I inspect every inch of his sun-kissed skin. It's instant pleasure those massive hands give with a simple touch. The erection bobbing below his waist is a work of art.

The totality of Braxton makes me feel safe and, most of all, seen. Unlike my ex, he appreciates my ambition and doesn't hone in on my faults. I even welcome the way his full lips twist into a smirk whenever he's about to check me on something. The snide remark I expect doesn't come.

"Tell me you'll give us a real chance," Braxton whispers as he kneels in front of me and places a kiss on my thigh. "Say it."

I stare down at him and can't deny the all-consuming need for him. "Yes" is the only word my brain can manage.

A surge of bliss overcomes me as Braxton's tongue leaves a trail of magic down the length of my body. He focuses on the most sensitive area buried between my legs. The sweet torture causes me to back away, but he holds me in place with a firm grip on my buttocks.

I moan his name as he brings me close to the brink.

Braxton answers my plea by intensifying his stroke. This time he doesn't stop until I spill over the edge and allow the strength of the orgasm to take me. Braxton is amazing. Sometimes I even hear bells ringing.

When my heartbeat slows and I can see clearly, Braxton is lying beside me with a satisfied grin. "Want to join me in the shower?"

"Sure. We should probably get back to the office. But I need to come down first. Do you hear that?"

"It's your phone," he says when it chimes for a third time. "Someone is determined to reach you."

I roll over and search the surrounding surfaces. My first thought is something must have happened to Olivia. My anxiety level mellows when I see the missed call from my lawyer.

"Let me return this call," I say. "I'll meet you in the bathroom."

My stomach growls as I hit the button to connect with the woman who rang. The room service order of fruit and pastries we shared earlier was long gone. I grab the bottled water left on the tray and take huge gulps while waiting for the call to go through.

"Margaret Warner," my attorney answers the phone with a brisk, no-nonsense tone.

"Maggie." I use the familiar nickname to greet my friend and lifesaver. "What's going on? I thought we were getting together later. Has the time changed?"

"Something has changed, but it's not that," Maggie replies with her usual bluntness. "Are you sitting down?"

The comment causes me to stand oblivious to the lack of clothing. My stomach now clenches in knots. I picture the renowned divorce attorney in her usual uniform of navy tailored suits and signature pearls. Margaret is an old college roommate who made her reputation in LA by winning the maximum amounts for her women clients dealing with their scheming former spouses. She has assured me that if I decide to get out of my marriage, I'll come out of it with most of my assets intact. A major undertaking, as Melvin will probably want an obscene amount of money to maintain his lifestyle. Words he actually said during an argument.

"Just tell me."

"I've been going over your finances," Maggie says in a measured tone. I recall the information submitted to get an overview of my status. Tax returns, bank statements, CDs, 401ks, etc. "Your records aren't syncing with what you told me. The numbers don't add up."

My mind races. I've worked hard to build a financial portfolio so I would be comfortable. It's a source of pride to provide for my daughter without needing Melvin's money. "What do you mean?"

"It means you can't afford to get a divorce."

Chapter Three

Braxton

A glimpse in the rear-view mirror causes me to downshift. The last thing I need to cap off this shitty day is an interaction with LAPD. My dream car, black Mustang GT, can be a magnet for unwanted attention from law enforcement. The white racing stripe down the side, spoiler on the back, and black leather interior seems to always fit the description for some undefined crime.

But I had to have it. When I saw it on the showroom floor at the dealership a year ago, it was leaving with me. I've been driving manual cars since my dad taught me how to steer in his old 1973 Impala sedan. And I've loved them ever since. And once I love something or someone, it's hard to give it or them up.

Especially Carmen. Our conversation replays in my mind like a rap music mixtape on a torturous loop. She's right. We shouldn't be together. All the reasons she outlined while standing naked in the bathroom are true. The major one being she's another man's wife.

I respect marriage. My parents have been married for over thirty years. Watching them raise three kids and make it work through difficulties was the perfect model for me. The ties that bind a marriage are strong. And I told myself we should only remain work friends. But then Monte Carlo happened.

Working with her for months, my admiration of her accomplishments grew to respect for her ambition to show corporate her abilities to lead. Then it grew into an attraction that spanned more than her physical gifts. Once we crossed that line, it was hard to hold back. To be unable to touch her again, the disappointment weighs on my chest and strains to be released.

A car horn blares behind me. Some jerk in a silver bus of an SUV makes the "hurry and go" gesture with his hands before swerving around and cutting me off.

My foul mood will not take this slight, and I shift gears and punch the gas. I blow past him, giving the one-finger salute and rocket through the next intersection.

Blue lights flash.

Inwardly, I groan and my body goes into autopilot. Pull over quickly, wallet placed on dashboard, radio off, hands in clear view.

I've been pulled over a time or seven. Black man plus sports car equals fitting the description. My Dad gave me the talk as soon as I got my license.

"The objective is survival." Dad used his massive hands to punctuate the last word.

I wiped my palms down a pair of black track pants and fought to maintain eye contact. Master Sergeant Bernard West, Sr. commanded respect at all times. Especially from his three children. As the youngest, I'd heard this speech before, but it felt urgent when all a sixteen-year-old me wanted to do was pick up my boys and go to the mall.

"You don't argue," my old man continued. "Even if they bait you."

"I know, Dad."

A look shut down any further comment from me.

"I've given this speech to your brother and sister. Hated to do it each time." Dad scratched his beard, then dangled the key. "But if you want these, you going to hear it."

I stood up straight. "Yes, sir."

Dad's eyes softened, and he touched my shoulders. "Bottom line, you take the ticket like a man. Justified or not. You come home and let your mother and me fight in the courts. Do you understand, son?"

The memory of that sweltering August day helps to calm my nerves. But as the officer approaches the driver's side window in this day and time, I can't help wondering if I'll make it home.

"Where're you racing off to this afternoon?"

The sunlight glares off the silver tag on his uniform, and I squint to make out the name. Officer Albert sports a blonde 'high and tight' or military haircut. His clean-shaven face has a scar from his nose to the top of thin lips.

His hand rests on his gun.

I clear my throat. "Heading to work."

"You must really be late," he quips. "License and registration."

To avoid any back and forth, I don't respond and simply give him the documents I've already pulled and sat on the dash to avoid reaching for anything in his presence. My hands are returned to the steering wheel.

"So, Mr. Frazier," Officer Albert studies my license and grins, showing crooked teeth. "You're awful quiet. Not going to ask what I stopped you for?"

"Just waiting for you to tell me." I can hear my father's voice. *Don't give him a reason to escalate.*

"Witnessed you reckless driving. You were clearly over the posted forty-five miles."

Traffic whizzes by. I spot at least two other speeders, but this guy wants to mess with me.

"Where do you work?" Officer Albert taps my license on top of the car to a rhythm that sounds like harassment.

Why does that matter? "Parker & Kramer."

Albert snaps to attention. "If you work there, you're going in the opposite direction. It's a couple of miles back that way. You need to come up with a better lie."

"Damn." *Carmen got me all messed up.*

I don't realize I've said the word out loud until Albert puts a hand back on his gun.

"So, where are you really going? Late for a drug deal?"

My mouth opens, but the ability to form a coherent response fails me.

"Is there anything in your car that I need to be aware of?" Officer Albert is no longer grinning.

"What?" I croak out. Now, I'm frowning, and he has my full attention.

He steps away from the car door. "Do you consent to a search of the vehicle?"

How did this day go from bad to 'about to be a trending hash tag'?

My jaw clenches and a headache tingles at the base of my skull. I take several deep breaths to regain control. Dad's words replay in my head. I want to survive this day and be able to call my parents. I need to make it back to Carmen, even if she thinks it's over.

"Sir, there's no need to search my car. I just got dumped by my girl and I need to get back to work." Pain radiates from my jaw from clenching my teeth. "You caught me in a moment of frustration when some guy cut me off and I sped around him. You can give me a ticket and I'll try to focus on getting to work. Maintaining the speed limit this time."

Officer Albert examines me for a moment. "I'll be right back." He strides to the patrol car.

Feeling like I dodged a literal bullet, I rotate my shoulders and run a hand over my face. Keeping tabs on the officer in the mirror, I check my phone. No message from Carmen.

When Office Albert sprints back to the vehicle, I resume the position with my hands in clear view.

"You're lucky I got a serious call." He tosses my license into the car where it lands in the cup holder. "Slow it down."

The officer jogs back to his vehicle and hits the siren as he peels into traffic.

It takes a few minutes before I'm able to drive and do a u-turn, aiming toward the office. Playing back the interaction with the cop, I imagine all the ways the incident could have gone.

Through it all, one thing occupied my mind more than my safety.

Carmen Miller.

Chapter Four

Carmen

What has Melvin done with the money? Why is $10,000 missing from our joint saving account? Melvin promised never to touch our savings. He claimed to have his spending under control. Like everything else with that man, the truth reveals something different from what it appears to be.

A few deep breaths help me to relax before the transformation back into a respectable woman begins. Using the blow dryer and a comb to lift and lengthen the natural curls of my hair, I gather it into a fashionable ponytail. A touch of cosmetics enhances my brownish-peach unblemished skin, the gift from my mother and Puerto Rican father. I slip on the navy pantsuit, white blouse and silver necklace representing the Director of Public Relations. Heels slide on my pedicured feet. A check in the full-length mirror anchored to the wall signals a job well done. The image reflected reveals no traces of unexpected infidelity. My mask hides a multitude of sins.

An internal struggle remains. I'm not usually the compulsive, spontaneous type, no matter how strong the attraction. My obsession with checking things off my checklist is a goal to avoid any moral dilemmas. People claim some things just happen, and I never believed it until it happened to me. I knew this thing with Braxton had an expiration date. There's no way I can continue sneaking around.

But I can admit the rush is intoxicating. How strong can a marriage be if someone else can cause temptation to be acted upon? I wonder if this is what my father felt as he began a relationship with my mother. She didn't know he was married until I was growing in her belly. Then she learned his wife was pregnant, too. Being the product of an affair, maybe cheating is embedded in my DNA.

All traces of Braxton are gone when I come out of the bathroom. My eyes sweep the room to ensure we left nothing behind. The toiletry bag goes back into an oversized tote. Braxton has already taken care of the room, so I toss the key card on the nightstand.

Feeling my cell phone vibrate in the purse thrown over my shoulder causes me to pause during the walk to my BMW sedan parked behind the hotel. If this is Maggie calling with another legal update, blowing up my carefully prepared life, I will lose it for sure. The name displayed across the screen causes my heart to stop. *Berkeley Hall School.*

"Hello." The word squeezes past the knot of dread in my throat.

"Oh, Mrs. Miller. This is Mrs. Lyons. I was going to leave you another message."

Mrs. Lyons is a short, round bundle of energy who works in the main office. *Another message?* "Is Olivia, okay?"

"Umm, a minor case of a stomach virus," she hedges. "We tried to call your husband as well and didn't get an answer there, either. I know it's close to the end of the school day, but Olivia goes to aftercare. We need her to be picked up. Can't have her around the other children, you know."

The woman rambles on as my steps pick up speed. "I'm on the way."

Mrs. Lyons is still speaking but juggling the keys and my bag requires an end to the call to unlock the door. Everything is thrown on the passenger seat and the ignition is engaged. Nothing. Happens.

Another try, but the thing refuses to start. I slap the steering wheel and curse.

A press of the lever pops the hood. I study the various parts which make a car run without a clue about what's wrong. For a day which began with so much pleasure, it has quickly turned into a shitshow.

And why isn't Melvin answering his phone? Running back the conversation from this morning, he mentioned nothing out of the ordinary. But most of our conversations haven't really been conversations. More like updates on pick-up/drop-off schedules and meal plans.

I contemplate calling my best friend Gayle. The call log shows I also missed one from her, too. But I haven't shared Braxton with her yet.

My heels tap a frantic pace as I go back and forth, debating whether to call Braxton. Then a big, brown truck comes barreling around the building. The logo for the APD announces that my husband's company is making a delivery to this hotel. Time stops and sweat forms under my arms faster than a celebrity viral video. The need to hide is overwhelming, but my legs are frozen in place. The driver jumps out with several packages, glances my way with an appreciative once over, then disappears into the building.

My breath comes out in a whoosh and my legs finally remember how to move. What if that had been Melvin? His normal route is on the other side of town, but what if he switched? This cannot be the way for him to discover my indiscretion.

The clock is ticking, and Olivia needs me. I have no choice but to call Braxton.

"That's a good-looking ride you got there."

A look over my shoulder confirms the baritone voice of the same APD driver. "No disrespect, ma'am, but I'm partial to BMWs. I got this 1998 M5 that I'm rebuilding. It's a beauty." His broad smile is meant to disarm as his gaze sweeps over the red exterior. "Though not as fine as you. Let me guess. That's a 328i, right? With the sports package, of course."

Before a response can slide past my lips, he continues, "I know this car isn't giving you trouble. That's another reason I love BMWs. Reliable cars. Do you mind?"

APD dude moves toward the driver's side door and is behind the wheel before a protest is formed. He listens for a second, jumps out, leans under the hood and starts fiddling with things.

"You think you can fix it?" This lanky, quick talking man may need a haircut and a gold tooth, but he may also be the answer to getting me out of this mess.

"Just what I thought. It's probably your battery," he answers. "Maybe a weak cell. We're not really supposed to do stuff like this, but I can give you a jump. You got some cables?"

There is a pair in the trunk, along with a first aid kit put there by Melvin when things were good between us. The guilt continues to piles on, but I push it aside along with the questions about where he is and focus on leaving to get to Olivia.

The driver maneuvers his truck in front of my vehicle and hooks up the cables. He lets it run for a few minutes, then instructs me to try it. The sound of the engine turning over gives me hope I can make it out of this situation unscathed.

"Thank you so much," I say, reaching back in the car to grab my wallet. "You were a life saver."

A church van pulls into the parking lot and beeps as it backs into a space. A hotel employee strolls out and lights a cigarette while tapping on his phone.

"The name's Jay. And you are?"

I am eager to leave and don't notice that Jay has turned his attention from the car to me. He gives me the same appraisal he gave the vehicle.

"Married," I say. "Can I give you something for your trouble?"

"A fine lady like you can give me your number." Jay licks his chapped lips in what I'm sure he considers a seductive tease. Since it would be impolite to check him, the cutting retort is tucked away. "I don't think my husband would appreciate that."

His bushy eyebrows wing upward. "If you won't tell, I damn sure won't."

Frowning, I retort, "Excuse me?"

"Well, you are in a Hilton parking lot *without* said husband. I know BMWs and I've seen this one here before."

All gratitude slithers into the pit of hell. "Look, Jay." I speak slowly so this man can understand the dangerous game he's playing. "You don't know me and it's none of your business why I'm here."

My index finger corks in the air. "And to be clear, my only interest in you is that you helped get my car started. You can try your pickup lines on some other woman."

He throws up his hands and steps back. "Oh, I see. You one of *those*. A bougie broad that thinks they too good for a blue-collar brother."

My body tenses since the insult is beyond ridiculous. Melvin is a blue-collar worker. "And you are one of those sorry ass brothers that can't take rejection without projecting your insecurities on any woman smart enough to see past your nice guy act. Here's some advice for you." Pausing to catch a breath, I continue, "If you want one of us 'bougie broads', you better step your game up. It's not the blue collar that's a turnoff. It's the dog collar."

Jay glares like he wants to put a fist through my face. Instead, he turns and snatches the cables off his truck, slams the hood, and storms to the driver's seat. The smell of burned rubber permeates the air when he tears out of the parking lot.

I clear my head by counting to ten, remove the cables from the battery, and toss them back in the trunk. Now the focus is on getting to my daughter. At the next red light, tension causes my hands to grip the steering wheel so tight, the muscles cramp. Flexing my fingers to get the blood circulating helps me to relax. By the clock on the dashboard, I will get to Olivia in twenty minutes.

Along the way, I promise to be a better mother. God knows, I won't win any Wife of the Year awards.

Not that Melvin would be nominated for Husband of the Year, either. Usually when he disappears by not answering his phone, it means he's up to his old tricks. He promised the gambling would stop, but I've learned not to believe that statement. The man refuses to get help and insists it's not a problem to bet on a few games. A few games almost caused him to file for bankruptcy last year. And Maggie's call is concrete evidence something is going on.

I met Melvin later in life. A few of my friends had found their forever partners, but the rest of us were struggling with the Jay's of the world. Men who only wanted women for one thing, had low-paying jobs and even lower credit scores. I was relieved when I met Melvin. My most serious long-term relationship ended with the ring but no walk down the aisle after wasting five years of my life. He Who Shall Not Be Named proved the fairy tale wasn't for me. Focusing on my career helped me advance at Parker & Kramer. Then Melvin came along and blessed me with my greatest achievement. My beautiful curly-haired daughter, with a bright smile and an even brighter disposition.

Rushing into Olivia's school, I power walk toward the office. Mrs. Lyons meets me in the hall. Her mouth opens and closes before she speaks.

"Mrs. Miller, I saw you pull up."

Olivia is asleep, curled in a ball on a chair in the office. The blanket wrapped around her legs bears the school's Bobcat logo.

"The nurse checked her out. No fever, so like I said, it's probably a little stomach virus."

The knot in my middle unravels as the worst-case scenario is relieved.

Mrs. Lyons hugs the manila folder she's carrying to her chest. "Since you're here, I wanted to remind you of your balance."

"Balance?" She must be mistaken. Most of our household bills are handled by me. But Melvin is supposed to take care of this one. He knows the tuition payments are due weekly. I take a deep breath and try to get my mind and heart rate to slow down without revealing this is news to me. *Has he gambled away Olivia's tuition money?*

Was that judgment or the fluorescent lights reflecting off the woman's thick glasses?

"I can settle that right now." Fumbling for my checkbook keeps me from having to make eye contact.

Mrs. Lyon quotes the amount, two months of tuition plus a month of extended care. The $4,000 hit isn't budgeted, but I'll transfer some funds later. Once I find out why Melvin hasn't paid.

A bell rings, announcing the end of the school day. Students and teachers filter into the hallways. The chorus of voices laughing and book bags banging on the floor cause us to step further into the office.

"You know if you're having financial difficulties," Mrs. Lyons begins.

The pen is used to punctuate the point. "No difficulties here." I interrupt her pity policy spiel before she can cast us as a family in need. Not a financial need here. I could use a reliable co parent, though. "Simple oversight that won't happen again."

Mrs. Lyons' smile fades, and she takes a step back. "N-no offense meant," she stammers. "You've always been an awesome parent, and I knew it had to be a something like that."

"Thank you," I accept the receipt when offered and gather my daughter and what's left of my dignity to head home.

Chapter Five

Braxton

Using my employee badge, I buzz into the building and head for the bank of elevators. The marketing team is located on the third floor and I step into a maze of cubicles. Late afternoon, the energy is a low hum of clicking keyboards and occasional ringing of phones. The mornings are more frantic and filled with meetings and strategy sessions.

The ninja ability developed from being an annoying little brother allows me to cross to my desk without being seen and collapse in the leather chair. Waiting on my laptop to power up, my thoughts return to Carmen. The best parts of the afternoon replays in my mind and I smile despite the way things ended.

I was drawn to Carmen from the first day we met. The physical traits were on point. Full lips, skin the color of a ripe peach, and a curvy shape that the conservative suit she wore couldn't constrain. But it was her mind that sealed it for me. Working with her on the Seduction campaign was challenging. She taught me how the company likes things but demanded I over deliver for the higher ups.

"Make them see our value to the team," she tells me one night as we fine-tuned our presentation. "Prove that you belong here. We can't afford to coast on past success."

And yeah, I pursued her because I had to know this woman. Even though she was married. Some attractions can not be denied.

Unhappily married.

Does that make me a bad person? A sinner in some people's opinion? I haven't been a regular churchgoer since I left my Momma's house, but I'm a firm believer in a higher power. I also believe that some people are made for each other.

My favorite poet, Rumi, has a quote about love which defines this relationship. Something about lovers not simply meeting but being meant for each other all along. Carmen and I have a vibe that I haven't found with anyone else. Her being my mentor was luck of the draw. The business trip to Monte Carlo sealed my fate.

Licking my lips, I can still taste her essence on my tongue. Carmen may have tried to end things today because of her situation. And I'll back off even though I love the woman.

My life is officially a Carl Thomas song. But I'm not ready to sing the chorus yet. Even if this is the end, I can't say I wish I *never* met her at all.

The nearby copier-printer spits out paper, and I enter my password on the screen. After scrolling through email, I craft a response to a question about proposed meeting dates when I'm assaulted by the potent scent of her floral perfume. Kayla Pearson has entered my cubicle.

"And where have you been?" she asks.

"Why?" I continue typing. "You need something?"

Kayla perches on the edge of my desk and folds her arms. "Actually, I was looking for Carmen. Figured you'd know where she was."

My heartbeat surges. "Why is that?"

"You're her favorite. Always in her office and stuff." Kayla tugs at the short black skirt that is not budging past mid-thigh.

I focus on the computer screen. "Carmen's my assigned mentor. Same as you."

"Yeah, I know. I'm glad she's out of the office though." She shrugs when I glance her way. "Hey, what happened to you hanging with us for drinks the other night? One of my friends scored tickets to the J. Cole concert."

Kayla rambles on about the show and some celebrity sighting. She punctuates every other sentence by touching my arm. It's obvious she wants my full attention, so I hit send on the email and swivel around to get the full view.

"Why so serious?" she asks. "A hard-working man like you can use a night out. You don't know what you're missing."

What am I really missing? Kayla pouts her red lips and twirls a strand of long-weaved hair. Her ample breasts strain against a white low-cut blouse. She notices me looking and slides completely back on my desk to cross one leg over the other and brush against my thigh.

I slide my chair back. Kayla is a good-looking woman, but everything about her is loud. Her perfume, her clothes. Her intentions.

She's not what I'm looking for. I've dated girls like Kayla. Girls who are flirty and fun. Until you try to have a conversation about something real. All things can't revolve around reality shows and getting "turnted up" in the club.

Besides, no woman, no matter how short her skirt or flawlessly makeup is applied, can compete with Carmen.

"Listen, Kayla," I begin, but I'm cut off by another visitor.

"What's up, my man. No wonder you didn't respond to my email," my buddy Devon Johnson leans against my cubicle.

I'm glad for the interruption. "D.J. What's happening?"

"Rude." Kayla is not happy with the intrusion and rolls her eyes.

D.J. extends a hand. "Apologies. It's Kayla, right?"

She gives him a blank stare.

"I'm Devon. Work down in HR, remember? We met at the Summer Fling last month. B introduced us."

Kayla ignores his hand and hops off the desk. "I'll talk to you later, Braxton."

Devon watches her swish down the corridor. "Damn, that chick is cold. She reminds me of that character from the show 'Living Single'." He snaps his fingers. "Regine. The one Kim Fields played. Man, watching those reruns had a teenage boy ready to do things."

"You have serious issues, my friend." My computer chimes with an incoming email but DJ straddles the chair in the corner. No work is getting done right now.

"Why she always treating me like I'm short though?" Devon straightens his signature bow tie and runs a hand over a low caeser haircut.

I laugh at him, trying to impress a woman who couldn't care less. "Because you *are* short, fool."

Devon straightens up to his full 5'8" height and puffs out his chest. "I'm not short. I'm compact. The better to wax that ass. She don't know about us corporate thugs."

"What's a corporate thug?" Devon is always coming up with a new way to describe himself. In high school, he was DJ Mustard because his skin is the color of the yellow condiment. In college, he was the 'Da D Man. I'm still trying to figure that one out.

"You know how honeys love a thug but not necessarily want to make trips to jail? Well, I'm the best of both worlds. You got the businessman up top." He fiddles with his bow tie. "And the thug attitude." He points to his Timberland boots.

I give Devon dap on that one. "What kind of business attire you got going on, man?" He is always on a different level.

"Hey, I got a date tonight with Sharon over in Research. Corporate thug is the way to go. If things go well, I might get to Form 54A her."

Human Resources makes all workplace romances sign a standard Consensual Relationship Agreement, or Form 54A. Of course, Carmen and I don't have one on file for several reasons. P&K strongly discourages relationships between Management and subordinates.

Devon has made it a working goal to have a form on file. This is his third attempt to date someone who works here. He makes himself more comfortable by leaning against the fabric wall. "But back to 'Regine' though. Is that you?"

"Naw, bruh." Kayla is not the one for me.

Devon raises both eyebrows and stares at me, but I don't elaborate. He slaps my arm. "Take a break. Got some news for you. That's why I came by."

After locking my computer, we take the elevator down to the basement. P&K has a full-size cafeteria complete with various stations such as a salad bar, grill, and a deli. The main kitchen features a special of the day and there is a small canteen stocked with assorted snacks.

The walls are decorated with painted murals of the various Parker & Kramer nationwide and global offices. The tabletops are a mixed hue of greens, blues and reds.

We both grab drinks from the store – Gatorade for me (must replenish those electrolytes) and settle in a booth on the back wall. The scent of garlic and oregano permeate the air, remnants from the daily special, and my stomach growls.

"So, what's the news?"

Devon gulps almost half the bottle of Coke and burps. "You got in, man."

"In what?" Two women come into the canteen laughing and their voices echo throughout the empty space. It's not unusual to not recognize them. P&K employs over 95,000 people with about 3,000 in the headquarters compound.

"I saw your name on a list in Engelman's office." Robert Engelman is the Director of Human Resources and DJ's supervisor. He makes the announcement with a flourish and a wink but I'm not making the connection to a list.

"What are you talking about?"

Devon rares back in the booth. "You know how he's always calling me in to fix something on his computer." He shakes his head. "Like I'm IT instead of getting one of those guys."

"You did save him by recalling that email. The man knows he could've been fired for sending that out before the Board had their final meeting." Engleman had mishandled notice of pending layoffs when the Board decided to change course. Carmen told me all about it.

"I get that. Right place, right time. But now the man calls me in his office for everything." Devon gets up to toss his empty bottle before sliding back into the booth. "Today he called me in there to set up an Excel spreadsheet. He wanted to create a formula to average out salaries. The man needs classes."

"Why doesn't he just use admin staff?"

Devon pounds the table. "That's what I'm wondering."

Laughing, I swivel the remaining liquid in the bottle. "So, what's this list?" Time is passing and there's still work to be done.

"The PK Management Associate Program. You got in, man. The notifications go out next week."

The last drops of Gatorade go down the wrong way, causing me to choke. "S-say what?" I stammer.

"You got in. Congratulations." Devon's smile shows all thirty-two teeth and his gums.

This is a big deal. The PK-MAP program is a highly competitive employee program which provides a framework for leadership development. Applicants must secure endorsement from upper management or someone who has been through the course. Everyone knows that in order to succeed and get promoted here, you will need to complete this program. No one gets in on their first application. But I just did.

"Wow, this is major," I say.

"You damn right it's major. But you can't say anything." Devon glances around at the empty cafeteria. "Don't get your boy hemmed up."

We stand and give each other dap. "I got you. Not a word."

But there is one person I have to tell. The person who helped me write the application and wrote an endorsement on my behalf. The woman who makes me better but can't be mine. Carmen.

Chapter Six

Carmen

This is the last lie.

I am no longer a cheater. I am a mother and wife trying to figure out what's going on with my husband. He promised the gambling would stop. There must be a completely rational reason he was missing in action today and not paying Olivia's tuition. I know I'm within my rights to leave him and his issues behind. But the rearview mirror reflects my greatest dilemma.

Pep talk complete, a turn of the handle opens the garage door.

The scent of lemons greets me and helps take the edge off the anxiety settling in my stomach.

"Smells good, Mommy," Olivia says wiping sleep from her eyes.

Coming into a clean home gives me pleasure. Especially since this ranch-style house was my first major purchase after being stood up at the altar. My focus turned to work, and the first bonus earned was the down payment I needed to close on this house.

Melvin's truck is parked on the street, which is the first clue that the man is inside. Tripping over his work boots at the doorway is the second. Every time Marie cleans the house, Melvin finds a way to let me know he doesn't like it. He thinks it's a waste of money. My sanity has no price. Superwoman exists in comic books. Not in Sherman Oaks.

Olivia's book bag, my purse and laptop slide on the bench before I place Melvin's shoes on the shelf underneath and go in search of this man.

We find Melvin in his favorite leather recliner. Olivia and her dad share a bond that makes me smile despite my disdain for his actions. Seeing them together makes me realize what my daughter will lose.

"Hey, Daddy." Olivia perches on the arm of Melvin's chair. I've told her about sitting on the furniture that way but because she's sick it can slide.

"Hey there, baby girl." Melvin returns our daughter's greeting but doesn't even glance my way. Shaking my head, I step over an empty pizza box and note the beer bottles on the end table. The smell of musky socks undoes all of Marie's cleaning in the family room.

Olivia climbs on Melvin's lap and puts her head on his shoulder. "My tummy was hurting. Then I threw up."

He pats her back and finally turns his attention to her and hugs her close.

Leaving the room, I shed my clothes and put on yoga pants and a t-shirt. Olivia's khaki shorts with blue polo shirt she wore is dug out of her backpack and thrown in the wash.

Olivia hops in my lap when I return to the couch. She leans close and cups her hands around her mouth. "Guess what? Daddy said I can have applesauce for dinner." Her wide hazel eyes dance. Applesauce is her favorite.

"That was supposed to be a secret." Melvin tears his gaze away from the television and tickles Olivia's foot. "How you gonna tell your Mom?"

"Sorry, Daddy." Olivia giggles, and the sound is pure joy. At least my daughter has the one thing missing from my childhood. A father. My own sperm donor wasn't the only man to cast me aside. But he was the first.

No need to dwell on ancient history. Olivia knows both parents love her.

My focus shifts to Melvin. "The school tried to call you. Where's your phone?"

Melvin is the type to purchase the newest model as soon as it's released. The latest iPhone he purchased is not in its usual location. His hand.

"Must be in the truck. Yeah, in the truck." He always repeats his lies.

Melvin takes a swig of his beer and flips the channel between SportsCenter and the NFL Network.

His salt and pepper beard is trimmed neat and he runs one hand over his balding head. Another of his tells. He sinks further into the chair and tugs at his black sweatpants. His brow has permanent worry lines.

"Well, the school tried to call you. I was stuck in a warehouse downtown. There was an editorial short to shoot for our new product." I wait for a beat. This is really the last lie.

He doesn't respond, as usual, when the conversation is about my work. He has no interest whatsoever in what I do all day. Unless it's something where I'm getting praised for an achievement. But then his only interest is knocking me down. For my own good, of course.

It takes a moment to tamp down my aggravation. Using the breathing technique the failed marriage counseling taught allows me to continue. "Then, when I got in the car, it wouldn't start. One of the guys had to give me a jump."

"Something wrong with the car?" Melvin looks at me with eyes that match Olivia's. I remember getting lost in those eyes. The promise they held offered the one thing I was missing. A family. Now his eyes only sparkle for our daughter.

"I don't know. It wouldn't start." My fingers stroke through Olivia's braided hair without me looking up. "My co-worker thinks it's the battery."

"I'll check it later."

His focus returns to the television. Olivia busies herself with a doll baby she retrieves from the toy box in the corner.

I know what's expected of me, but I have to ask the question anyway. Things were supposed to change after the last round of counseling.

"Did you start dinner?"

Melvin sighs, and a vein throbs on his forehead. "Are you going to start that foolishness again?"

"You agreed to help more." A simple statement, but it sounds more like a plea. *How can I manage an* entire department *but feel helpless in my own home?*

"I took a sick day, remember?" Melvin drains the last of his beer and sets the bottle on the end table. "Momma sent over a pot of chili. And some cookies for Livvy."

Olivia perks up at the sound of her name and bounces off my lap.

"Daddy's going to let me drive to Grandma's house." She dances in front of me mimicking the steering motion.

Melvin has one of those big pickup trucks. A black Chevy Silverado. When they're together and Melvin gets in the neighborhood, he puts Olivia on his lap and "allows" her to drive home. It's a cute ritual for them. But I know he's trying to change the subject.

"How was I to know you took a sick day when you didn't tell me? But you felt well enough to go to your mother's, yet couldn't answer a call to pick up Olivia?" The breathing exercises are not working now.

Melvin shifts in his chair. "When you're so busy working, you can't prepare a meal..."

The unspoken comparison is always present. His Mother.

Low blow but a glance at Olivia now sitting at my feet flipping through a book stems the cutting remark I want to make.

"The counselor suggested we stop being bound by traditional gender roles." Melvin refused to do any housework during our marriage. He took weaponizing incompetence to a new level. "We work together. Pick up each other's slack."

"What's that supposed to mean?" Melvin sits up straight. "I don't carry my weight around here. Last time I checked, I'm still the man."

Olivia taps my leg to look at a picture. I help her sound out a word and then turn to Melvin. "So?"

"So, we each got a role to play." He grunts and his knees crack when he stands and heads out of the room. Tossing the empty bottle, he returns from the kitchen with another beer.

"You knew it when we got married. You handle the house and stuff. Cooking and all that. You already got somebody to clean the house for you when my Mom did it all with no complaints." Melvin nods like everything is settled.

Are we really going there? "Your Mom didn't work."

"That's the natural order of things. The man is the king of the castle." Melvin shoots me a look. "You're the one that has to prove you can do it all. Well, do it then."

"I know you aren't going to sit there-" My voice raises and Olivia looks up at me.

Melvin cuts me off. "Ain't that right, Luv Bug. Dad is the King and Mom's the Queen. Kings rule and Queens make dinner."

Olivia stands and strikes the Superhero pose. Hands on hips, feet spread.

"No, Daddy. Kings and Queens both rule. Boys and girls are the same."

My daughter looks at me for approval and all aggravation drains away. The crestfallen look on Melvin's face helps. I suppress the urge to stick out my tongue.

"That's right, baby. Girls and boys are equal."

Olivia jumps up and down. "Mommy, can we do another girls' trip? Remember when we went to the hotel and Daddy couldn't come?"

The temperature in the room drops several degrees as Melvin's eyes narrow. The 'girls' trip' Olivia recalls is a point of contention, and we agreed never to speak of it. Things got so bad between us that I left, taking Olivia with me. We were on our 'girl's trip' for two weeks before I gave in to Melvin's pleas and promises and came back.

Olivia notices Melvin sulking. "Don't be sad, Daddy."

"He's fine," I say. "Let's get you something to eat."

"Yeah, applesauce." My girl made me proud. She has more sense than the both of us. She's getting a big helping of dessert.

Olivia follows me into the kitchen, but I swear the heat of Melvin's gaze is on my back. I'll save my fury for later. He's going to have to answer for the missing money when we can talk without an audience.

Chapter Seven

Braxton

The best part of coming home greets me at the door. His collar jingles as my two-year-old border terrier/boxer mix, Maxx, spins in a circle then balances on his hind legs.

"Hey, boy. What did you do today?" I scratch behind his ears and get down on one knee. If Maxx could talk, he would probably say that he spent the day playing with his toys, going for a walk with the hired dog walker, and snoozing. I envy his simple life.

After a quick change into a pair of black running shorts, a gray t-shirt, and sneakers, Maxx and I head out. We follow our usual route. Living in the Vinz @ Fairfax apartment complex means being in the middle of the Miracle Mile neighborhood of LA. It was a deliberate decision to live here which grants easy access to Museum Row and the convenience and proximity to Hollywood or Downtown LA in under twenty minutes. Even with traffic.

The eighty-degree temperature is perfect for a quick jog, and Maxx is an always willing, running partner. Dodging the tourists milling around, we run a little over a mile and under 22 minutes straight down Fairfax Avenue to the LA Farmers Market at The Grove.

The Grove is a popular outdoor mall with a mix of retail shops and restaurants. It can get crowded on the weekends, but during the week, the fountain in the center of the plaza is great for people watching. You can spend all day out here shopping, catching a flick at the 14-screen Pacific Theatre, or power walking. The dancing water show, which plays every half hour, is reminiscent of the Bellagio in Las Vegas. The adjacent Farmer's Market is a favorite of Mom's. She has Pop bring her up every couple of months.

I read somewhere that Walt Disney sat at a table in the Farmer's Market and designed Disneyland. Sometimes you can see a group of writers or Hollywood executives here in the mornings. This evening, there's not much to see as Maxx and I meander past the stalls of bakers, butchers, and ice cream shops. The smell of Bob's Donuts makes my stomach growl and I stop at a fresh produce stand.

After purchasing an apple, a piece of cheese for Maxx and bottles of water for us, I forgo the red vinyl stool at the counter and find an empty spot among the green painted folding chairs. Maxx sits at my feet and waits for his treat.

"Here you go, boy," I feed him pieces of cheese and then sit a plastic cup of water on the concrete.

Taking a deep breath, I bite into the Golden Delicious apple and contemplate the whirlwind day I had. The situation with Carmen was the best and the worst parts. To have Carmen fully mine in that hotel room had a brother making plans. Then it was snatched away by illegal paperwork. The encounter with the police runs a close second.

Without hesitation, my phone is out and I'm Face Timing my Dad. His US Air Force cap comes into view after one ring.

"What's going on, son?" The booming baritone voice makes me sit up straight and turn down the volume in my Air Pods.

"Ran down to the Grove," I say. "Sitting in the Farmer's Market and thought of you and Mom."

He laughs. "Don't get that woman started. She'll have me on the 405 right quick."

"Pop, hold the phone down some. All I see is your hat."

It took a few lessons to get the old man used to the video feature on the phone, which was a Father's Day gift from me and my siblings. I'm still seeing his hat and part of our house in El Segundo. We moved there right before I started high school. Lucky for me, it was the only place we stayed longer than two years. Pop ended up retiring during my junior year and wanted to stay near the LA Air Force Base.

A face that resembles my own lights up the entire screen. "This better?"

If I ever wonder what I will look like in my 60s, all I have to do is FaceTime Pop. We both have the same wide nose, hooded eyes and deep umber skin. The only difference is his salt and pepper hair and missing goatee. "Yeah, man. I can see your nose hairs."

"You got jokes?" Pop extends his arm so his face doesn't take up the entire frame. "Better?"

"Yeah, that's more like it. What are you doing? Did I catch you coming or going?"

The scenery changes as Pop walks from the garage and through the alley toward the house. "Was about to run to the auto shop. My part came in for Sally."

"Sally" is the 1969 Ford Mustang Mach 1 that Pop has been restoring off and on since I can remember. It's a dark blue hard body with light blue reflective striping. He named the car Sally after the Wilson Pickett song, Mustang Sally.

Maxx tugs at his leash and puts his front paws on my lap. I give him the last bite of my apple and he resettles at my feet.

"We're going to have to celebrate if you ever get that car running. Remember the time Bernie tricked me into breaking one of Sally's window. I don't know why I believed it was made of bullet proof glass. In my defense, I was four at the time and Bernie gave me the bat and threw the ball. It was a swing and a miss. Man, you were so mad I thought you would kill us." I ramble on about some of the situations my older brother, Bernard, Jr. or Bernie, got us into. The fourteen-year age difference between us made me naïve enough to follow him up and believe everything he said.

"What's on your mind, son?"

He could always see through my stalling tactic. "Ever have one of those days that make you question everything?"

"Sure have." He lifts his cap and scratches his receding hairline. "What's her name?"

My laughter mimics a bark, causing Maxx to stand, tail wagging, and lick my hand. "What makes you think it's a woman?"

Pop pauses at the back door and with a straight face says, "They're the only ones can give a man 'one of those days'".

"Ain't that the truth."

"Go on and tell me about her." The telltale crackle announces when Pop opens the French doors leading into the family room. We could never sneak in after curfew without that door giving us away. Pop refused to fix it no matter how much Mom fussed. He settles in his favorite black leather lounge chair and puts his feet up.

"She's everything," I begin and glance up with the vision of Carmen making me smile. "She's so smart. The first time I saw her making a presentation to the marketing team I knew she was special."

"So, you two work together?" Dad asks.

"You can say that. She's in a higher position then me." I don't tell him she would be considered my boss. "But we have this connection, and I can't get her out of my mind."

Pops repositions the phone by propping it on the armrest. Now I can only see the angle of his face. "Then what's the problem. And what's her name, son?"

"Her name is Carmen."

"This Carmen ain't *checking* for you?" He laughs.

Shaking my head at his attempt to be cool, I ask, "My nephew teach you that?"

"Yeah, Brody tried to catch me up with that slang mess when they were out here this summer."

Bernie has two kids with his wife, Laura. They met when Bernie followed in Pop's footsteps and joined the service right out of high school. He was stationed in Oklahoma when he met his soulmate. They married when Bernie was nineteen against Mom's wishes. She got over it when Brody and Brianna were born. Brody's seventeen years old now. Brianna is three years younger.

"Anyway." I shift in the chair and get the conversation back on track. "Carmen *is* checking for me. The feeling is definitely mutual. But it's complicated."

Pop takes off his cap and runs a hand over the tight military cut he still sports despite the receding hairline. Gray patches are prominent on his temples.

"You young people and your complications. Only thing that matters is if you love each other. The rest of the mess will work out."

Easy for him to say. Bernard, Sr. and Hannah were high school sweethearts and married right after graduation.

"Well, sometimes there are other considerations besides love."

He grunts as if to dismiss that statement and then asks, "Like what?"

I stretch my legs and debate telling him the entire story. Falling for a married woman. Trying to end it weeks ago, but we couldn't stay away. Her ending it this time. My inability to let go. Maybe he can give me some judgment free advice.

"Here's the situation," I begin.

The reflection from a silver cross flashes on the screen, and Mom appears behind Pop's chair. "That was a quick trip."

"Braxton caught me before I could leave." Pop passes her the phone and Mom's face brightens on the screen. Her brown eyes widen and crinkle at the edges, showing off otherwise flawless skin. She's the first woman I fell in love with.

"Hey, baby," she says.

"Mom, guess where I am?" Flipping the screen, I extend the phone and do a slow show of the stalls like a game host. "Can you smell the donuts?"

Bob's Donuts start making their pastry treats at 4:30 in the morning. Their glazed donuts are one of Mom's favorite.

"Boy, you going to make me get your Dad to bring me down there before the weekend."

Pops mumbles something in the background and Mom bumps him with her hip and walks away.

"How you going to take the phone? I wasn't finished talking to my son."

She ignores him and the view changes as she walks towards the kitchen.

"I was going to call you," she says. "Guess who I saw today."

"Why are you whispering?"

Mom looks over her shoulder and then leans against the granite countertop. "I saw Leslie. She's back in town."

Despite the warmth, my body shivers with a sudden feeling of icy dread. Leslie Adams. My first in so many ways. First girlfriend, first love.

First woman to break my heart.

"Um, okay. That's nice," I say.

Mom scrunches her face. "Nice? Is that all you have to say? She's back home for good. Left New York and took a job here to be closer to her father."

I stand to relieve the tingling and stretch my legs, and Maxx does the same. We head back through the Market toward the exit. Mom is really gearing up. My lack of questions doesn't mean she doesn't have all the answers.

"She came to Bible Study last night. Surprised Pastor so much, he dropped his tablet. I was able to get my hug after the session ended. She asked about you."

"Oh, yeah?" Maxx stops to sniff around a planter and circles it a few times. My mind races. Did Leslie mention to Mom the way she dumped me over the phone? The way she led me on and then left. Not for another man. I may have been able to understand that one. She left me for a job. Like we couldn't have worked that shit out.

"I always liked you two together." Mom's smile is so bright I look away from the screen.

"Why's that?" Maxx and I cross the street, dodging a group of joggers, and continue the trek home.

"You guys were such a cute couple. And she's a good Christian girl. Her Dad being the Pastor of our church, I guess that goes without saying."

Little does Mom know the 'good Christian girl' taught me a few tricks. The Metro bus blows by and drowns out Mom's next comment.

"I gave her your number," Mom repeats.

Maxx yelps when I stop short, yanking his leash back. "You did what?"

"Why would you do that, woman? Braxton already has a lady friend he was just telling me about." Pop's voice asks the question I would like an answer to.

"She asked for it." Mom shakes her head like it's obvious she would meddle in my love life.

"Mom, I wish you hadn't done that. I'm seeing someone. And Leslie and I haven't spoken for years."

We started dating Senior year in high school. It lasted throughout college. After graduation, while I was thinking about the best way to propose, she was planning her escape to New York. It took weeks for her to return my call. She couldn't stay in LA anymore, she said. The city was smothering her. I caught the veiled reference to me and her father being the someones confining her.

"I have her number too, if you want it."

Mom will not be deterred from playing matchmaker. I release a heavy sigh and run my free hand over my head and listen to her ramble until the light changes from green to red. A teenager waiting at the intersection gives me a head nod. He's probably had to endure a meddling conversation with his mother too.

"Speaking of numbers, Debra asked me if you got the check she sent you for your birthday last week."

There is no better change of subject than bringing up my one and only sister. The rebel in the family. Debra and Mom were never close. As long as I can remember, those two rarely agreed on anything.

It got worse once Debra came out as gay. Mom's been trying to pray it away ever since.

Mom wrinkles her nose. "I suppose. There was some mail or something your dad said I had. She could have called her mother."

"She tried. The seven-hour difference between here and London makes it hard." Debra is a software engineer for Microsoft. We normally talk when I'm getting ready for work and she is on her lunch break. Any other time, we are left to communicate via email or text.

"Lord, just protect my babies," Mom says. "I'm praying she stops sinning, meets a nice man and come from over there."

An ambulance siren screams through the intersection, causing a tow truck to slam on brakes. The smell of burned rubber pollutes the air.

"She likes it there, Mom." I don't add that Debra has already met a very nice woman and they're happy. I want to get the focus off me. Not give Mom a heart attack.

"And you, too. Bernie has his wife and kids. It's time you settle down. That's why running into Leslie was a blessing. He's a right on time God. Yes, He is."

Before I can reply, Pops walks into the kitchen. "Hand me my phone, woman. You always trying to set this boy up. I told you he was telling me he got a woman before you took the phone."

"Is she a good Christian girl?"

Before I can answer, Mom continues. "Even if she is, I bet she can't hold a candle to Leslie."

I'm so involved on the phone that I almost walk past my building. Maxx stops and pulls on his leash to get my attention.

"Listen guys, I'm back home and I'll lose you on the elevator. Talk to you later."

Mom and Pops continue talking and now the phone is on the counter, staring up at the ceiling.

Ending the call, I'm left with one thought. Mom would never approve of Carmen.

Chapter Eight

Carmen

Exhaustion overcomes me when I recline on my side of the king-sized bed, but the urge to turn on my laptop to check emails is too great to resist. Maggie has already drafted a new motion to contest the judge's action. We plan to meet tomorrow.

The dark wood floor and light gray walls with an aqua blue accent usually offer calmness to the end of a stressful day. The Mediterranean decor reminds me of my favorite vacation spot, Aruba.

"Luv bug is out." Melvin saunters into the room like he hasn't blown up my 'after divorce' plans. "Only took one story tonight."

I scan through my messages and wait. Melvin glances at me and goes into the closet. He's been sleeping in the guest room, but his clothes are still in here.

"And checked out the car." Melvin places his work uniform on the bench at the end of the bed. "Seems to be running fine now."

"Umm hmm." Missing work has my inbox full of unread messages. My hours will be long tomorrow.

Melvin's lengthy silence followed by a cough causes me to look up. "Did you hear what I said. The car is fine."

Returning focus to the screen, I reply, "Yeah. Thanks."

He grunts and pulls his shirt over his head, tossing it on the bench before storming into the bathroom.

My cell phone buzzes in time with the shower spray.

> Braxton: You didn't come back to the office. Is everything okay?

> School called. I text back. Olivia was sick. She's fine now.

Watching the dots on the screen blink in time to my heartbeat, I wonder if he will still send his nightly text. From the beginning, it's been our ritual. His goodnight messages usually include a quote from the poet Rumi. My favorite is 'You are not a drop in the ocean. You are the entire ocean, in a drop.'

When the text comes, it's only four words and I'm transported back to the carefree hours in that hotel room.

> I miss you already.

The finality of what I've done hits me like an elbow to the stomach. Am I fooling myself to think I can pretend Braxton and I never happened?

A swipe of a finger deletes the message. That part of my life will have to wait. My daughter, who is fast asleep on the other side of the house, deserves an intact family, at least until things are finalized. It's my obligation to provide the one thing I longed for as a child. A loving father. For all of Melvin's shortcomings, he tries to be a good dad.

When Melvin emerges, I am buried underneath the clean sheets wishing sleep will come to allow me an escape from this situation. I won't allow myself the luxury of mourning my relationship with Braxton.

Melvin collapses on his side of the bed after tossing the decorative pillows on the floor. Wrestling with the remaining pillow completes his bedtime routine.

"What are you doing?" The need to confront our issues will not let me rest.

Melvin pounds the pillow and wraps an arm around it. "Going to sleep if you would stop talking."

Heat flushes through my body, and I sit straight up. "Were you planning to tell me about the money? And before you lie, I already know about it. Are you gambling again?"

Melvin rolls on his back and laughs. "Don't know what you're talking about. You're losing it, babe. Losing it."

"I'm losing it?!" Pain shoots from my jaw as I clench my teeth. "I'm losing it, alright. Losing a lot of money because you won't deal with your problem."

He looks at me with a blank expression. "I made an executive decision to take out some money. Ain't that how you like to say it?"

I kick the covers off and stand. "That's the problem. You think you can make decisions and I have to fall in line? How can our marriage work like this? Maybe we should talk about ending things for good."

The weight of my proclamation is a boulder pressing on my heart. I fight the tears that threaten to fall and mark a trail of disappointment.

"It would work if you let me be the man around here." Melvin sits up and scratches his head. "Stop trying to manage everything and everybody."

The smirk on his face causes a surge of adrenaline to flow and settle in my hands and curl into fists. I cross my arms to suppress the urge to fight and glare at him.

Melvin rearranges the pillows and props himself up into a sitting position. "Okay, okay. Calm down and let's work it out."

My eyes narrow. "Work it out how?"

"What 'cha mean?" Melvin feigns confusion by scrunching up his face and widening his eyes. Olivia pulls the same move when I catch her sneaking extra snacks.

I place my hands on my hips and take a deep breath. "For the past two years, all we've done is argue over gender roles like the one tonight. And my job. You try to ruin any good news I get when it comes to my work. I received an award for excelling in my profession, but you couldn't even let me have that bit of recognition. The other day, you called my mom to upset me before my big presentation. And you didn't even ask me how it went."

Melvin protests, but I cut him off with a wave. "It's what you intended. I've made peace with it. The only thing that matters now is the little girl asleep on the other side of this house. I think we may be done."

We stare at each other. Melvin fidgets with the covers and throws his legs out of bed. He runs a hand over his balding head. "I need money."

It shouldn't be about money. We both make good salaries. Mine happens to be more than his. Much more. A fact Melvin struggles with even after six years of marriage. I never understood his problem. Our money was combined in a joint household account, and the monthly expenses were easily covered. I thought combining our incomes would erase the gap in our take-home pay, but Melvin kept a running tab in his head. I learned to have HR shift bonuses and raises into a separate private account.

"Nothing for you to worry about." Melvin turns away from my glare.

"What do you need the money for, Melvin?" My mind races and I don't want to believe he's resorting to old behavior. He promised to stop gambling. "Why didn't you pay Livvy's tuition?"

He is quiet, so I repeat the question. *Why is everything so hard with this man?*

"I need to help my mom with a new roof. A new roof," he says after scratching his head.

That's another of his tells. Silence followed by a head rub clues me in that he's hiding something.

I must have loved him once. My mind recalls memories in the story of us. The Melvin I fell in love with is a good son to his mother. He's been helping take care of Ms. Barbara ever since his father died in a car accident when Melvin was a teenager. We bonded over missing our fathers. His was a victim of a drunk driver. My father only pretended to be dead.

"Are you sure it's for Barbara? Did you lose money on that game you were watching?" The way he cursed at the television, it was obvious the team he was rooting for didn't win.

"Don't start, okay?"

I suck in a deep breath and release it through clenched teeth. And that's the quality about Melvin I can't stand. He's so damn stubborn. Without thinking, I cross the room to stand in front of him.

"Look, I need you to be honest. You're talking about money for your mom and I get embarrassed at the school because you didn't make Olivia's tuition payment. What's really going on?"

He punches the pillows and gives me his back to ponder. "I didn't gamble away the tuition money, if that's what you think. The payment was made, but you want to believe that woman at the school over me. I'm done talking about it."

I am a volcano ready to erupt at his attempt to gaslight me. When I first discovered Melvin's secret, his bad habit of gambling, I blamed myself. If only I didn't make so much more money than him. If only I hadn't insisted on living in the house I bought before we met. If only I could conform to his ideal of a perfect wife. But I'm growing tired of trying to make myself small not to challenge his ego. I've been suffering for over a year now, and he still finds fault. It's become obvious my husband has problems beyond me. Too bad he won't admit them.

No one told me marriage would be having the same argument over and over again. I lean over him, and my voice is as hard as his head. "Did you ever apply for the supervisor position we talked about?"

Melvin pretends not to hear me and gets up from the bed. He goes back into the bathroom when the question is repeated. The lack of ambition is mind numbing. He says he wants, no; he needs to make more money, but he'd rather gamble his way into a payday. I return to my side of the bed and try to calm down. The air changes when Melvin returns to the room, causing my stomach to flutter.

"That little stunt you pulled earlier, questioning what I do around here in front of Olivia. That's the reason you're going to end up alone."

Caught off guard, I'm speechless but I should have been braced for the attack. Melvin would not let the simplest slight go. Along with the gambling problem, I think he's bipolar with the way his moods change.

Having gotten the reaction he wanted, Melvin crawls back in bed and pulls the covers over his head.

He must have loved me once. Now it's hard to recognize the man who shares our bed but sleeps with his back turned to me. Melvin's words echo within the walls. Not only from tonight, but from all the years before. How many times has he told me and shown me I wasn't good enough? Always falling short of his expectations and demands.

Night settles in the room, and the quiet allows me to play my favorite game of 'what if'. *If* Braxton was here, we would have a conversation. *If* Braxton was here, I wouldn't have to dumb down my work efforts and accomplishments. *If* Braxton was here, I wouldn't be shaking with rage at the audacity of this man.

But I sent Braxton away before he could figure out I'll never be good enough for him either.

Chapter Nine

Braxton

I miss you already.

My stomach knots with the push of the arrow on the screen. Too late and it's sent through the ether to show up on Carmen's phone.

She didn't come back to the office, and I had to know if everything was okay. The walk and conversation with my parents served only as distractions. Everything comes back to that woman.

Maxx senses my mood and hops onto my lap, almost causing my drink to spill. He nuzzles his head under my chin and tries to lick my face.

"I'm okay, boy," I tell him and put the phone and glass on the patio table. My small balcony overlooks the busy street with the lights from the city reflected in the night sky. My fourth-floor location minimizes the sounds of traffic and the ceiling fan offers a refreshing breeze. After a shower and a meal of baked fish and salad, it's my go-to spot to unwind from the day. The cushion on the rattan wicker sofa creaks when I readjust to shift Maxx's weight.

Staring at the phone, those three dots indicating that she has seen the message and is composing a response torture me.

Does she miss me too? What is she thinking about us?

I swallow the last drop of wine, put Maxx on the floor and stand, tucking my phone in the pocket of my shorts. Grabbing the empty plate, I step through the sliding glass door into the living room.

Maxx trails behind me into the kitchen.

The plate joins the other pots and utensils in the dishwasher. The sink and stove are wiped down, and the towel is hung up to dry.

I grab Maxx's leash and we go out for his final walk so he can relieve himself. Ten minutes later, we're back and ready to shut it down for the night.

Still no response from Carmen.

The built-in wine cooler hums as I kneel to remove the bottle of Sauvignon Blanc wine. This feature alone was enough to sell me on this apartment along with the covered parking, security-controlled access, and location.

The pungent scent of berries mixed with something acidic hits my nose while the liquid swirls in my glass. The smell induces the memory of sharing a bottle with Carmen. One of the few times we could go out for a meal. We were in France at the P&K offices for a training session. After the afternoon workshop, we snuck away to visit a winery.

Just the two of us.

We strolled through the vineyard hand in hand. We cuddled in the wine cellars for warmth with whispered promises of lustful activities to enjoy. And we sampled wines while going through a maze of grapevines. The wine tasting introduced us to this brand of wine. Carmen said it smelled like cat pee, but we both loved the flavor. It's been my favorite ever since.

I take out the bottle of Chablis Chardonnay. The buttery oak flavored wine is a perfect complement for seafood. The unopened bottle is returned to the cooler because it's only for special occasions. It's Carmen's favorite.

Maybe one day we'll get to open it. Glancing at my cell phone, that day is not looking good since there is still no response from Carmen.

"Let's go to bed, Maxx."

The usual nighttime check of locks and lights are performed. Maxx circles on his dog bed and then settles. I pull back covers and sink into my usually comfortable queen-size bed. It feels particularly lonely tonight.

I replace the book on the nightstand with my cell phone to charge and try to get engrossed in the latest Ta-Nehisi Coates novel.

The sudden blaring ringtone makes me drop the book in my haste to grab the phone. A 212-area code followed by a foreign number shows it isn't the call I'm expecting. I let the call roll over to voicemail and then play it back.

> Um, hey. Thought I'd take a chance and give you a call. I'm back in town. New York ran its course, so to speak. Um...I realized sometimes the best place is home. I hope you're doing well, and we can link up. So, call me when you get a chance...I'd love to see you.

Damn.

Leslie's voice, which could arouse me with her trademark "Um, hey" no longer has a hold on me. The sultry, sensual sound I really want to hear belongs to a woman with more baggage than an overbooked flight.

A rush of heat at the thought of Carmen causes me to kick away the covers. Even after the events of today and Carmen backing away from this relationship, I can feel her essence or spirit calling to me. She belongs with me.

I'm a patient man. If Carmen needs to end things for the moment, I won't push. Relaxing back under the sheets, my heartbeat lulls me to sleep with thoughts of Carmen back in my arms again.

Chapter Ten

Carmen

A glance up from my laptop and my heart quickens. Braxton stands in my office doorway.

"You wanted to see me, Mrs. Miller."

The man even makes the standard work attire of navy slacks, crisp white shirt, and tie look sexy. "Yes, come in and close the door."

He takes a few steps in but doesn't sit down and stands behind the visitor's chair. "I think it's best we leave the door open. Keep things professional."

I lean back in my chair, stunned. This is new.

"Did you finish the social media plan we discussed yesterday?" Shuffling the two pieces of paper on my desk helps me try to maintain command of this situation.

"Emailed you this morning." Braxton puts both hands in his pockets. He looks past me out the window at the pristine view of the parking garage next door.

Truthfully, his email was the first to be read, but I needed a reason to get him alone. After the disaster of last night with Melvin, a part of me wants to know that Braxton and I are okay. Even though I told him it's over, I need to maintain his friendship.

The walk around the desk to perch on the edge leaves only a few feet between us. "I wanted to congratulate you on getting into PK MAP. They notified the managers this morning. You'll get notice next week."

Braxton takes a deep breath and gifts me with a smile. "Thanks to you."

"No, it was all you. You really came through for us. Stepping in to assist on that presentation to the Board in Monaco."

"Yeah, Monte Carlo was some of my best work." Braxton licks his lips.

It really was. The mention of the district of Monaco takes me back to the scene of our first indiscretion. The ocean breeze, a hint of champagne, and Braxton's touch caused me to lean into that first kiss. Braxton has been making me crave him ever since.

We stare at each other, and the silence between us dances on an electric current that pulsates and twirls in the air. I clasp my hands to keep them from reaching out and losing every ounce of control I'm struggling to contain.

Braxton shuffles his feet and rubs a hand over his hair. He takes another deep breath. "Why didn't you respond to my text?"

His piercing gaze sees into my soul and the warmth I feel is like bathing in the rays from the sun. He knows the answer. He just wants me to say it.

I want to tell him I miss him, too. Want him to grab me and ravish me on top of the desk. Want to scream his name. Over and over again. I want him. All of him.

"I would like for us to remain friends." As soon as the words leave my mouth, I want to snatch them back.

"Friends, huh?" He grimaces and pats his chest. "If that's all I can have of you..."

"No matter what's happened between us, we still have to work together."

Braxton nods. His eyes say he's no more convinced than I am.

I return to my seat without embarrassing myself. My legs tremble as I collapse in the chair. "Let's schedule a time to get together. To discuss our next steps."

Braxton leans across my desk and winks. "We can do that. Or we can just go have a long lunch and work out our issues now."

A long lunch is code for meeting in a hotel room. The only issues that we'd work out would be which position to try and how many orgasms it takes to get to the center of my soul.

Warmth spreads between my thighs. That he still wants me brings delight. His hand snakes across the desk and his fingers trace my own. The energy between us sizzles like grease on a hot stove. It takes every ounce of strength to move my hand away.

"We can't do this," I whisper, repeating the mantra in my head: *I can't get him caught up in my mess. He deserves someone free to be with him out in the open.*

"I know. And I'm trying to do the right thing here and respect the new situation." Braxton's smile doesn't meet his eyes. "Do you want me to wait?"

I sigh, cross my legs, and follow his gaze to the divorce papers on my desk.

My early morning meeting with Maggie wasn't encouraging. Bottom line, California is a community property state, meaning all assets and debts are divided equally. I can prove that my home was a premarital asset, but knowing Melvin, he will fight for his share. Plus, his gambling debts may become my problem if he's amassed huge losses and used any assets to cover them. It will take time and resources to sort through everything. Maggie's last piece of advice was to maintain a lifestyle which won't be used against me.

Looking at Braxton, I know he could be used against me. That's exactly what I want. Him to wait. But I can't ask him to put things on pause while I continue in my sham of a marriage.

"I'm not asking you to do anything but your job." My fingers fly across the keyboard. "What time are you available to discuss the media plan?"

Braxton lifts an eyebrow. "Whatever time you say, Mrs. Miller."

He turns to walk out, and I stand to call his name. A knock on the door and Kayla sticks her head in. "Carmen, do you have a sec?"

"Sure." I slip on my professional mask and make my expression neutral. "Braxton was just leaving."

Kayla blocks Braxton's exit. "Hey, you," she says, and twirls a strand of hair around one claw-like finger. "When are we ever going to get you to join us after work? Thought you were coming yesterday."

"Something came up," Braxton mumbles and flicks a quick look at me.

Watching Kayla trying to engage Braxton in conversation is nearly painful.

Despite how many times she's been counseled by management on the appropriate way to dress for work, Kayla walks the line. Today, her most valued assets are on full display, and she practically shoves them in Braxton's face. Her form-fitting dress accents her curves and straddles the line between work and the club. *Young women try too damn hard.*

"You should at least come to lunch with your co-workers. You can't hang out with management all the time." Kayla touches Braxton's arm and her lashes flutter. "Give someone else a chance to impress the boss."

"Kayla, did you need something?" Hope she doesn't notice the edge to my voice, but I've enough of watching her antics.

She doesn't. Instead, she blinks as if she forgot they are standing in my office. Braxton takes the reprieve and dashes out.

Kayla watches him walk away with a look I recognize.

Lust.

"I'll just email you," she says to me over her shoulder as she hurries to catch up with Braxton.

Too. Damn. Hard.

Chapter Eleven

Braxton

Her words may have classified our relationship on the friend level, but this thing we have won't turn off that easily. I wasn't a chemistry major in school, but I know all about the laws of attraction. Every time I see her, my hands ache with the need to touch. My thoughts are fully tuned to every movement she makes, and my nerves seem to fire all at once.

But maybe she was communicating something more. My man Rumi has thoughts on friends that I can attest. He wrote that friendship goes beyond the heart and mind. It is the soul that survives them all. *The soul never stops or forgets, he wrote.*

My mind can't focus right now, so I walk past my desk and head toward the employee parking lot.

Kayla catches me at the elevator.

"Whew, slow down." She puts a lone hand on her chest in an exaggerated gesture. "What did boss lady do now to get you so heated?"

"I'm cool," I say and stab the down arrow.

"She did something." Kayla slides past me when the doors open. "You can tell me. We all have to suffer under her whims."

I'm in no mood for Kayla right now. But no way I'm letting her get away with disrespecting my lady. "She's actually the best mentor to have. Maybe you can learn something from her."

Kayla crosses her arms. "Don't tell me you actually like her."

I shrug, hoping the nonchalant posture won't betray my true feelings. "What's not to like? Strictly business wise, the woman is sharp. She had to be to advance as a woman of color in this company. You should be eager to learn from her."

"Sounds like you're a member of Carmen's fan club. But she can learn from me." Kayla's hands move to her hips. "She's always on me about the 'proper' way to appease a client. I have old man Sullivan in check."

Sullivan as in Sullivan Communications. Our marketing client on the East Coast. I was working with them until Carmen moved me to the Seduction campaign.

McAllister Sullivan is known for being uncooperative and supplying the bare minimum when it comes to feedback from our agencies. He only keeps the contract with P&K because of good old-fashioned nepotism. He's married to the daughter of one of the owners. The P in P&K, I think.

"All I had to do was meet with him one time," Kayla continues and details her recent trip to New York with Carmen. "I was able to get him alone and use my assets to make him to agree to all our terms."

I avoid eye contact by staring at a flyer displayed on the opposite wall. Carmen told me about that visit. Based on her assessment, Kayla was unprepared and resorted to flirting and flattering to make an impression on Sullivan. Carmen was going to write her up but was overruled by the higher ups when Sullivan gave Kayla rave reviews.

A response is avoided when the elevator dings, and a group enters the car. The blonde-haired woman requests the lobby, even though it's clearly illuminated on the panel. A visitor badge sways from one of the gentlemen's coat when he shakes it off and folds it over one arm.

Kayla and I are pressed against the wall so close I feel her breath on my neck. "You still didn't tell me what got you so twisted?"

"It's not work related. Just got some things on my mind."

"Sounds like you need a distraction. Know what I'm good at? Being a distraction." Kayla bats her long, fake eyelashes. Taking advantage of the opportunity to invade my personal space, she runs a finger down my arm.

"Listen," I begin the awkward conversation to let her down again when the elevator grinds to a halt, and the door squeaks from its opening.

Following the shuffling of feet, I maneuver around a man putting an obstacle in Kayla's path.

"I'll talk to you later," I toss over my shoulder and hurry past the guard station to head outside.

Kayla pouts, but she doesn't follow me.

First, Leslie calls out of the blue thanks to Mom and now Kayla is offering the goods. I've never been more popular.

It's nice to have options, but they pale in comparison to the one woman I want.

Chapter Twelve

Carmen

Burying myself in work means taking lunch at my desk. When my bladder is about to pop, I make the dreaded trek down the hall past Braxton's cubicle. I could go to the single bathroom that's closer to my office but the Executive Assistant, Ruth, uses that one and she has Irritable Bowel Syndrome. No one wants to follow her into an enclosed space after an episode of IBS. Especially since she refuses to utilize the air freshener I've discreetly placed there.

Laughter echoes down the freshly painted hallway, and I remember the days when I paid my dues in one of these smaller spaces. I breathe in the familiar scent of cardboard boxes and markers and march in time to the click of a stapler.

Braxton's cubicle is the last one on the left. It stands out in the sea of padded fabric that divides the walls. The cardinal and gold USC flag decorates one entire section. But it is the man himself that draws my attention.

He has the phone in one hand and scans the computer screen with the other. When our eyes connect, he swivels in his chair. Braxton gives me his back instead of the smile I've come to depend on. That's twice in twelve hours a man has done that.

Guess I've really ended things.

The door slams back on its hinges when I enter the bathroom. I lock myself in a stall, line the toilet seat, and plop down. *Get a grip. This is what you have to do.*

Two women enter. They keep up a steady stream of conversation. Their flushes don't cause them to miss a syllable. My plan is to sit quietly and wait them out. But then I figure out the subject of their gossip.

"There is no rule against dating co-workers," Kayla says. "I checked."

"I bet you did. But maybe the man has a girlfriend. Have you thought about that?"

Kayla and her friend are at the sink primping in the mirror when I walk out.

"Ladies." I wash my hands at the lone sink not blocked by their bodies. Kayla is studying me as though she needs to pass a science test and dissecting me will get her the best grade.

She puts the cap on her tube of bright red lipstick and turns to me. "Can I ask you a question?"

After grabbing some paper towels, I lean against the sink. "Sure. As long as it's work related."

"We were wondering about Braxton. You're his mentor too. Has he mentioned if he's seeing anyone?"

Crossing my arms, I peer down at the shorter woman. "How is that work related?"

She meets my stare and doesn't blink. "Well, he works with us, doesn't he?"

"Our relationship is strictly professional. We don't discuss our personal lives."

Kayla lifts a penciled eyebrow. "Maybe you can slide that in. Hook me up with that fine piece of man."

This little girl is working my nerves.

She makes a face and shrugs. "No disrespect, Carmen. But don't act like you hadn't noticed. I know you married and all but you ain't blind."

Kayla's curly-haired friend nudges her. She must work in another department because I would know her name if she worked in Marketing. Whatever her name is, she must recognize Kayla has crossed a line. Unfortunately, Ms. Fass & Nosy, like my mother would say, is oblivious and raises her chin in a challenge.

I crumble the paper towel in my hand, wishing it was Kayla's shirt, and toss it into the trash. Checking my reflection in the mirror gives me pause before turning to face Kayla. "I think it would be better for you to focus on the agency feedback I gave you. We're going to discuss it later this week."

Kayla absorbs the iciness in my tone and her expression changes from hesitation back to defiance. "I got it. I got it." She turns to her friend. "I'll just have to make the first move. The brother is not taking the hint."

They leave and I grip the sink to steady myself while swearing under my breath. All the ways in which I could sabotage Kayla's career flash through my mind. The thought of having her outside the company door makes me smile.

My jaw unclenches, and my shoulders relax. This is the price I pay for getting involved with someone at work. My feelings can't compromise all the strides I've made on the job. I earned my current position by having laser sharp focus on the work.

Braxton and I have a connection, even though things are now complicated. Competing with younger women isn't necessary. As Shug Avery said in the Color Purple - "I's married now".

Damn shame I have to remind myself of that fact. Getting through this divorce with my reputation and child intact will take all my willpower. I told Braxton I wanted us to remain friends, but my heart wants much more than that.

Chapter Thirteen

Braxton

She walks by my cubicle, and my body responds on its own. The agency contact on the other end of the phone is rambling on about consumer feedback, but like a magnet, all my senses are heightened in her presence.

My natural reaction is to drink in Carmen's physical form as it glides by. The woman is pure perfection, from the curve of her hips to the fullness of her lipstick-stained lips. The navy-blue wrap dress she's wearing is screaming for me to take it off.

Then I remember.

Turning my chair back to the computer screen helps me refocus. But her scent, a calming essence mixed with vanilla, lingers long after she disappears around the corner.

"Mom." Tossing my keys in the yellow ceramic bowl on the wooden console table by the front door, I unhook Maxx's leash and look around for my mother. Dad called me on his way to a meeting with the other deacons at their church, so I know he's not here.

I walked into my apartment after work, and the emptiness of the evening stretched before me. A quick change of clothes and Maxx and I were out the door. Called Mom on the way and she promised to have a plate of her famous homemade lasagna ready for me.

There's no answer to my greeting, so my nose follows the scent of oregano, tomatoes, and basil to the kitchen. Maxx pads beside me, but we both stop at the entrance.

"Hey, baby." Mom stands from her chair at the table and makes a game show hostess flourish. "Look who stopped by."

Mom is a lot of things. Generous. Nurturing. Bossy. One thing she isn't is an actress. The setup is reflected in the nervous burst of laughter she releases and how she busies herself wiping nonexistent crumbs from the table.

"Hello, Braxton." Leslie puts down her fork and smiles. "Your Mother was kind enough to offer to feed an unexpected visitor."

No, the acting is Oscar worthy from the woman I once thought would be my forever. I surmise her pursuit of the stage was worth breaking my heart.

Surprise glues me to the spot.

Leslie Adams still sports the "girl next door" look, which made her the most popular girl in our high school class. Her long, black, shoulder length hair frames a sienna-colored face. The wide brown eyes appraise me from head to toe. She's probably comparing the boy she used to know to the man standing in the doorway who still hasn't responded to her voice mail.

"Now you know better." Mom breaks the awkward silence. "That dog can't come in my kitchen."

Maxx wags his tail as all eyes turn toward him. Whenever we come home, Maxx knows not to enter this room. There is a blanket for him stored in the laundry room.

"You have a dog? He's cute." Leslie walks around the table, but before she can kneel, fur rises on Maxx's back and he stiffens.

That snaps me out of the trance. "Come on, boy."

Maxx follows me into the next room, where I rub him between the ears. "Good dog. I don't trust this situation either."

Returning to the kitchen doorway, I watch my mom and Leslie work side by side at the sink. They always shared a certain mother/daughter bond. Leslie lost her mother when she was thirteen years old and before we moved into the neighborhood. Mom and Debra couldn't be in the same room without tension brewing beneath the surface. When we began dating, it was understandable Leslie and mom would be drawn to each other.

"What's a guy got to do to get some of that famous lasagna? I braved the 110 on a Friday night to get here, lady."

Mom laughs at my teasing and dries her hands on a dish towel. "Poor baby had to sit in traffic on the interstate. Small sacrifice to see your mother."

I assume my usual chair at the well-worn wooden dining table, almost drooling in anticipation. Mom places a covered dish in front of me and hovers as I peel back the foil. The first bite is almost orgasmic as the flavors collide across my tongue.

"It was worth the drive." I salute Mom with my fork and continue to shovel noodles and cheese into my mouth.

Mom rubs the back of my head and plants a kiss. "Let me get out of here and let you kids catch up."

The food lodges in my throat, along with the uncomfortable silence.

"Um, well this is awkward." Leslie runs her palms down the legs of her skinny jeans. Something she used to do whenever she was nervous. "It's been a long time."

I watch her over the rim of the glass as I drink some iced tea to swallow an errant piece of Italian sausage.

"Are you going to say anything? Or continue to ignore me?" Leslie folds both arms across her yellow t-shirt with the quote 'Acting is my Superpower' emblazed across the front and frowns.

There used to be a time when seeing her looking sad would spur me into action. I wait to feel something. Anything. My past is staring me in the face, and I can't even muster up the anger I carried for months after she left.

"What do you want me to say?"

Leslie drops her arms. She looks everywhere but at me. "I thought we could...maybe you could start by saying hello."

Taking a deep breath, I push back from the table and stand. "Alright, hello."

"Was that so hard?" Leslie reaches for the plate and returns to the sink. "Remember the first time I made you dinner in this kitchen? Your parents were away, and we had the place to ourselves. Mrs. Hannah gave me her recipe for mac and cheese, but when I tried it..."

"It turned out dry." I finish the trek down the faded memory, then ask, "What are you trying to do here?"

"What do you mean? Simply catching up with an old friend," Leslie places the rinsed plate in the metal dish rack.

Leaning against the counter, I raise an eyebrow.

She blushes and looks away. "You could always see through my act."

Now it's my turn to fold my arms. "So, what's this all about? You're blowing up my phone now. Funny how I couldn't get a return call when you left."

Six years ago, Leslie ended our relationship with promises to call before she got on a plane to New York. After a week without hearing from her, my mind raced with different scenarios, each one worse than the one before. Once two weeks passed, I visited her father. He assured me she was fine, only getting her bearings in a new city. Another three weeks went by before she called, and I struggled to rein in my anger.

While she gushed about the part she got in an Off-Off Broadway play, her tiny apartment and getting lost on the subway, I paced back and forth in my bedroom. Photos on my dresser captured us at various times. High school prom. Road trip to Vegas. College graduation.

Leslie and Braxton. Braxton and Leslie. We'd been together so long you rarely saw one without the other.

"What the hell, Leslie?" I erupted, cutting off her diatribe praising all things New York.

"Don't be mad, B," she said. "I told you I wanted to focus on getting situated here."

"Understand focus. Not ignoring."

The silence on the other end of the line spoke volumes. I replayed the myriad of conversations we had before she left. There was no reason she couldn't pursue acting in Hollywood, but she insisted on making it in New York. The place where no one knew her as the pastor's daughter. Or a longtime girlfriend.

I was planning our future, and she was planning an escape.

Leslie draws my attention back to the present by tugging my shirt. "I was hoping we could be friends. We used to be good friends."

It's true we used to be great friends. Omar and Leslie were the only people in my orbit. Moving around from base to base with a military father made making friends hard or not worth the bother, since we always moved in a year or two. By the time I started high school, Pops was ready to retire, which meant we got to settle in El Segundo.

"Why now?" I take a step back. Her scent, a blend of mint and something floral, tries to stir a long dormant attraction. "You only came back to care for your dad. Aren't you going back to New York?"

Leslie crosses to the table and slides into a chair. "Dad's heart attack brought me home, but I've been thinking about moving back for a while now."

"Really?" A tilt of my head conveys my disbelief. Leslie's career may have slowed in recent years, but she got steady work. There were a few months when I couldn't avoid seeing her face in a national commercial on television. I knew about the sitcom where she played the recurring role of best friend to the main star. My Mom kept me up to date on the soap opera role until her character was killed off. She even landed a part in a few independent movies, though she was never the main character. Either she never caught the big break which would bring her back to Hollywood or she purposely avoided anything that would film here.

Leslie traces a finger along the lemon-colored vinyl placemat. "Yes, really. Sometimes you realize the thing you're searching for is something you already had."

The implication hangs between us. She lowers her head and looks up through long eyelashes. My face is a mask. There was a time when I ached to hear her say something along those lines and return to me. That time has passed.

Before I can respond, Mom appears. "Look what I found."

In her hand is an old VHS video. The label has faded with time, but I instantly recognize the blue and gold Eagle high school logo. Junior year. Leslie talked me into taking a drama class, although it didn't take much convincing. I would have done anything to spend time with her. At the end of the semester, we put on a play for the entire school.

"OMG," Leslie squeals. "My first starring role. I can't believe you kept this."

Mom beams. "Of course, I kept it. When the pastor announced his daughter would be in the production, the whole church came out to support. I got to see my son and his girlfriend up on that stage. Everyone knew right away you were going to make it big."

It was evident to me while watching from the wings of the stage that Leslie had talent. I don't remember the name of the play, but the character she played had this soliloquy where she took center stage. The spotlight shone on her and she captivated more than the audience that night. I thought we would be the high school couple that married after graduation, like my parents. Leslie may have chased her dream, but my heart was the casualty. It took months to get over her. This mini reunion only proves it was for the best.

"Well, Maxx and I need to hit the road."

Both women stop talking and say, "No" at the same time.

"You don't have to hurry," Mom recovers first. "It's so nice to see you and Leslie catch up."

Crossing to kiss her on the forehead, I whisper in her ear, "Thanks for dinner, but I know what you're trying to do."

Her eyes widen, then her brows furrow. Recognizing that look, I know this won't be the end of her meddling.

"How about you walk Leslie home?" Mom asks, loud enough for the entire house to hear it.

Didn't make it three seconds before Leslie starts gathering Tupperware containers. "That will be nice."

Shaking my head, I call for Maxx to come and walk outside. It seems the conversation that should've taken place years ago will be addressed now.

The neighborhood hasn't changed much over the years. Some families may have moved on, but the houses are mostly well maintained along with the lawns. My car is parked along the tree-lined street, and I attach Maxx's leash for the walk.

Leslie joins me on the sidewalk, and I automatically reach for the bag to carry it. We set out on the path I've walked a million times before.

"It was so sweet of your mother to send food over for Dad. He loves her lasagna," Leslie says. "The doctors said he's recovering nicely. I even got him to walk over here last week."

"Good to hear the Pastor is recovering." Mom has been giving me regular updates. The heart attack happened during a nightly Bible Study. One of the members is a registered nurse and began the lifesaving procedure, giving the ambulance a chance to get there.

"Hey, I wonder if Mrs. McCall still lives here." Leslie nods toward the white siding house with an American flag attached to the porch. The flower beds contain an array of colorful plants. Mrs. McCall was an older Hispanic woman who ran a small store out of her garage. It used to be the first stop on the way to school to get snacks for the day.

"No, Mom said her kids took her to live with them in San Diego."

Maxx stops to sniff around the stop sign at the corner.

We turn and continue up a gradual incline. Leslie rambles on about the weather and other families in the neighborhood. Glancing over at her, I try to imagine the life we could have had. Her face is animated as she changes the subject and describes an audition for a role on Broadway.

"Why did you leave me?"

Leslie stumbles and catches herself against a utility pole. "I didn't leave you. I went to New York to pursue my dream."

"Maybe I was dreaming when a certain someone finally returned a call to say it was over."

Maxx takes advantage of the grassy area around the pole and relieves himself. He looks up at me and I rub his head with approval.

This entire conversation is dredging up long dormant feelings that are best left in the past. My mind races with memories of a first love and I feel exposed, as if she can see the tears she made in my heart.

"No, I know I didn't handle that well." Leslie starts walking without making eye contact. "But I thought it was for the best."

We stop outside her house. The white stucco with brown trim looks exactly the same. A wooden fence encloses the front yard with a gate leading to the back.

"The best for who?" Laughter escapes like a bark, causing Maxx to mimic the sound and wag his tail.

Leslie glances at the two cars in the driveway. "Looks like Dad's nurse is still here, or I would invite you in. He would love to see you."

"That's okay," I say, shaking off any thought of getting an answer to my question. "Maxx and I need to hit the road."

I turn to go back, and Leslie takes my arm. Her face flushes and she fidgets from one foot to the other. "The truth is, I did leave you when I went to New York. I felt...suffocated here."

"Wow, suffocated?" I step back, almost tripping over Maxx's leash to get away from her touch.

Leslie shakes her head. "Maybe that's not the right word, but I needed to get away from the expectations of being a preacher's kid."

My shoulders relax. "I can understand that." The life of a PK can be stifling. The constant pressure to be perfect is applied by an entire congregation.

"And being your girl." Leslie sees me tense up and talks fast. "We were so young, and it felt like you were ready to settle down and get married. I wasn't ready for it then."

She's right. I was ready to get married, but we didn't have to do it right away. I wasn't working at Parker & Kramer then. My first job after college graduation was as a temporary glorified assistant with a smaller marketing company, but I knew it was the first step for my career.

"Thanks for finally being straight up with me." Her admission resolves something long dormant inside. The reason Carmen is my first serious relationship since Leslie is my inability to fully trust someone. She taught me it was best to leave them before they found a reason to leave. My guard was lowered with a married woman. Analyzing what that says about my emotional state will occupy me back down the 405.

I'm two houses down when Leslie calls after me. "Hey, um, I was wondering if I call you later, will you answer the phone?"

Chapter Fourteen

Carmen

Saturday morning, I'm up early and out the door. Melvin is going to his mother's and Olivia, who adores Nana, begged to tag along. I take advantage of the rare free weekend and track down my friend Gayle. R & B songs drift in from 94.7 - The Wave as the BMW cruises 'over the hill' to the Beverly Center.

The escalator up from the parking garage takes only seconds and I'm gliding through the sliding doors. The soothing background music does not match my sullen mood.

Gayle, the one person to trust with this burden and vent to, is in the Dolce & Gabbana store, modeling a pair of polka dot sandals. She has changed little from the girl I met freshmen year in orientation. Replace the expensive shoes she now wears with Converse sneakers; beige linen slacks for sweatpants and her new sleek bob with box braids, and you have the same girl. She started as my roommate at UCLA and grew into my best friend.

"Looking good, Dr. Peters." I move a stack of boxes out of a chair and claim a seat near the clerk, who hovers close by.

"Living good, Mrs. Miller." Gayle winks and twirls in front of the mirror. "This must be serious if you came across town to see little old me. What is it you always say?"

"I don't leave my footprint on the weekends." A mantra that means no one likes the traffic in LA. Like the natives, who avoid major highways on the weekends for sanity's sake. "But this required a face to face."

Gayle slips off a shoe and points it at me. "What can top being blindsided and not getting your promotion? Dish it, bitch."

My cringe is a natural reaction. Gayle throws the word 'bitch' around like a term of endearment. The salesperson's ivory skin reddens, and I smile.

"How about you wrap up your transaction first?"

Gayle purchases three pairs of heels and we exit the store and walk toward Bloomingdale's. The yeasty smell of fresh pretzels wafts from Wetzel's and my stomach growls.

"Let's grab brunch at Toast."

My favorite restaurant is a few blocks down 3rd Street. The weather is a sunny seventy degrees, so we leave our cars and walk.

A small group mingles at the entrance but we luck up and get a table for two right away. After we order our usual mix of scrambles, turkey sausage for Gayle and pork bacon for me, we get coffee and a pancake to share.

"I slept with someone new." The words tumble out in a rush. "So, does this mean I'm having an affair? I think I'm having an affair."

Gayle adds creamer to her coffee and stirs it slowly. Like I didn't just confess to the worst sin a married person can commit. "Good. It was only a matter of time before you met someone better. Told you those divorce papers were a good thing, right?"

I'm unable to suppress my flinch and twist the napkin on my lap. "Why would you say that?"

"Face it. You married down." Gayle takes a sip, looking at me over the rim. "I knew you'd get bored, eventually."

Now, I'm speechless. My girl is the reason I met Melvin. Gayle's family was everything my family wasn't. Big. Loud. Loving. I jumped at every opportunity to be around them. The annual family barbecue that year offered a respite from the long hours I was putting in forging my path at the company. Plus, I was hoping Gayle's cute cousin Paul would be there. Months had passed since the word date and my name were in the same sentence.

When I arrived, the backyard was swarming with people. Kids ran through the sprinkler in one corner and the grill was smoking in the other. The music was blasting, and people busted a move between tables filled with trays of food and the makeshift bar. Gayle's mother took the pound cake out of my hands and planted a kiss on my cheek. I offered to help, but Gayle swooped in and pulled me aside. "Okay, Paul's not here."

My heart sank at the chance to spend time with the only handsome, single and employed cousin in the family was out the window.

"But I got you." Gayle gestured to a group of men congregated near the bottles of rum, cans of soda, and a keg of beer. "Uncle David brought a friend. He's single with no kids. A little older than you like, but I figured he can get the job done and knock some of the dust off your lady parts."

I elbowed her in the side. "I'm not desperate. Just been busy."

"Whatever, bitch," she shot back. "Your career is going gangbusters, but you can't replace heartache with work. You have mourned 'Him Who Shall Not Be Named' long enough."

A twinge ran down my spine at the memory of my ex-fiancé, Daryl, and my scalp itched. "Why did you have to bring him up? I was in a good mood."

Gayle feigned innocence. "That's what I mean. He shouldn't be affecting moods anymore. It's almost been a year. I told you I was going to hook you up and there's a contender out here."

She tried to ignore my death stare, then crossed her arms and stared back. It was too hot outside to prolong this conversation. Especially when a breeze blew the scent from the grilled food my way. "You make me sick."

Gayle ignored by comment and grabbed my hand. "I know."

She led us through the throngs of family to the card table and stopped beside a tall, husky brother with a complexion the color of golden-brown biscuit fresh from the oven. "Look who finally arrived. This is Carmen."

He turned and hit me with a sly grin that would win my heart. "I'm Melvin. You're going to be my partner."

"Excuse me?" I took a step back.

"Spades partner." Melvin raised both brows. "You do know how to play the game, right?"

"Yes." I folded my arms across my chest. No one dared question my card playing skills.

His eyes shone with promise. "Good. 'Cause I got to prove to my man over here that he ain't got no game. And seeing how you're the only woman here not related to this clan, I can trust you not to throw the game."

Striking my superhero pose with hands on hips, my brows furrowed. "I play to win."

He nodded and those full lips lifted even higher. "Me too, young lady. Me too."

We made excellent partners that day. A successful game led to us spending the rest of the night talking about everything from Melvin's love of sports to the popular action movies he introduced me to. When we delved into views on family, I was intrigued by a man who knew he wanted kids and wasn't looking to play games in a relationship. After that day, it was a whirlwind of daily phone calls and nightly dates.

Melvin asked me to marry him three months later. The overwhelming chemistry wasn't there, but he was a good man offering the thing I longed for. Marriage and children. Time was ticking.

"Now don't get all quiet on me," Gayle's breathy voice brings me back to the present. "I didn't say that to make you feel bad."

The perky waitress returns, interrupting my response, and places our food on the table with the flourish of a game show host. "Enjoy, ladies."

Once she turns her attention to a man snapping his fingers for more coffee at the next booth, I dismiss Gayle's comment with a wave and grab the pepper shaker. "It's okay. I'm fine. Just thinking about marriage and the choices we make, you know?"

"Believe me, I know." Gayle slathers butter on the blueberry pancake. "Marriage is something you have to work on every day. Like this shit is hard sometimes. You remember the hours of therapy we went through when Wayne confessed he cheated?"

My girl is preaching the truth. I nod as the first bite of the fluffy golden eggs crosses my lips. They spent half a year going to couples counseling.

"But since we're sharing messed up marriage stories, I can admit to my affair last year."

A piece of egg lodges in the wrong place. Coughing clears my airways. "What?" I croak. Gulping coffee helps push the food down, while ignoring the burning in my throat. "And you didn't tell me?"

Gayle shakes her head. "Girl, I didn't know how to tell you. Still had to process it myself first." She looks down at her plate. "Plus, I didn't want you to judge me."

"I would never do that. You know that, right?" I reach for her hand and her eyes water before she takes a napkin to dab at the corners.

"You wouldn't. I know. I judged myself. It's a horrible thing to do to someone you love, but I had to get his back for his mistake." Gayle sniffs and adjusts her eyeglasses.

"Does Wayne know?" A couple settles at the table behind us. Lowering my voice, I ask, "Are you thinking of leaving?"

"Of course not." Gayle cuts the pancake in half and butter drips off the sides. A reminder that she can get away with all the fattening stuff and still maintain a size six figure. "Wayne and I are good now. Besides, it would tear him apart if he knew and wouldn't take back what I did. This burden I'll carry alone as my secret. Most of the time, I'm happily married. We have the twins and a life together. I'm not trying to go anywhere."

The second bite of eggs manages to get down without strangling me. "I can understand that. I'm feeling some type of way that you didn't tell me, though."

Gayle drops her fork and takes both her hands in mine. "Don't get in your feelings. I'm sorry. Just didn't want you to look at me different."

I slap her hand away. "We used to live together, remember?" My girl went through a whole trifling ways phase. We both did.

Only favor saved us from negative consequences. There was a time we broke into Gayle's ex boyfriend's apartment to get evidence of his cheating. Or the time we spent the night before finals getting wasted while 'studying'. Still passed exams, although we were so hung over afterwards we stayed in our room for two days.

"Yeah, but I'm a respectable doctor and mother now. I'm your role model." Gayle sits up straight in the chair, purses her lips and peers at me over her glasses like a librarian chastising a child with overdue fees.

That makes me laugh. "Whatever. You just need to give me the details. I'll tell if you tell."

While we finish our meal, Gayle shares how she went to the annual ophthalmologist conference in New York. The man of the night was a presenter on the program and a professor at Duke University School of Medicine. They became acquainted at the Meet the Faculty Reception and spent the entire weekend exploring the city and each other.

"Do you plan to see him again?"

Gayle shakes her head. "Never. It was a onetime fling." She pauses before adding, "I needed to do something just for me, you know? At least that's what I tell myself."

I lean back and think about that for a second. "So, things between you and Wayne..."

"Are good."

Tilting my head and narrowing my eyes, the question must be asked again. "Really?"

Gayle nods so fast she looks like a boat caught in a hurricane. "I know it sounds like some typical bored suburban wife mess, but I like my life. Sometimes you have to settle for what you already have, right?" She shrugs and swirls a piece of sausage in the syrup. She seems to have a handle on things, and it makes me wish I could dismiss my indiscretion so easily.

"Your turn. And don't leave out any details." Gayle motions with her hands for me to tell the story.

My fork is positioned on the edge of my plate, signaling my need to unburden my spirit. From beginning to end, it feels good to tell someone else. I start with that first kiss in Monaco, which was a combination of weeks of working together on the "Seduction" campaign and getting to know the man. Being there with Braxton, the ocean breeze and the hint of the forbidden led to a memorable night of talking and getting to know each other. I conclude the story with the events from yesterday and how things ended.

"Uh, uh. You in trouble, girl."

"What do you mean?"

Gayle waits until the waitress clears the table. "You messed around and fell for the guy?"

"Don't be silly," I say, trying to keep a straight face. "What makes you think that?"

"The way you say his name." Gayle clasps her hands together, bats her eyelashes, and in a breathy whisper says, "Braxton, my sex slave. You make me want to divorce my husband and run to your bed."

I wave her off. "You're crazy."

"I'm crazy?" Gayle places her hand over a perfect B cup bosom. "No, ma'am. You're crazy. See, you can't even cheat right. I had a one-night stand out of town with a man I'll never see again."

"What does that have to do with anything?" I toss my napkin on the table. My girlfriend was supposed to give advice, not a lecture.

Gayle rolls her eyes and lifts an index finger. "First, I'm glad you finally got some good sex. You deserve to be set free after the mediocre loving you've had to endure all these years. "

Another finger goes up. "Second, you're allowed to do something for yourself. If punk ass Melvin wants to play dirty, then we'll get in the mud." And yet another finger, "But aren't you moving a little too fast? He's single with nothing to lose, and you still have Melvin in your house."

Nothing to lose.

My stomach's full of good food, but I suddenly feel empty. How can I fight Melvin when the rules change?

"I broke it off so none of that matters."

Gayle studies my face for several moments. "Doesn't matter, huh? Bitch, you can lie to yourself, but you can't lie to me."

Dismissing Gayle's comment, I shift my hips in the chair. "Are you ready to go? Where's the waitress with the check?" I look around, trying to make eye contact with our server.

"So, what are you going to do?" Gayle doesn't go for my attempt to change the subject.

Staring into space, the truth of the matter elicits a heavy sigh. "It's like you said. I'm moving too fast, and I'm still married. Maybe I should focus on making things work. Olivia deserves a complete family."

Gayle peers at me over her glasses. "Are you *that* woman? You'll use your child to stay in an unhappy relationship?"

"I'm not using Olivia. It's called being an adult and making sacrifices for the benefit of raising a happy child. Like you said, maybe I should settle for what I already have."

Melvin is far from perfect, but he did choose me. At least in the beginning. Maybe the money issues is a sign to give us another chance. He never has to know about Braxton.

The server appears and asks if we need anything else before leaving the check. Dishes rattle and the smell of fresh baked chocolate chip cookies make my mouth water even after finishing my meal.

Gayle crosses her arms. "You're a mother, not a martyr."

Every cell within me goes rigid. "Whoa. Where did that come from?"

"Your mother. You sound like Katherine."

The room spins, and it takes a few minutes to regain focus. My mother's constant belief was spoken often during my childhood. 'Children need their fathers in the house.' My own father decided he wouldn't be there, so Mom went out and found a replacement. A stepfather to fill in for a non-engaged biological one. Not that he was any better.

"This is different." Mentally removing any comparison to my mother is a challenge. "I can't upend my daughter's life for a new relationship. Who knows if things would even work out? Besides, Melvin will flip out if he learns I'm seeing someone new."

Gayle sips her coffee and glares at me.

"Don't give me that look. I know what I'm doing." The waitress leaves the bill folder on the edge of the table and I rummage in my purse for my wallet.

"I can't believe it," Gayle says, her tone surprised. "You actually think you can make this thing into something real." She laughs and leans back in her chair.

My stomach clenches. Truth just did a sneak attack and delivered a full body blow. I'm frozen in the realization that I want Braxton in a real way. Gayle is right. And she can't be right.

"Hey, don't get all quiet now." Gayle picks up the dessert menu. "Think I'll get some cookies for the kids. You want to order something?"

"Alright. You win. Bitch," I snarl through clenched teeth.

Gayle raises an eyebrow, impressed that I finally used her word.

"Your marriage is good and mine isn't," I growl. "You can cheat and still have a good, boring marriage while mine blows up. Guess you showed me."

"It's not a contest," Gayle says and looks around. My outburst has attracted some attention, but I don't care.

The money in my hand is tossed onto the table. "With you, everything's a contest."

Having said the last word, I turn and march out the door, pretending not to hear Gayle's last comment.

"You need to stop lying to yourself, girlfriend. Your marriage may be over, but you need to focus on yourself and not some new man."

Chapter Fifteen

Braxton

Weekends are the worst. After seeing her five days a week, thinking about Carmen at home with *him* can drive me insane. So, I don't.

After dropping Maxx at the groomers, the gym is the focus. The former warehouse, turned boxing gym, is located between an auto body shop and a building materials store. I love the simplistic nature of this space. No fancy slogans or classes. In this place, the three boxing rings dominate the center of the floor. Scattered around are heavy bags, weight benches, and free weights. The mirror lining the length of one wall is cracked in some spots and peeling in others. The smell of sweat and bleach combine and circulate through the air with metal industrial fans, which wobble with each rotation.

I place earbuds in my ears to drown out the sounds of shouts, metal clanging, and other chatter. My workout mix is set to play while I wrap my hands and warm up by shadow boxing for five minutes. From there, I do fifty jumping jacks. After a brief rest, I'm on the floor to crank about at least fifty pushups and roll over to do fifty crunches. Three rounds of this and sweat is pouring. Frustration still simmers beneath the surface, and I pace back and forth while lacing up the gloves. The heavy bag absorbs each jab, cross and hook punch. I need to resolve this thing with Carmen. How can I live without her? How can she choose him over me?

And does Leslie want to reconnect after all this time? Our conversation trended friendly, but there's an undercurrent to her words. I used to be able to read her emotions. Now it feels like getting to know a stranger.

The bass booms through my ear buds in time with each strike of the bag. My arms feel like noodles after thirty minutes of grueling work.

I collapse on the bench and lower my head into my hands. Taking deep breaths helps to slow my heart rate. When I look up, a mountain of a man stands in front of me with his beefy arms crossed.

Shaking off the gloves and removing the ear buds, I stand. "Lieutenant Colonel Monroe."

He's able to maintain the grimace, but a smile threatens to break through, and he pulls me into a bear hug.

"Come here, nephew," he says, pounding my back and then holding me at arm's length.

"What's up, Unc."

Lieutenant Colonel Clarence Monroe is not a blood relative, but he is Pops' oldest and dearest friend. They grew up together, joined the Air Force, and served together until retirement. Pops is an only child and Monroe has filled in as a surrogate uncle who was present at every childhood milestone. He's the owner of this gym and was the one to train me and Bernie on boxing techniques.

"I can't call it," he says and fakes a punch that I easily dodge.

"Take it easy, old man," I bounce on my toes. "You don't want any of this."

He dismisses my boast with a raised fist. "Saw you tearing up that heavy bag. It doesn't hit back. One lick of this and you'll be on the floor."

It's the truth. My jaw aches with the memory of Monroe's famous right hook connecting during our last sparring session. He may have slowed down from his prime, but that punch can still be lethal.

I grab a towel out of my gym bag and wipe my face. "How are things going? Business seems to be good."

A group of teenagers announces their entrance in a whirl of shouts and catcalls. One of the trainers corral them around the far-right ring.

"The boxing clinic you suggested seem to be popular with the young'uns. At least it gives them something to do besides run the streets." Unc's knees crack when he sits on the bench.

"Young'uns? Man, you been in Cali too long to still speak Southern."

Monroe was born and raised in Alabama like Pop. He grunts like a bear and shakes his shiny bald head.

"What got you out here pounding my bags like you got something on your mind, anyway?"

I lean against the wall to stretch my calves and hamstrings. "Just getting my exercise in."

When I turn around, Monroe hits me with his death stare. The one he uses on knuckleheads that come in here thinking they're Rocky Balboa and trying to dominant ring time. He calls it his bullshit detector.

Since my hands are still wrapped, I hit the heavy bag. Monroe gets up after one failed effort and holds the bag steady.

"Don't drop that left. Lead with your hips."

Adjusting my stance, I land a blow that pushes Monroe back.

He nods his approval.

"Why didn't you ever get married?" I ask between punches.

"Never met the right woman," he answers, then turns to shout instructions across the gym.

Now I shoot him a stare.

He throws up both hands. "Alright, you want to get real? I never married because the woman I loved...she had her eyes on someone else."

"And you never met anybody new?"

Monroe steps back from the bag and releases a hearty laugh. "Now you know the ladies love me."

"Yeah, you're a real chick magnet."

"Trying to keep up with you, playboy." He motions for me to continue hitting. "Got to be woman problems got you pounding the bag like this."

I drop my hands and step back. "Man, it's like you said. I love a woman...that has someone else."

"Chin up, young blood," Monroe says and places one large paw on my shoulder. He lowers his voice. "You know what they say. If you can't be with the one you love..."

"Yeah, I know." The conversation has taken a serious turn and I'm ready for it to be over.

"Settle for whoever you can get." Monroe's roaring laugh causes a few guys to stop and look our way.

I knock his hand away. "You got jokes."

"Don't worry 'bout it, nephew. Serious talk, if this gal can't see what you putting down, you might need to let her go."

My mind knows this to be true, but the heart wants her, which leaves me dealing with messy emotions I would rather avoid. "Thanks, Unc."

Satisfied that he's solved my problem, Monroe yells across the gym, "Who think they can land a punch on my boy, right here?"

Choking on water I'm guzzling, I protest. "I just did an hour-long workout, and you want to put me in the ring?"

"Aw, you can handle these chumps. Besides, I know you still thinking about your situation. You need to work out all that frustration. No better way than knocking a young punk on his ass."

The guys that came in earlier are shadow boxing and bouncing around, hyping themselves up. Leaning my head to each side, I rotate my shoulders. Monroe is right. Maybe schooling these boys will take my mind off Carmen.

"Hand me my gloves."

Chapter Sixteen

Carmen

Focus on yourself and not some new man.

I smack the steering wheel and maneuver my vehicle onto the ramp as Gayle's words follow me back down the 405. She has some nerve trying to get me to admit to something this life changing. Melvin has issues, but it's a big decision to walk away and uproot Olivia's life. It's not like my situation with Braxton could dare be called love.

Besides, it's over now. I did the right thing and ended it.

When the Bluetooth screen lights up, I push the answer button before it announces the caller. I knew Gayle would apologize.

"Had your sister look for flights on that internet." My mother's Jamaican lilt flows through the car stereo speakers like a wave and extinguishes my anger.

Mom isn't one for small talk. She launches into every conversation without a greeting. "The little one is still coming for summer break?"

"Yes." I clear my throat and speak, clearly falling into old habits. "Olivia is coming."

"Good. I already have plans to teach my girl how to make fried plantains."

Second only to applesauce, Olivia loves plantains. But only the ones prepared by her grandma.

"We have plenty of time to buy the ticket, you know. Summer is still a good five months away."

The background noise changes from the blare of the television to the ticking of the old grandfather clock that stands in the house's foyer. I picture Mother sweeping through the compact three-bedroom home I grew up in Columbia, South Carolina, doing her Saturday morning cleaning. The woman is never still for long. Mom is constantly in motion, moving from one area to the next. I've only witnessed her rest longer than seven minutes when she retires for the night.

"You know I don't like to wait until the last second," Mom continues. Now there's water running in the kitchen sink. The dishes clatter as Mom gives me a rundown on the happenings at home.

She tells me that Ray is finally going to retire this year. Ray is the man she married to have a father in the house. She once confessed she married him because of his 'shine head'. Her way of saying she was attracted to his bald head. I later learned she was trying to replace my birth father with one that chose to be there.

"That's good for Ray," I reply and switch lanes to pass a brown VW beetle spewing toxic fumes.

"I still don't know why you never call the man 'Dad'. Him raised you up along with your sister."

For ten years it was me and Mom. My own father appearing and leaving so quickly, he could have been a mirage. And then Raymond 'Ray' Washington gave Mom the ring my father didn't.

Mom introduced me to my new baby sister and her new husband on the same day. I knew her growing belly meant a baby was in there, but I didn't associate that with having a live-in dad.

Having a man in the house required some adjustment. I had to learn not to climb into bed with Mom in the middle of the night anymore. His razors cluttered the bathroom counter, and the stench of cigarette smoke hung on his clothes.

Cassandra was about three or four months the day Ray set me straight. I was 'helping' Mom change the baby. Helping consisted of me making faces to get Cassie to laugh and handing Mom whatever item she needed.

"Run tell your Dad that we're almost ready. Tell him to put the car seat in the van," Mom says.

I found Ray in his usual spot, outside on the carport, smoking a cigarette. This area was his hangout since he wasn't allowed to smoke in the house. He was sitting on a lawn chair in the corner where he kept a small table to hold his ashtray and a boombox that he blasted Motown hits.

"Dad," I said, after jumping down the three steps from the kitchen door. "Mom said put the car seat in the van."

Ray blew a smoke ring and stubbed out the butt. He beckoned for me to come stand in front of him. After a glance toward the door, he leaned in so close I could see his nose hairs.

"I don't want there to be any confusion now. I'm going to always take care of you cause you're Kat's daughter. But you don't need to call me Dad."

My stomach curled and it wasn't from the smoke on his breath. It had taken me a while to even call him Dad. Mommy didn't say he was only Cassie's Dad. She always referred to him as my Dad too.

"In fact, you should just call me Ray and let that be good, okay?" He stood and went to his black Camaro parked in front of Mom's silver minivan in the driveway.

I was still standing in the same spot when he finished transferring the car seat. Ray paused on the bottom step and pointed at me. "Don't you dare tell your mother what I said."

And I never did. No need to do it now. Instead, I change the subject. "What's Cassie up to? Did she start the beauty school classes yet?"

"That girl? Now it's bartending school she wants." Mom clicks her tongue when she's annoyed. "I wish she would decide on something. She has Jalen to take care of, you know."

This is true. My baby sister has a nine-and-a-half-year-old who she had at seventeen. She's been floundering ever since. Cassie dropped out of college after one semester and has had a string of different jobs.

"Who you telling my business to?" My sister's voice blares over the speaker. I turn down the volume as I stop at the light on the off ramp.

"Mind who you're talking to," Mom chides Cassie. Their conversation is muted with occasional words breaking through.

I flick the signal to make a right turn and head home, but at the last minute, continue through the intersection and head toward P&K. My laptop is already at home, but the charger cable wasn't in the bag. It's probably still plugged into the wall at the office.

"You need to go down to the church in sackcloth and ashes," Mom's voice is clear, using the popular phrase from her birthplace. She pulled it out any time Cassie and I did something to displease her.

"Here, talk to your sister," Mom says, and then Cassie is on the line.

"What's up?" I prod once it's obvious this girl will hold the phone without speaking until I say something.

"Nothing," she says.

Cassie and I used to be close. She was the annoying little sister that always followed me around. The seven-year age difference didn't matter to the little girl with long pigtails.

Things changed once I went away to college. My visits home dwindled to once or twice a year. A teenage Cassie became sullen towards me. I chalked it up to teenage angst. Then she got pregnant with my nephew. The connection between us has been on life support ever since.

"How are the classes coming?" Trying to make conversation, I scramble for something we can talk about. "What made you decide on bartending?"

Cassie takes a deep breath. "Is something wrong with making drinks? I know it's not what the perfect executive would do."

"Nothing wrong with it." I fight to quell the anger that percolates into the start of a headache. "It's just the last time we talked, you were excited about doing hair and owning your own shop one day."

"Changed my mind."

I swear I can hear the eye roll from 2,250 miles away. "Just like that."

"Yeah, just like that. Not everyone has their lives mapped out since they were thirteen years old."

Ignoring the attempt at a slight, I pull into a spot and throw the car into park without cutting off the engine.

"How is my nephew? Did he get the shoes I sent him?" Normally we can find common ground in our love of my cornrow wearing, basketball loving nephew.

Cassie refuses to lose the attitude and sucks her teeth. "He's with *my* dad at his basketball game. Thanks for the shoes, though."

Button pushed and all patience gone. "What's your problem?"

"No problem over here," she snaps.

"Then why does every conversation with you turn into an argument?"

There's silence on the other end.

"You're giving me all this attitude," I continue. "When did I become your enemy?"

"You're not the enemy," Cassie mumbles.

Rolling my shoulders releases the tension building there. "Then what is it, Baby C?" I hope referencing my childhood nickname for her will remind her of our past connection. "Why don't we talk more? I'm always here for you."

It's so quiet on the other end, I check the call timer on the Bluetooth display to make sure we haven't been disconnected.

"It's just…" Cassie stops, and I hear Mom's voice in the background.

"Girl, how many times must I tell you not to bring this mess in this house? You should be more like Carmen and …" Mom's voice trails off.

Cringing at Mom's constant comparisons, which isn't fair to Cassie, I try to get back to her to focus on our talk. "What were you about to say?"

"Nothing," she says. "Talk to you later."

I hear the phone hit something and then Mom is on the line again.

"That child will put me in an early grave. Always angry about something. She needs to get her life together. Jalen needs his mom to step up for once."

"Maybe you can back off a little." I try to bite back the words, but they have already escaped. A quick prayer is sent that mom's hearing fails for two seconds.

There's a sharp intake of breath. Prayer unanswered. "Back off? Is that what you say to me?"

"No, Mom." Unsnapping the seat belt, I shift in place. Being a grown woman doesn't stop the familiar churning of unease when crossing my mother. "I'm stressed right now. Trying to decide how to proceed with something."

She stretches her silence for a few more seconds before moving on from my comment. "It's not like you to be of two minds."

"I know. I'm just not sure what to do." Mom doesn't need to know the issue involves another man. She's already disappointed about the divorce and keeps advocating for me to stay with Melvin. The only time she ever said she was proud of me was the day I got married. I have two degrees and worked to become an executive at one of the largest companies in the country, but in her eyes, my highest achievement was becoming someone's wife.

"You do how I raised you," Mom says. "You do what's right."

The question is, do what's right for who? Me or my family.

Chapter Seventeen

Braxton

Maxx gallops after the raggedy tennis ball and catches it on the first bounce. He trots back and drops it at my feet with his tail wagging. "Good boy."

Scooping up the semi soggy ball, I toss it again. Maxx could do this all day. We are at our favorite hangout, Hermon Dog Park, which is about 20 minutes from my spot. The dog run area is an off leash, mud free and quiet place I discovered by accident. Came to test out the bike trail and wandered under the bridge to the dog area. We get out here at least once a week. And even though Maxx just got groomed, he deserves a treat for enduring the nail clipping he hates.

I toss the ball a few more times until Maxx is distracted when his doggie friend, Oscar, arrives. Oscar is a black and brown beagle whose owner is an elderly woman. She nods an acknowledgment to me and sits on the opposite bench.

We've never spoken. She continues her routine of pulling a pack of yarn out of her bag and starts crocheting.

The large tree offers shade from the bright sun but feels chilly in the seventy-degree weather. Slipping a hoodie out of my backpack causes my arms to ache. The extra workout of schooling Monroe's students pushed me past my normal levels. I'll be sore for days.

Monroe's comment about settling for whoever you can get makes me wonder if that's my fate. Based on his comments, he seems to have accepted the bachelor's life because his love chose someone else. It makes me wonder about the identity of this mystery lady was. And was she worth it?

Before I can stew over Monroe's lost love, my phone rings and Debra's name flashes on the screen.

"What's going on in London town?"

She laughs. "My silly little brother." Debra's term of endearment was stamped on me when I was ten and went through a joke telling joke phase. She returned from college and I was glad to have a sibling in the house. Debra had the patience for me I needed and was the only family member entertained by my comedic pursuits.

"Is everything okay? It's kind of late in your part of the world." Glancing at my watch confirms it's after ten p.m. there. The eight-hour difference makes telephone conversations hit or miss. We normally text or email each other.

"Things are good. In fact, they are great. I have some news, and you were the first person I wanted to tell." Debra's happiness emits through the phone. I don't have to see her face to picture the joy sparkling in her large brown eyes.

Checking on Maxx, who is now wrestling with Oscar while they double team a brown and white cocker spaniel, I lean against the large oak tree, "This must be huge. Spill it."

"We're engaged!" Debra shrieks.

I wince before turning the volume down in my ear buds. "Wow, that is major. Congratulations. How did all this happen?"

Debra gushes about how her girlfriend, Imka, planned the perfect proposal during dinner at the scene of their first date. When I visited over the holidays, they took me to The Kudu restaurant located on Queens Road. The South African inspired shareable dishes were as delicious as watching the chef, Imka's cousin, prepare each edible creation.

The pair entertained me for a week, and I knew Imka was the one for my sister. They even looked good together. My sister is a lanky brown skinned woman who's taken to wearing her natural hair in twists with red-rimmed eyeglasses. Picture a sexy librarian and you get Debra. Although her chosen profession is a mechanical engineer. Imka is an ebony skinned queen with long braids. She's an artist who supplements her income by working as an exhibit designer in a museum.

"She barely let me finish the question before she said yes." Imka has joined the conversation. Her soft South African accent soothes my ears after Debra's high-pitched tone.

"My sister knows what's good for her. Welcome to the family, Imka."

I'm happy for my sister. I really am. But I can't help but wonder when it's going to happen for me. Listening to them tease each other back and forth makes me long for that type of relationship. Someone only for me. No sneaking around. No more sharing stolen moments. No more wondering what's she's doing this weekend with her not ex-husband.

"Braxton, are you still here?" Debra calls.

Maxx runs over to nuzzle my leg. He's panting, so I walk over to the large blue drinking fountain and rinse one of the bowls to put down fresh water. "Right here. So, when are you planning the wedding?"

"No firm date yet. I want to enjoy this moment first." Debra says something to Imka in the background and then pauses. "What's wrong?"

Setting the water down, I stretch, releasing pent up tension in my shoulders. "Do you plan to tell the parents soon?"

By parents, she knows I mean our mother.

"I doubt Hannah will congratulate me," Debra says. Her voice lowers and pain radiates through the line. "She didn't get to pick my spouse like she did with Bernie. She was always trying to set me up with some guy from the church or a son of one of her friends."

Mom's rejection of Debra's true self contains a sea of disappointment and resentment. I know it's at least partially the reason Debra took the job in London. She figured the Atlantic Ocean would shield her from Mom's judgement.

"That's what she gets for not listening. I tried to tell that woman all her kids liked girls. Shoot, you made it easy for her."

Debra's laugh signals my mission to bring her back to the present moment was successful. "I have better taste than her, anyway."

"Now that's true. Bernie's wife is a tad uptight."

"Well, she is a younger version of Mom. I don't know what that says about our brother, but he seems happy."

I call for Maxx to come and secure his leash for our walk back to the car. "He is. He found his soulmate at an early age and now you're about to get married. I'm the last one to get set up. No wonder Mom gave Leslie my number."

"She did what?"

Filling Debra in on Mom's latest scheme covers the walk to the car. Maxx is strapped in the back with the seat belt leash attached to his harness. I settle in the driver's seat, allowing the call to switch to Bluetooth.

"So, let me get this straight. Mom wants you to reconnect with the woman who left you and broke your heart?"

Debra has a way of drilling down to the pertinent fact of a situation. "That's the gest of it."

"And what do you want?"

The question gives me pause. I want the stability of knowing someone has my back. I want the all-consuming feeling of protecting and providing for a woman. Someone who makes me believe I can conquer any problem. I want an intelligent, challenging, and fine as hell woman.

I want Carmen.

Maxx curls into a ball on the back seat, and I recline and take a deep breath. The sunlight warms the arm I have propped on the open car window. Families pass by on the walking trail or sit beneath the canopy of trees. The smacking sound of a tennis ball being hit travels from the nearby courts.

I'm lonely. And I'm tired of being alone.

"Hello, are you still there?" Debra brings me back to the present.

"Yeah. Let me tell you about the woman I love."

After listening to me pour out my messy situation, Debra says, "You're making things complicated when it should all be simple. You love her and you believe she loves you. But if she truly did, you wouldn't have to ask to be chosen."

"But it's not simple. Did you not hear me say the woman thought she was divorced but is still married?"

"Marriages end all the time. And I'm not trying to trivialize it. But…it took me twenty years to find the love I have with Imka. Nothing would keep me from being with her. Nothing and no one."

My chest tightens. "You think I should let her go."

"I think you shouldn't waste time waiting on her to realize what a good man you are. Let her fix her life before you make her the end all."

Shaking my head at the thought of letting things end with Carmen, I change the subject instead. I tell her about the management program at work and how this is another step to learn all I can before thinking about branching out with my own firm. Debra offers her advice about navigating corporate dynamics.

"So, back to this wedding. Am I the best man or maid of honor? I can be either one, you know."

"My silly little brother," Debra teases. "You'll always be the best man I know. Besides, Dad. And maybe Bernie."

Throwing the car in gear, I back out of the parking space. Time to run a quick errand and get home. "I have to be ranked higher than Bernie. Did he come see you and meet your lady? Nope, that was only me."

"You know you're my number one. And I'm going to end this call. Imka went to bed a few minutes ago. But remember this: you don't have to settle. If this Carmen woman won't make a move to be with you, you need to move on."

Chapter Eighteen

Carmen

I cut the ignition in the P&K parking lot, ending the call with Mom. A dog barks when I walk behind the car next to mine. Closer inspection reveals the vehicle is Braxton's. The personalized license tag of B Man 1 is his shout out to the Jay-Z lyric about being a business, man. Braxton has big dreams and I know he'll get there. We spent a lot of hours talking about his plan to conquer the business world. Ambition is so sexy on a man.

The day has improved. A chance to see Braxton helps to shake off the argument with Gayle and the depressing convo with Mom. My face relaxes at the certainty of getting to see him.

"Well, look at this. Who knew I would see you again?"

Happiness is short-lived when I turn and see that APD driver. *What was his name?* Jay. Crusty lips and all.

"Are you stalking me?"

He gestures at the truck parked at the side of the building. "Not at all. I'm on the clock. Unless you want me to. I'm guessing you work here, right?"

My gaze darts around the parking lot. There's no one here but a barking dog. A pricking sensation crawls over my scalp.

Jay takes a step closer. "Yeah, I know where you work." He rubs his crotch. "And where you play."

I flinch then lift my chin. There's no way I'm letting this guy intimidate me. "Do I need to remind you I'm married?"

He laughs and leans in close. The sandwich crumbs dangling off his unkempt beard shout his love of oil and vinegar. They make a nauseous harmony with the stale coffee breath to assault me. "We both know you're not above stepping out."

Now I'm pinned between the car with Jay blocking a clean exit without me touching him.

"How about you run me your name and number? Your husband obviously ain't handling business properly. And I won't tell him if you don't." Jay's eyes are slits.

My heart pounds and I tighten the grip on the keys in my hand. Damn a key fob. I need something to fight with.

The dog in the car is now pawing at the window and growling. The only witness to what's about to happen.

"Hey, is there a problem here?"

Braxton appears behind us looking like a pissed off Superhero. A Superhero in a pair of gray sweats and a white t-shirt that flexes when he squares his shoulders.

"No problem, my man." Jay moves away and throws his hands in the air. "Just speaking to the lady."

"Doesn't look like she wants to talk to you. You need to back the fuck up." Braxton moves to stand in front of me. A human shield.

Jay looks at us both and lowers his hands. He walks backward toward his truck and points at me. "It's cool. Maybe I'll see you around."

Braxton's hands clench into fists and he stomps toward this fool, but I grab his shirt. No need to escalate things, since Jay is climbing into his truck.

Jay watches us while he starts the engine. He leans over and spits on the asphalt before driving away.

"Are you okay?" Braxton's body is tense but relaxes when the UPS truck is out of sight.

I bow my head with closed eyes and breath in and out my nose. My heart rate slows as the natural scent from Braxton acts as a balm to my frayed nerves.

"Do you know that guy?"

I've never lied to Braxton before but there's no need to revisit what happened at the hotel the last time we were together.

"Thanks," I croak and shake my head.

"Hey, no need for that. I got you. I'll always be there for you, Carmen." He touches my cheek and pushes a wayward curl behind my ear.

Now my hands are trembling, and he pulls me close. "It'll be alright," he whispers.

Basking in the warmth of his body, his heartbeat soothes me and my muscles relax. He encases me in the cocoon of his arms as he rubs my back.

A blaring car horn brings me back. The traffic noise and the dog barking again make us both step away. We're in a public place and we're at work. Someone might see.

Standing in front of each other, the connection between us sizzles like a downed power line. The energy humming between us is almost visible.

Braxton wipes his hands down those sweatpants and clears his throat. "I see you met Maxx."

He uses the car remote to lower the window, so the dog can hang over the edge.

"Nice to meet you, Maxx." I scratch him behind the ears and his tail wags faster. He tries to lick my hand, and I pull away, laughing.

"He likes you," Braxton says. "But I knew he would."

Maxx bounces on the seat and spins in circles. My thoughts go to Olivia. She would love this little dog. "Really? How did you know?"

"He recognizes good people." Braxton waits until I look up and wink. "Besides, he likes whoever I like."

"Smart dog."

Braxton surveys the parking lot and leans against the car. "What are your plans for the rest of the day?"

"Just had lunch with Gayle. I only stopped by here because I forgot my power cord. Then heading home."

He nods. "Came by to sign some stuff. Sent off that email for the Cooper account and forwarded you the cost estimates. The training program starts Monday, so I'll be tied up most of the day."

Raising my eyebrows and nodding my approval, I feel a rush of pride. Braxton will make an excellent executive. He has the strong work ethic and ability to over deliver that will get the attention of the higher ups here. "That's good."

"So, are you free this afternoon?" Braxton licks his lips. "Can we go somewhere and talk?"

My stomach flutters. All background noise goes still and the atmosphere dances with an intoxicating rhythm that will lead to us ending up naked. I want this man so bad it's taking everything in me not to reach for his hand.

You do what's right.

My mother's words help me fight through my physical need. I nod even as I reply, "I don't think that's a good idea."

Braxton's shoulders drop and he sighs. "We're really over then?"

"We can't keep doing this. It isn't fair to ask you to wait until I sort out this mess." Olivia deserves a two-parent home and maybe this situation is a sign to work things out. Even if it hurts me.

"I'll see you around then." Braxton runs a hand down his face and pushes off the car.

Shielding my face, I move toward the building. He can't see the regret in my eyes.

"Carmen," he calls.

When I turn, he is in front of me. His hands caress my face and then he pulls me in. Our lips connect and heat flares throughout my body. His tongue parts my lips and seeks to tangle with my own. He presses closer and my hands stroke his neck.

All too quickly, the connection is broken and Braxton retreats to his vehicle. I'm lightheaded and stumble as I turn back to the double doors.

It seems a fitting end. Our relationship started with a kiss. The affair should end with one as well.

Chapter Nineteen

Braxton

I open the door to my apartment and walk into a disaster zone. A duffel bag spills its contents across the chocolate-colored leather love seat. A pair of shorts are in a ball on the floor and one size sixteen Air Jordan sneaker is perched near the sliding glass door.

The cause of this mess is Hurricane Omar. My best friend since high school showed up this morning looking for a place to crash for a couple of nights.

Omar is exactly where I left him. On the couch playing Madden 2K.

"What's up?" he says without taking his eyes off the screen.

"Same ol' thing." I release Maxx's leash and he wrestles with a sock and drags it to his bed in the corner.

I sink into the couch, but not before tripping over a toiletry bag and stepping on a bottle of cologne. "Man, why haven't you put your stuff in the guest room?"

"There you go," he says. "Always so particular. I knew I should have stayed at Devon's."

"You know Devon is a worse slob than you. That's why you came here."

"I know growing up with Master Sargent got you being a nag instead of a gracious host."

He spent enough time at my house to know the particular way Pop's liked things done. He was worse than Mom when it came to doing Saturday morning chores. Some habits are hard to break. I like my place a certain way. Omar's things all over the room throw off the whole vibe.

I toss a brush at him and he blocks it with one hand. "Quit playing, man. I'm about to score."

"Clean this mess up. I'm serious. My parents will be up in a few days."

The television blares out 'Touchdown' and Omar pauses the game. "Relax, man. I'll be gone by then. Keisha is tripping. A couple of days living outside my love will have her calling. She knows she misses her big teddy bear."

I laugh. "You guys do this all the time. How does that work?"

"It's our thing, man." He tosses the controller and leans all two hundred and twenty-five pounds of his frame back, spreading his legs. I swear I hear the seat groan.

"You know, I got released by the Raiders last week," he continues.

"Yeah, but that was expected, right?"

Omar Jackson is a practice squad player for the NFL Oakland Raiders. He played wide receiver at USC and was drafted in the seventh round. He played one season until he tore ligaments in his ankle and knee. Things never truly healed right, even after a ton of rehab and at least three surgeries. He's been on the practice squad ever since.

"Expected? Yeah, I knew my time as an athlete was getting short. I can't continue to subject all of this to the punishment." Omar stands to his full 6'5" height and stretches. He pulls his locs back and ties them with a band he takes from around his wrist. After a brief disappearance into the kitchen, he returns with a Gatorade.

With an exaggerated gesture, Omar places a coaster down before sitting his drink on the coffee table.

"See you still moping over ol' girl." Omar stuffs his gear back into a duffel bag.

A wave of my hand dismisses the statement. He knows all the details of my short-lived relationship, so there's no need to elaborate. "Nobody's moping."

Omar takes the bag into the guest room and returns to his spot on the chair. "Oh, you moping. She got you all twisted. You sure it's over?"

The kiss in the parking lot sealed the end. I must accept it. "Yeah, she found out she's still married and shut things down. Who knows, they might work things out." I blow out a breath. "Got to respect that."

Omar shakes his head. "That shit not going to work. My parents divorced. Keisha's was never married. We came out alright. If two people are miserable, it only makes it worse."

I shrug in agreement. My feelings on the state of Carmen's marriage are well known. It's her choice to stay when she knows she wants to be with me.

"Now you know the best way to get over a woman," Omar grins.

Groaning, I rub my goatee. "Don't say it, man."

"Get on top of another one." Omar punctuates his statement by gyrating his hips.

I point at the door. "Get out."

"Naw." Omar laughs. "You set yourself up, though. How you get involved with a married woman, anyway? That don't seem like you. That's some shit Devon would do. He grimy like that. You the poetry reading, sensitive brother."

The laughter dies on my lips and turns into a frown. "You calling me soft?"

"Not at all," Omar gets serious. "You came through for me on several occasions. Whether that involved busting some heads or talking shit. What I mean is that you aren't afraid to show your feelings, but you play it smart. This seems a bit reckless for you."

Reckless isn't the word I would use to describe my relationship with Carmen. Magnetic, passionate, consuming, maybe. But not reckless. There was nothing impulsive or wild about it. Two people got to know each other and developed a bond. And now it's over.

"Maybe." I unstring my sneakers and toe them off. "But she had left the man before things got physical."

Omar leans forward. "So, she was really feeling you if she left her husband."

Carmen didn't leave for me. At least she never confirmed that fact. She wasn't even aware I knew. Working late one night, I left the conference room we were using on another floor to retrieve something from my desk. When I returned, she was on the phone with her friend, Gayle. Lingering outside the doorway, I eavesdropped on her, thanking Gayle for babysitting her daughter. She mentioned Olivia thought they were going on a girl's trip, but she was really contemplating leaving her husband before he served the divorce papers. It was another three weeks before we shared a kiss on the beach.

Some things need to remain between lovers. Omar doesn't need to know everything.

I ease my cell phone out and open the text message app. Wonder if Carmen will let me know she made it home safe. Something about that guy in the parking lot seemed off. "Debra called while I was out. How about she got engaged today?"

"Congratulations to big sis, but don't try to change the subject?"

"Naw, I'm sharing some good news, man. You know she's been through it."

I continue fiddling with my phone and only look up when there isn't a response.

Omar raises an eyebrow.

"What you want me to say?" I ask.

He continues to study me.

"I know you trying to do the whole 'get inside your opponent's mind' thing you swear by, but there is nothing left to say."

"Are you sure?" Omar asks.

The only thing I'm sure of is that I want to taste her one more time. But it's not going to happen. Sitting the phone on the table, I rear back on the couch and put both hands behind my head. "Yeah, man. It's a done deal."

He looks at me a moment longer and then picks up the video controller. "Cool. Then we're going out tonight."

"No way. I'm planning to chill right here. I had a hell of a workout fooling with Unc at the gym."

"It's my duty to get you back out there. Besides, I want you to check out this sports bar I'm planning on investing in. Remember I told you about my phase two?"

I nod. Omar has always been clear that football was a short-term gig. He majored in finance in college with the goal of being an entrepreneur. Owning a sports bar is his first venture into new territory.

Before I can answer in the affirmative, my phone rings. 212 area code again.

Omar laughs. "You jumped like you saw a ghost."

"Mom gave Leslie my number. I actually saw her yesterday when I dropped in to get a meal. Mom had that planned, too. She's been blowing up my phone ever since."

He knows the history, so there's no need to explain, although I share the conversation had during our walk.

"Damn." Omar pauses the game again. "Well, you could set up a little something. Deal with your present woman by getting revenge on your past."

"What are you talking about?"

"You can get Carmen out of your system by hooking up with the woman who left you. Then you ghost on her ass. It's genius."

The call rolls over to voice mail and I stand. "Not sure about all that. But I will hit up the spot with you tonight. It's time to get back out there."

Chapter Twenty

Carmen

He walks out of the bathroom reeking of cologne and I know the drill. Melvin expects me to endure my wifely duty and have sex with him. It seems our argument hasn't detoured his disillusion of reconciling. Besides, it is Saturday night, after all. It's always on a Saturday.

I tried to spice things up a few times. What's wrong with wanting to feel close to your mate on, say, a random Tuesday? There was always an excuse. Either he was too tired, or he would remind me not everyone has a cushy desk job. Or my personal favorite: What's wrong with you? Something I didn't factor in by marrying a man sixteen years older than me was the incompatible sex drives.

That was BB, Before Braxton. Once I was intimate with Braxton, any memories of Melvin were erased.

After the events of the day and the past few months, the last thing I want to do is have sex with him. Even when our marriage was on better terms, Melvin would only agree to fulfill my needs once a week. But if I refused his advances, it was considered a divorce level transgression. The one time I turned over and went to sleep, he didn't speak to me for a week.

Melvin cuts off the light even though I am reading a book. He gets under the covers and slides close to me.

"Come on, girl." He gives me a peck on the lips before I can turn my head. He doesn't take the hint and starts on his routine. First, he nuzzles my neck and tells me I smell good. Then he palms my breast and tells me I feel good.

I feel nothing. Our sex life was mundane before he served me with divorce papers but my body would respond to the physical touch. Right now, even the thought of having sex with him leaves me as cold as an air conditioner set to the Artic.

Melvin chuckles as he kicks off his boxers. "Let me give you what you been waiting for."

I slide out of bed. "Are you kidding me right now? Have you lost your mind?"

He looks baffled. "You're still my wife and I have needs."

I think back to when Melvin and I first started dating. We were seeing each other for about four months before he made a serious move. The chemistry between us wasn't sizzling, but I told myself it didn't matter. I was ready for a serious relationship, and I wasn't going to cloud things with something as simple as damn good sex. Melvin was respectable and dependable. He told me he was in the market for a wife, and I was ready to be one. I figured the sex would get better with time.

And for a while, it did. I could get my needs met any day of the week. Melvin was a willing partner, if not the most thrilling one.

Until I got pregnant.

Melvin's grunts bring me back to the present. He strokes himself and looks up at me.

"What are you doing?" I ask, taking a step away from the bed.

"Getting it ready for you," he mumbles and reaches for me.

I can barely make out his face in the glow from the alarm clock, but the frown doesn't hide in the shadows. "You're still my wife."

"You've made it clear I'm not a good wife, so you need to go somewhere else with that." I gesture to his now flaccid penis. It would have only been a few hearty thrusts and the whole thing over in three minutes, anyway.

Melvin's jaw tightens, and he speaks through clenched teeth. "Are you going to relieve me or not?"

This can't be happening. I ease away until the wall is at my back and flip the switch, illuminating the room with light.

Mistake.

Melvin bounds off the bed and presses his body against mine. The cologne cloud isn't the only thing suffocating me. I've never felt afraid of Melvin, but this situation could escalate beyond my control. The bedroom door is to my right, but it might as well be a mile away.

Images flash through my mind of every fighting move I can make, but my body is frozen in place. Knowing Olivia is asleep in her room helps calm my nerves. Melvin wouldn't dare cross the line and force himself on me. I squirm and cough until Melvin moves.

He kisses my cheek. "You know you want it."

I push him away and point to the door. "All I want is for you to get out."

He looks confused for a moment but drops his head. "I wasn't trying to—"

This is my own fault. I've allowed things to spiral beyond my control with Melvin and Braxton.

"Just go sleep somewhere else." I cut him off and move to the other side of the room. "I may still be your wife on paper, but what kind of marriage is this?"

Melvin nods and then squares his shoulders. "It's not over. We can fix things."

I don't respond and stare at him until he leaves. My heartbeat returns to normal and locking the bedroom door helps ease my thoughts. Cutting off the light, I replay the interaction with Melvin. I can't help but wonder if my marriage is truly over, why did I end things with Braxton?

Chapter Twenty-One

Braxton

"Surprised Omar got you to come out," Devon shouts over the canopy of piped in music, multiple conversations, clinking glasses, and shouts from an ongoing pool game.

"Me too." I swallow the remnants of beer and set the bottle down. It is immediately replaced with a new one. The skinny server with braces looks too young to drink herself, but she is working hard for a major tip.

We are in the heart of Inglewood, the majority Latinx and Black community that is slowly being gentrified. The strip mall where Practice Squad Bar & Grille is located sits on the corner of Century Boulevard. Planes taking off from LAX can be heard between the mix of today's hits. Big screen televisions cover almost every inch of wall space and the wide glass mirror behind the wooden bar highlights the small stage, which hosts local acts and karaoke battles.

Devon moans at a missed free throw on the screen and reaches for the last lemon pepper chicken wing. "Nice crowd tonight. But where the fine women at?"

Scanning the crowd, it appears the genders are equally represented. "What are you talking about? Plenty of ladies in here."

"Yeah, but they all booed up. Where can I find a single, lonely woman with low self-esteem? A brother needs some action." Devon extends his greasy fingers for a high five.

I leave him hanging and take the last bite of a beef slider before moving to the fish tacos. "What happened to girl you were taking out the other night? The one you said worked in Research."

"She was tripping." Devon crumbles a napkin after wiping his fingers. "We had a nice time. Comedy show and dinner. She invites me back to her place. Things get heated, and she throws on the brakes."

"Got to respect a woman's right to change her mind." I add more salsa to the taco between bites.

Devon leans back. "No doubt. I dipped." He takes a drink and swirls the liquid in the glass. "She's nice and all. Maybe I'll ask her out again. But she left a brother in a bad way."

"If at first you don't succeed..." I begin the college mantra we adopted back in the dorms.

"Then you got to beg and plead." Devon slaps the table and roars with laughter.

We turn our attention back to the game and discuss USC's chances this year against Villanova. But the college dating philosophy nags at me. Getting back into the dating scene isn't appealing at all. The dance of getting to know someone feels draining after being with Carmen. I was ready to settle down with the woman and she chooses to stay with him. My shoulders tense at the thought of her at home playing the happy wife.

"Alright, the night just got interesting." Devon is focused on the entrance, and I turn around to see what or who has him showing all his teeth.

Kayla stands near the door with two other women.

"Damn, is this woman stalking me?"

I don't realize I expressed the sentiment out loud until Devon responds. "She can stalk the hell out of me. Pretty women do travel in packs."

Before I can stop him, he's basically jumping up and down, waving them over. Kayla frowns when she sees Devon, but when she spots me, says something to her crew, and they follow. Heads turn as the trio weave their way through the crowded space.

All three are dressed to impress and have forgone the standard sports bar apparel of jeans and jerseys. Kayla leads the group and is wearing a navy jumpsuit with an off the shoulder, breast enhancing cutout.

She stops in front of me. "So, you do come out at night?"

"Yes, I do." I stand and take in the ladies with Kayla. One is a Latino beauty with brownish orange skin and wide expressive eyes. Her name is Elena, and she's rocking a burgundy form fitting dress with her back out. The golden goddess bringing up the rear is introduced as Savannah. She balances on black thigh-high boots and strikes a pose. The harsh lighting can't diminish her aura and her grayish blue eyes survey the scene with attitude.

I've seen her somewhere before recently but can't remember it.

Devon is awestruck. "Damn, baby," he slurs, but tries to correct himself. "Please join us."

I offer Kayla my seat and she smiles while motioning for her friends to sit. Devon grabs another chair from a nearby table, but we're still one short.

"What brings you ladies out?" Devon asks.

Kayla answers after ordering a drink from our efficient waitress. "We're celebrating Elena passing the bar exam. Just stopping through before we head to the club. Savannah wanted to make her ex jealous."

We offer congratulations and then follow Savannah's glare to the muscular blonde bartender. She tosses her long brown tresses over one shoulder and winks. He is not happy to see her.

"Your ex is an idiot," Devon says. "But I'm willing to be used to help you out. Let me buy you a drink."

Savannah plays along and moves her chair closer to Devon.

Elena rolls her eyes.

"How about you come out with us?" Kayla asks.

Before I can respond, Omar taps me on the shoulder. "I want you to meet my partner."

Introductions are made again. Omar makes sure to mention he's an owner and instructs the waitress to put the ladies' drinks on his tab.

"D, you're straight?" Devon is about three mojitos deep, and I'm not sure he should be unsupervised with the opposite sex.

He waves us away and turns back to the three ladies. "Listen, I got an idea."

That can't be good.

I leave them to it and follow Omar as we maneuver around several tables and people mingling around the hostess stand waiting to be seated. We find Ryan standing in an alcove between the bar and the kitchen.

"My man," Ryan shouts and grabs Omar into a bear hug.

"Ryan, this is Braxton," Omar extracts himself and tries to make introductions.

I extend my hand, but Ryan slaps it away. "Naw, man. If you're a friend of O, then you're like family." He pulls me into the same rough hug he gave Omar.

Ryan Kelce is Omar's business partner and former teammate. He played as an offensive lineman and was touted as one of the best. A reputation I learn is well deserved when I try to loosen his hold on me.

"Yo, Ryan, you're not running a blocking play. Let my man breathe." Omar laughs.

I'm suddenly released and can feel my arms again. "Good thing you and Omar were on the same team. Where were you when he got body slammed to the turf?"

"On the line keeping the quarterback from getting crushed so he could get the ball to our best receiver," Ryan's voice is as big as his massive chest. The man must be a good three hundred pounds and at least 6'5" in height. His stringy black hair is pulled back into a ponytail and his beard is giving me ZZ Top vibes.

Omar steers the conversation to business. "This the friend I was telling you about. He's a big-time marketing exec. About to start his own agency."

"Well, good thing you a friend of O's. Probably won't be able to afford you when you get your firm up and running." Ryan leans against the wall. "What do you think of the place?"

Scanning the area, I nod in time to the music. "It's nice. In an excellent location. Clientele is diverse. Various activities to keep people engaged, and the food is on point. With the right marketing, Practice Squad can become 'the' sports bar."

"That's what I'm talking about," Omar raises both fists and Ryan taps them with his own.

"When can we sit down and talk? We're planning to open another location downtown near LA Live."

I'm about to respond to Ryan's question when the karaoke machine screeches with feedback. We turn to see Devon on the stage.

"Here we go," Omar says.

The track drops, drums and horns sound and the 80s classic by Jermaine Stewart blares. Devon is hamming it up for his audience of three, and everyone stops to watch the show. "We Don't Have to Take Our Clothes Off" is a song about good, clean fun, but Devon changes the words.

"We don't have to take our clothes off, but we should," he sings and points to Savannah. "To have a good time all night."

The entire bar joins in the chorus and starts screaming, "Hey, hey, oh hey, hey. Na na na na nnaaa."

Savannah jumps on the stage and dances around Devon, which gets the bartender to throw down a towel and leave the bar.

"Hold up there, Brent." Ryan calls. "Where you going?"

Brent points at Savannah. "That's my girl up there."

Not according to Kayla and crew, but I don't interject.

Ryan punches Omar's arm. "That's her. The Peak Model Winner, Savannah Simmons. My wife is crazy about that show."

Peak Model is the current reality show craze which features around ten ladies battling for the number one spot. They are judged by former models, current stylists and makeup artists and are put through weekly challenges. Past winners have gone on to land coveted deals with major designer labels and fashion houses.

I may have watched an episode or two with Carmen. No wonder she looked familiar. Plus, we passed her billboard on the drive over here.

Devon finishes the song with a flourish and twirls Savannah into a dip. The crowd applauds.

Brent charges the stage.

Ryan displays the speed he used on the football field and blocks Brent from advancing.

Devon loses his mind and tries to kiss Savannah. She pushes him away and Elena stands over him, berating him for his actions.

Kayla stomps over to me. "Get your boy!"

In three strides, I'm helping Devon up. "What's up, man?"

He staggers away and collapses in a chair. "It was part of the show. Look, ole boy is going crazy."

Devon points and we watch Brent almost lose his job because he is causing a scene. Ryan and Omar have him blocked in the corner. Savannah is laughing and taunting the man. "Remember, you're the one that left. You're the one who couldn't handle it."

"Kayla, get your girl," I take her hand. "This is my man's place of business."

She looks at our hands intertwined and runs a manicured finger across my wrist. "Only if you come out with us. We're going to hit a few clubs. It'll be fun."

I raise an eyebrow, and she turns to gather Savannah before things get out of hand.

Brent is taken to the back and Omar returns after a few minutes. "We got him cooled out in the office, but it'll be best if the ladies leave."

Omar scans the crowd, which has gone back to watching the game, eating, and talking. Devon is slumped over in a chair. "I'll take D home. His ass can't ever hang, anyway."

"Naw, let me take him," I say. It's a good excuse to ditch Kayla.

"Why would you want to deal with a sloppy drunk when you got a trio of ladies looking at you like you the last Louie Vuitton bag on display?"

The ladies are gathered near the hostess stand. Kayla motions for me to join them.

"Remember when we talked about your options? I'm locked down. Devon messed up his chance. All these dudes in here trying to get noticed, but I can tell Kayla got her eyes on you. Do your thing and forget about your married fling," Omar says.

There are a few dudes hovering around the ladies trying to get their attention. Savannah ignores them all and is tapping on her phone. Elena has her arms crossed. And Kayla, well, she stares at me.

"I don't think that's a good idea. Kayla and I work together."

Omar catches the implications. Messing with a co-worker is bad enough. Adding a third into the mix is asking for a disaster.

"Then hook up with Elena. Savannah seems messy as fuck, although she is beautiful. Just go, man. And don't hurry home."

He's right. Why not go out and have some fun? A guy couldn't do better than escorting three fine women.

"Ladies, ready to celebrate?"

Kayla hooks her arm through my right. I offer Elena the left. Savannah leads the way, a golden beacon toward my options.

Chapter Twenty-Two

Carmen

I've been a faithful wife for over a month. And I'm miserable.

Usually, I can get some solace from work, but dealing with Susan and knowing I was denied her job, grates on me with every meeting and microaggression she throws. Today she told me I always "dress very nicely" and "always look the part". I was too shocked to respond to the"compliment".

Because of her, my meetings ran long today, and I had to ask Gayle to pick up Olivia from school.

"You ever have one of those days?" I ask. Crossing from the fridge to the stove takes two steps. A skillet is taken from a low cabinet and my knees crack when I stand. What my kitchen lacks in size is made up with character. The cabinets are painted a bright red to highlight the cream pimpled backsplash. The stove sits on an island and Olivia spins on the bar stool at the opposite side.

"You love that corporate grind," Gayle says and slides to the side when I reach for a knife out of the butcher's block. "Remember, you used to always tell me you were going to show the head honchos that a Black woman can run things."

Today was about more than the usual corporate micro aggressions. "You know I got that part on lock. Today has been on a ten and I need it to level down. Thanks again for getting Livvy for me."

"Girl, no problem. You know I got you," Gayle answers.

I ran out of the office so fast a broken heel couldn't stop me. An unexpected meeting running long almost made me miss the pickup time at Olivia's school. I called Gayle for back up. No way was I calling Melvin.

"Stop twisting in that chair and go clean up those books." I point at Olivia and she hops down to get her coloring books and dolls off the couch.

The open floor plan allows me an unobstructed view of Olivia as she gets distracted and picks up a crayon. Shaking my head, I return to browning the hamburger.

"But you know I got you." Gayle's promise is about more than the occasional after school pick up. We didn't speak for two days after our confessional lunch where I stormed off.

Gayle broke the stalemate by calling me and delivering her signature line. 'Bitch, you still mad?'

Chopping an onion, I launch into a venting session. "Should have known this day was going to try me when the car wouldn't start making me miss my morning meeting. Melvin claims there's nothing wrong with it but there I was waiting on Triple A. He had already left to take Olivia to school and then I couldn't reach him on his new cell. Once I got into the office, it was one disaster after another."

Things had been cool between us. He hasn't tried to sleep with me again and we've been cordial. But this week the surly mood returned.

Gayle starts to speak but I hold up a finger. "Get to work and the system is down. Couldn't log on until noon, at which time I learn the photo shoot has been rescheduled to two o'clock today."

I take a plate from the cabinet and a knife from the butcher's block. "When I get there the talent, some B-level celebrity whose cable series is going off, picks that time to renegotiate her contract."

Gayle shifts on the bar stool and rests her head in her hands. "Ooh, now this is getting good. Who is it? One of those reality housewives?"

Shaking my head, I grab the pack of tortillas from the pantry and put them on a microwaveable plate. "No, she's in some ensemble cast of a show on HBO. She's the breakout star. Getting a lot of praise from the Hollywood press. We signed her based on some modeling work she did. I'm working on launching a new hair care line. Anyway, she's pitching a fit because she wants higher compensation."

When I arrived on set, the actress was in the middle of a full-blown tantrum. My team of wardrobe, camera, and makeup crew were in panic mode.

"What did you do?" Gayle pops a cherry tomato in her mouth and turns down the offer of wine. *Who turns down a glass of Provence Rose?*

"Since she was behaving like a child, I treated her like one. We went to her dressing room, and I reminded her of our agreement. Spelled out the terms and broke down the ramifications of her breaking said agreement."

"Ha. Wish I could have seen that. Did you do the fast talking, finger pointing thing?" Gayle says I got my business argumentative style from the Scandal television show.

"Went full Olivia Pope." I laugh. "Had her sitting there with her mouth hanging open. Then I turn to leave and run smack into a crew member bringing the star coffee. My black and which Dolce & Gabbana suit was ruined."

"Damn, babe," Gayle says. "That had to hurt."

We share a moment of silence for departed couture.

"Anyway, I decide to race home and change. Traffic was terrible as always but there was an hour before I needed to get Livvy." Pouring another glass, I continue. "Now my cell phone's blowing up and Paul's on the line."

Gayle points a finger and bobs her head. "Boss, right?"

"Yeah, seems as if the little superstar's agent called him. Now I'm trying to smooth things over with him and get out the door. And now the bumbohole car won't start."

Gayle raises her eyebrows. "Not you're pulling out the Jamaican curse words. What's really going on?"

"Mommy, can I have three tacos?" Olivia has changed into a pair of blue shorts and a black t-shirt. The coloring book and box of crayons are in one hand. She joins Gayle and climbs on a stool.

"Three? Remember what happened the last time you asked for three?"

Her face falls and turns serious. "I couldn't handle it."

I stifle a laugh and Gayle has to turn away. "Go wash your hands and come set the table."

While she runs to the bathroom, I take out some plates. "Joining us for taco night?"

Gayle picks up her purse and stands. "No. Wayne and the kids asked me to grab a pizza on the way back home."

I walk Gayle out to her car. She gives me a hug and then holds me at arm's length. "Is everything okay? With Melvin still living here, I mean?"

Melvin has tried to resemble the man I married years ago. The man before the gambling started. The man who chose me. He took 'his ladies' out for dinner one weekend. Didn't criticize when I had to travel to New York for a couple of days last week. I'm not fooled by antics, as he insists, he can change. The mask will drop soon enough.

Cracks are already beginning to emerge. This morning the surly mood returned. He went back to only smiling at Olivia and ignoring me.

Waving at a neighbor walking his dog past the house, I shrug. "Everything's okay."

Gayle gives me a look but doesn't push. "And things with lover boy?"

"Definitely over." We haven't spoken in weeks. Braxton has been busy with the management training program, so I haven't seen him in the office much. His absence hits like a softball to the chest, causing me to close my eyes and take a deep breath. Picturing his smile helps clear the dizziness and I'm centered back in the driveway.

Gayle studies my face. "Are you alright? I ask about that man and it's like you went somewhere else."

"I'm good." I wave my hand to cool a sudden surge of heat caused by the mere thought of Braxton. "No need to worry about me. It's only life doing its thing, but you know I'll figure it out."

Without saying a word, Gayle's eyes communicate she is here for me. I return the sentiment by wrapping her in a hug. It's reassuring to know someone supports me through this mess.

Gayle slips into her vehicle. "Love you, girl. Call me later."

Olivia sits beside me at the table, mirroring the preparation of a taco. We both scoop a heaping spoon of the spicy meat onto the shell, followed by cheese, tomatoes, and lettuce. She bypasses the sour cream and asks for more salsa. We toast our tacos and take a bite.

"So good, Mommy," she says with a mouth full of mouth.

My baby's happy, I think while she swings her legs under the table and tells me about the secret club she and her friend Destiny are starting. It's all worth it to sit here with my baby girl.

I get up to grab some paper towels when the doorbell rings.

"Maybe Gayle forgot something," I tell Olivia and go to the door. A glance through the peephole reveals the last person who should be on my porch.

Anger makes me open the door before better sense can prevail.

"What the hell are you doing?"

Jay's eyes widen and he laughs, displaying a dull gold tooth. "Well, ain't today my lucky day."

My hands curl into fists and I plant my feet. "What the fuck are you doing here?"

He sniffs. "Seems like I'm just in time for dinner. Smells good."

"Are you crazy? My husband will be home soon."

"I hope so," Jay's beady eyes narrow. "The man owes me money and I'm here to collect."

My chest tightens. *Money?*

Jay rocks back and forth on his heels and grins. "I'm on a winning streak. First, I win five hundred dollars off Mel. He really shouldn't bet on college basketball. The man can't pick a winner to save his life. I already got this phone off, old boy." Melvin's missing iPhone protrudes from the pocket of Jay's shirt.

My tongue is frozen, so Jay continues, "I knew seeing his wife at that hotel would one day be useful information for me." He snaps his fingers. "You and the youngster from the office parking lot. No wonder he stepped to me like that."

My body trembles from the host of emotions that assault me since I opened the door. This man knew who I was from the beginning.

My body trembles from the host of emotions that assault me since I opened the door.

"He has a uniform like Daddy's." Olivia peeks around my legs.

"Well, hello, little lady," Jay bends over to peer at my child.

I block his view with my body and send Olivia back inside. Stepping out on the porch causes Jay to back up. "Why are you here?"

Jay scratches his head and nods. "Oh, yeah. My luck is getting better and better. I guess I saw that BMW at the hotel at least two, three times that week. Piece of advice, if you're doing dirt, you should change up locations."

"What do you want?" I don't have time to listen to words of wisdom from this man.

"I did want your number, but seeing how I got you in a bind, I'll settle for cash."

Is he crazy?

"And seeing how Mel already owes me five hundred and been avoiding me for a few days, you need to cover his tab too. A cool thousand ought to do it." Jay stuffs his hands in his pockets and waits.

My mind races and my thoughts are scattered. Jay being here can't be real. *This* can't be real.

I don't realize the words are spoken out loud until Jay repeats them.

"This is real, sweetie. Pay me the money or I'll tell Mel about your car at the hotel."

Everything slows down. This can't be happening. Who knew my reckoning would come in the form of a sleazy UPS driver with halitosis and a knack for showing up at the oddest places?

"You know nothing." My eyes narrow and jaw clenches. Beads of sweat form on my brow.

Jay's face registers surprise, and he cocks his head. "That's where you're wrong. I know more than you think. I know you're doing the young dude that stepped to me in the parking lot. Knew something was up with that cat so I drove around the block. Saw you two lip locking all out in the open."

Anger deflects like a needle pricking a balloon and is replaced by something else. My pulse beats in my ears, blocking out any other sound.

Jay is still talking about what he knows, but all I can focus on is the life I built falling apart. Fear of losing my daughter if Melvin finds out and uses it as leverage in our custody fight. The nagging voice whispering, "I'm not worthy". It tells me I'm not good enough to keep the things I've worked so hard to achieve.

"Mommy." Olivia returns to the door, breaking the spiral of thoughts. "I'm finished eating. Can I watch tv?"

I turn and compose my face. "Sure. Mommy will be there in a sec."

When I return to Jay, my face is a mask. "How do I know you'll keep your mouth shut?"

"You don't," he grins. "But I'm a fair man. You pay me what's owed to me. I'm not in the business of busting up marriages."

I stare at him. He slides both hands in his pockets and rocks back and forth, trying to appear cool. But I saw a glimpse of fear in his eyes before he looked away. He doesn't really want to confront Melvin. He'll demand settlement of a gambling debt, but I imagine he doesn't want to tell him about his wife. Melvin is liable to crush him. Jay is a small man. His brown uniform pants hang off a narrow waist. His bony arms cross over a light bird chest. Yeah, Melvin would take him out.

Weighing my options and coming up with none, a numbness wraps itself around me like a vise. "Fine. I'll write you a check."

"This is a cash only transaction." Jay rubs his hands together. "You can stop payment on a check before I get to the bank."

"And once I give you this money, you need to understand that's it. No coming back." My hands rest on my hips giving my best Superwoman pose. I hope to project a strength I don't possess. A sense of dread crawls down my spine.

Jay's smile doesn't match the coldness in his eyes now that he thinks he's won. "Mel lost the bet fair and square. And your little situation ain't my business. I only want what's owed to me. Bring it on Monday at your favorite hotel. You know what time I'll be there."

The sun is setting when I return to the house and check on Olivia. She jumps up and down with excitement when she's allowed to watch an extra hour of television. The distraction allows me time to think.

Three things continue to nag at me. Why is Melvin betting on games with Jay? When did he start gambling again? And if I meet Jay at the hotel, can I trust him to keep quiet?

Chapter Twenty-Three

Braxton

It's been thirty-two days without Carmen. Thirty-two days and the ache in my chest isn't solely coming from driving through this last lap.

My sneakers pound the blue rubber track in the UCLA Drake Stadium in time to the beat pulsating through my headphones. It's a lazy sunny Sunday morning, and that's what I had planned for the day. Lying around doing nothing.

Until The Three called. Or B's Angels, a name given to the group by Devon.

"Try to keep up." Elena slaps me on the ass and runs past. Her long, black ponytail swings when she looks back and laughs. I speed up to match her stride.

We take the final lap together and stop in front of the bleachers where Kayla sits fanning herself.

"Can we go now?" she asks.

"How are you ready to go? You only lasted one lap," Elena grabs the top of one foot and pulls it toward her buttock, stretching the thigh muscle. She holds and repeats with the other leg.

Kayla pouts. "It was your idea to come out here. I wanted to sleep in after last night."

"What did you guys get into last night?" I ask and join Elena in doing a hamstring stretch.

The past few weeks, I've become the escort/bodyguard for the trio. After the introductions at Omar's Sports Bar, the ladies (or rather Kayla) made sure to keep me busy every weekend. Savannah's on again, off-again boyfriend, Brent, joined us a few times. Devon has begged to be included, but the ladies vetoed his participation down.

"It's Fashion Week. Savannah walked in the show and got us tickets. The after party was crazy. Got pictures with some celebrities." Kayla scrolls through her phone to show me.

Hanging with the ladies has its perks. Savannah has access to the best events. We went to a musical award show a few weeks ago.

"Where did Savannah disappear too, anyway?"

Kayla tilts her head, and we look up to see Savannah running the bleachers. She bounces up and down when she gets to the top and gestures for us to join her.

Elena hip bumps me. "Race you to the top."

"Sure." Extending my hand to Kayla, I ask her to join.

"I'm good right here," she says. "But watch out for El. She cheats."

Before I can acknowledge the comment, Elena takes off. Stumbling over the first few steps, I gain the advantage by leaping two stairs at a time.

Savannah cheers us on and slaps hands when we reach the top.

"Not bad, B." Savannah adjusts her red headband and bends over to tighten a shoestring. "Looks like you have some moves."

She's a shameless flirt, and I can't help but notice the way her fair skin glistens under a sheen of sweat. She abandoned the track after a couple of laps and must have been running the stairs the rest of the time.

"We know he can hang," Elena adds and looks me up and down. "But what I want to know is when are you going to make a move on Kayla?"

"Wait...what?" I turn to look down at Kayla. *Did she set this up?* She's busy on her phone and doesn't appear to be concerned with her friends accosting me.

"Now you know that girl likes you," Savannah says.

Elena nods and adds, "Why do you think we keep you around?"

"For free rides and bum deterrent," I say.

Savannah winks at Elena. "Well, he *is* nice to look at, too."

"Yeah, he has that Obama swag. Even though he reps USC." Elena is a proud UCLA Law School alum. Like my Carmen.

The best way to get over a woman is to get on top of another one. Omar doesn't give the best advice sometimes, but if I'm being honest, Elena would be the one I'd choose. My motivation for indulging Kayla outside of the office means spending time with the smart-ass lawyer. I've hesitated to move beyond the friend zone though. She *is* Kayla's friend.

Shaking off those thoughts, I focus on what the ladies are doing. Trying to set me up. "Did Kayla put you up to this?"

"Like I said, you know she likes you," Savannah repeats. "So, what's the deal?"

Before I can respond, Kayla yells for us to hurry up. "Can we go now?" she adds.

"Go get your girl," Savannah says to me. She and Elena share a look and start down the stairs.

My phone buzzes, so I pause to check the screen. Leslie.

Again.

Figured I would be hearing from her after I left my parent's house last night.

The reason I wasn't with the Angels yesterday was because I rode up to El Segundo and spent the day with Leslie. After a few hours, it became clear that whatever chemistry we shared in the past was left there. No amount of reminiscing would bring it back. There was no spark when Leslie touched my arm to make a point during conversation. Whatever we could have been has been replaced by my need for someone else.

Commotion below draws my attention back to the ladies and Kayla lays in a heap at the bottom of the stairs.

I'm breathless when I reach the track. "What happened?"

"This chick takes one step off the bleachers and twists her ankle." Elena crouches beside Kayla who is writhing on the ground.

Savannah points at Kayla's ankle. "That doesn't look good."

It doesn't. Kneeling beside Kayla and gently taking hold of her foot, the skin is discolored and tender to the touch. "Yep. It's sprained."

Kayla props herself on both elbows, her voice wavering. "All I did was step down."

"While looking back at me," Elena adds.

"How is the one person who didn't exercise at all...," Savannah uses air quotes around the word exercise. "How is that person the one that's hurt?"

Falling back while turning the drama up to ten, Kayla whines. "It was your idea to come out here. I wanted to go to brunch."

"I think we need to get you to a doctor." Kayla's ankle is swelling. "Did you ladies all ride together?"

My Mustang is in the parking lot, but the ladies were already here when I arrived.

"Savannah drove," Elena says.

We help Kayla up, and tears well in the corner of her eyes when she tries to put weight on her foot.

Without thinking, I pick her up and carry her to Savannah's red Audi convertible.

"I'll follow you all to the Urgent Care," I say after buckling Kayla in the passenger side.

Savannah slides into the driver's seat and shoots me a wink. "Something sexy about a man taking control, right?"

After an x-ray and exam, Kayla's ankle is wrapped, and she's given a prescription for painkillers. I'm roped into taking her home while Savannah and Elena go to the pharmacy. Those ladies are not subtle in their intentions.

"We live on the second floor," Kayla announces when we pull into the parking lot of her building.

Elena and Kayla are roommates and have a spot in West Hollywood, or WeHo as it's called by the locals. Their home is near the famous Sunset Strip.

"You just want me to carry your heavy butt again." Exiting the vehicle, I open the passenger door and offer Kayla the crutches.

"I can't work those things," she whines. Her eyes widen and she pokes out her bottom lip. "You'll have to help."

Shaking my head, I offer her my hand and pull her up out of the car, then lock the door. She smiles as I lift her and walk up the sidewalk and stairs.

Kayla leans into me, genuinely enjoying playing the damsel in distress role.

The scent of her perfume heightens the physical touch of her in my arms. It's been a while since I've felt the softness of a woman and I'm relieved when we're inside. Placing Kayla on the sofa allows me to step back and regain control.

"Nice place." I take in the tasteful décor of cream painted walls with the gray sectional sofa as the centerpiece. "Is that a Charles Gaines piece?"

Kayla leans back on the chaise lounge and looks at the framed artwork on the wall. "I think so. Elena went to an exhibition and came back with a painting."

I move closer to get a better look. Carmen has one of his paintings in her office. She told me she supports the local artist because he's from her home state of South Carolina. We visited an exhibition last year at the Sculpture Center during a business trip to New York. It was nice being able to walk through the museum hand in hand without worrying about being seen.

"This is from his Trees-Central Park Series." I ramble on about the man's work while surveying the novels on the wooden bookcase in the corner. A vase of fresh flowers gives off the scent of lilac blooms.

Kayla shrugs. "You sound like Elena's girlfriend. She can drone nonstop about this stuff."

It takes a second for my mind to compute the nugget which was dropped. "Wait, Elena has a girlfriend? Girlfriend as in friend girl, or girlfriend as in gay?"

"Thought you knew." Kayla does a poor job of hiding her smirk.

"And how would I know? We've been hanging out practically every weekend and this 'girlfriend' hasn't been around."

She shifts her position on the sofa. "Sloan's been in New York. She's a museum curator. I think she comes back tomorrow. You can meet her then."

"Okay, I guess." There goes any notion of getting with Elena.

I'm still processing this new information when suddenly my shirt is tugged, and a pair of lips are pressed against mine. I step back. "What are you doing?"

Kayla balances on one leg and lowers her lashes. "I got tired of waiting on you."

"Waiting on me for what?" A part of me knew this situation would come up. Kayla has sent out more signals than an FM radio station.

"You know. Don't you find me attractive?" Kayla puts a hand one hip and runs the other down my chest.

Taking a deep breath, I study the attractive woman in front of me. Kayla is fine. That's not the problem.

"You're beautiful," I tell her.

"Then what's up?" Kayla pulls me into another kiss.

Hesitant at first, I allow the feel of her body pressed against mine to take over. My tongue chases hers and I run my fingers through her hair. It's been a month since I've had sex and the opportunity is right here to release. I could run to the store for condoms and take out my frustrations by sinking between her thighs. If only Kayla was the woman I wanted.

"We shouldn't do this," I say, holding her at arm's length.

Kayla frowns. "Why not?"

Adjusting myself, I move toward the door. "It's not right."

"Not right?" Kayla limps to a chair and places a knee on the seat to brace herself. Her nostrils flare. "I'm not good enough for you, huh? Are *you* gay?"

Things have escalated too fast, but I temper an angry response. "You can clearly see I'm not gay." I nod toward my groin, which is standing at full attention. "But we work together, and I don't want things to get messy."

Kayla exhales and relief spreads over her features. "That's all. You don't want to get involved because we work together?"

"And I need to shower. Not exactly at my best right now." Among other reasons I can't share.

"There are ways around that." Kayla looks down the hall. "I can show you my bedroom before Elena and Savannah get here. There's a really nice shower in there."

My body wants to walk down that hallway. Carmen has left me in limbo. She's put a stop to us because of a marriage based on obligation and an easily manipulated legal system. Which means I'm a single man, free to engage in grown man activities. Free to be a dog and sleep with other women. But my mind won't accept that Carmen is gone for good. It won't allow me to move on.

Kayla licks her lips and focuses on my hardness. "Come on. Let me help you with that." She crosses to stand in front of me again. Her hand grazes my manhood through the thin fabric of my running shorts and my breath catches.

"No one has to know," she whispers.

Chapter Twenty-Four

Carmen

"I'm speaking as your friend right now. Not your attorney. Are you sure you want to go through with this?" Maggie leans back in her leather chair and tosses her reading glasses on the wooden desk.

"Of course," I say without looking up from my phone. An early morning work email announces a mandatory company wide meeting to address rumors of a sale. One more thing to worry about.

Maggie flips through some papers on her desk. "I only ask because like I mentioned before, it's going to cost you. Do you think this is an opportunity to reconcile?"

The question causes me to fumble the phone in my lap. Recovering and clicking off the screen, I focus on my attorney or rather friend, wondering why she's asking me this now. Maggie's salt and pepper hair is brushed back into a sensible bun without a strand moving as she tilts her head.

I stand and walk over to the floor to ceiling windows.

Maggie's corner office is on the twenty-fifth floor of the Wilshire Grand Center building in downtown LA. The view allows me to study the various concrete, glass and metal structures encompassing the heart of the Central Business district. The traffic whizzing through the streets mimics the collusion of thoughts swerving through my mind.

"Melvin talks about reconciling but…" I turn away from the window and retrieve printouts from my bag. "But it seems as if it's mostly financially motivated."

"What's this?" Maggie flips through the bank statements.

I settle back in the seat in front of her desk. "Look at the highlighted entries. Those withdrawals coincide with Melvin's changed behaviors."

Last night, I spent hours going through Melvin's account. It helps that is used to be our joint account before I moved my direct deposit into another one at a different bank. Melvin forgot to reset the password, so I still have access.

"This is not solid evidence of a gambling problem, but it does show bad financial management. Did you ask him what the money was for?"

Shaking my head, I explain what I know. Those bank statements withdrawal dates line up with Melvin's mood swings. One hundred dollars two weeks ago when he came home with a gift for Olivia. Two hundred- and fifty-dollars last week when he insisted on taking the family out for dinner. And another five hundred when he came home sullen and short-tempered. Plus, it matches when Jay showed up asking for his money.

I update Maggie on my agreement with Jay to repay Melvin's debt.

"Make me understand why you paid this man." Maggie hits me with her serious legal face. I've seen her do this a time or two in the courtroom. She leans forward and crosses her arms while narrowing her eyes.

My stomach churns as the seat warms underneath me. I always fold when Maggie looks at me like that. "In my defense, it seemed like a good idea at the time."

Maggie relaxes her stance by shaking her shoulders and rearing back. "What did you do?"

I share the details of the relationship with Braxton, Jay seeing us together and the payment made for his silence. "But I've ended things with Braxton," I add.

She studies me for a beat, then gets up to take the seat beside me. "You met someone."

"Doesn't matter. I'm still married. Where's my attorney?" I grip her hand. "Can we fix this?"

She crosses back behind her desk. "First step is serving Melvin, and I'll send my process server out today. We'll try to catch him when he leaves work. Once that's done, I have everything ready to file with the courts."

I nod and check my phone again. The meeting starts in two hours and it's going to be a rush to make it across town in time. Replying to an email has me distracted, but I almost drop the phone at Maggie's next statement.

"You need to think about moving out of the house."

My body tenses at the thought of leaving the home I sacrificed and worked long hours to purchase. The house I had before the marriage.

"Why should I leave?" I ask, feeling a vein throb in my neck as I the push the words out. "He should leave."

Maggie doesn't acknowledge my emotional outburst and maintains eye contact. "It's best not to live together during this process. Someone has to move out and start the separation time clock. Are you thinking about living in the same house with him? Why?"

My shoulders slump. "To make things easier for Olivia."

"Nothing about divorce is easy." Maggie waits a beat. "But staying together sends mixed signals to the court. And to Melvin."

When I don't respond, she continues. "I asked you earlier if you were sure you want to go through with this. Because if Melvin finds out about the other man..."

I open my mouth to interrupt, but she holds up a finger to stop me.

"You say it's over, but it can still be used against you. I'm preparing for all contingencies because I'm going to win this thing for you."

My mind churns in anticipation of my life changing. Questions bounce off each other about the unknown, and I blink to bring reality back into focus. Compartmentalize emotions to be dealt with some other day.

The elevator doors open and Ruth's blue eyes widen in surprise. "I didn't know you were in the office yet."

Traffic was terrible, but I made the drive from downtown to the office with five minutes to spare.

"I'm here," I say, smoothing the wrinkles from my skirt. "You hear anything new about this meeting?"

Ruth crinkles her pug nose and smiles, taking delight in sharing office gossip. "Seems as if the boys in C suite want to address a rumor about the company being sold. I hear it's a done deal."

My face is a mask. "Paul mentioned it last week in our Team-10 Meetings."

Paul Jones is the Chief Communications Officer and our boss's boss. Every quarter, he hosts a virtual team meeting, which includes Susan, Doug and me.

My bluff works to shut down Ruth's glee and the ride to the fifth floor is quiet.

The 300-seat auditorium is filling up quickly and the hum of various conversations fills the space. I make my way to the front where Doug has saved me a seat. Susan acknowledges my arrival with a tight smile. The movie screen has been lowered, and the projector is being adjusted on the stage by a khaki clad employee with the signature phone clipped to his hip, which most of the IT division seem to favor.

"We're getting a speech straight from the CEO in New York," Doug leans over. His thin mustache matches his thinning hairline. "I guess the rumor is true."

I can only manage a nod because a tingle caresses the back of my neck and takes my breath away. There is no need to turn around to know when Braxton has entered the room.

Doug continues to speak, but my attention is drawn to the man several rows up. I haven't seen him in a few weeks and watch as he maneuvers down the aisle and stops to squeeze past someone seated on the end. The muscles in his starched shirt flex as he excuses himself past. Braxton speaks to someone and as he adjusts in the seat, our eyes meet.

We are separated by several rows, he is about eight or ten rows up, but it seems our thoughts are connected. I telepath my energy with a smile. He will always be the sexiest man I know. And I miss him like crazy. He returns the sentiment with his trademark smirk and double taps two fingers to his chest.

Braxton told me once that whenever he sees me, his heart dances. It's a simple gesture we worked out early in our relationship, but one which works on me every time. The familiar fluttering in my stomach returns, but soon turns into a pit that cramps.

Someone elbows Braxton and lingers a little longer than casual. He laughs at whatever she's saying, and our moment is lost.

Kayla. He's sitting with Kayla.

Turning back to the stage, I can barely focus on the presentation. Parker & Kramer's CEO, Steven Kramer, appears remotely to ensure us this new transition will be smooth. He keeps fidgeting with his salt and pepper beard, which doesn't exactly convey job security.

Now Gary Moeller strolls to the podium and takes command. "Here are the facts," he begins after adjusting the microphone and running a hand over his gelled hair. "One small part of P&K has been purchased by another company. This company is based in New York and is a leader in the beauty care business with global offices around the world, including here in LA. The Board is still negotiating the particulars, but I have assurances that every current employee will retain their jobs. Some of you may be relocated, but no one is losing their livelihood on my watch."

He pauses here for applause which doesn't come. The room is quiet until someone coughs. Gary's face reddens, but he continues. "Human Resources will be in contact with any employee who will need to shift to the new company."

Gary squares his shoulders. "I'm sure there are questions, but I'll ask that you save them for your Department Head. I'll be meeting with them this afternoon to go over specifics. Thank you for your attention."

He exits the stage and is surrounded by upper-level executives who whisk him out the side exit. People file out, but I'm unable to move from my seat. The plethora of sentiments weighing me in place.

Melvin's gambling must be addressed. The uncertainty of being moved to another company is unsettling.

But the major feeling that brings on sudden nausea is the thought of Braxton moving on with someone else. Have I lost him too?

Chapter Twenty-Five

Braxton

After making a detour to the Research lab, I dash into the auditorium to find a seat. This Management Program has a brother humping most days to meet the obligations of learning about every area and maintaining my usual workload. I keep reminding myself it will all pay off in the end. Playing the long game, so to speak.

But I am tired. And not in the mood for a long-drawn-out presentation. My feelings lighten when I see her.

Carmen gifts me with a smile and all the tension leaves my body. Those lips. She has taken her rightful place up front with the executives, and my face lifts into a smirk to hide the pride I feel for her. Carmen still has an effect on me, even from the other side of the room.

I tap out our signal. Let her know she still has my heart. Even though I must let her go.

Kayla leans over and makes a snide comment about the CEO looking like Colonel Sanders of KFC fame.

"You know I met him once," I laugh. "The CEO, not the KFC dude. He had on an all-white suit then too."

I'm relieved that Kayla and I are still cool after our close encounter last weekend. Stretching my legs under the seat in front of me, I replay the awkward conversation.

"I can't do it," I mumbled.

Kayla smiled. "Sure looks like you can. Looks like you got a whole lot to work with, too."

Removing Kayla's hand from my shorts, I fixed my clothes and reached for the doorknob. "No, I mean, I can't do this with you. I consider you a friend, so I have to be honest. There's someone else."

"Wow." Kayla hopped back to the sofa and propped her ankle on a cushion. "All this time and you've never mentioned a girlfriend."

"Yeah, well things are complicated right now."

"Tell me about it." Kayla motioned to the chair across from her perch on the sofa.

The memory of that conversation fades as Gary, the Operating officer, is on the stage now. "One small part of P&K has been purchased by another company."

Maybe getting transferred somewhere would help me get over Carmen. It's not like I can sit around and wait on her forever. Actual advice from Kayla, although she doesn't know the identity of this 'ex-girlfriend'.

"You can't wait around forever," Kayla said. "Either tell this woman how you feel and work it out or move on."

So, I took the first steps toward getting over Carmen by revisiting the past again.

"It's been a long time," I said when Leslie answered the phone. The lady was persistent. She had been calling at least once a week.

Leslie's voice pitches high when she raps. "I shouldn't have left you..."

"Bad joke. Don't use Rakim's lyric like that." Maybe it wasn't the best idea to call the woman who broke my heart while dealing with a broken heart. That song reminded me of memories from college. When I thought she was happy with me.

Leslie was quiet for a second and then cleared her throat. "Sorry about that. I had this whole speech planned for when we spoke again but...I'm glad you called."

"Yeah." I bit back a nasty retort. "You've been blowing up my phone. Do you need something? 'Cause we already talked, and I thought we were done rehashing things."

"I feel like something still needs to be said, though."

There was silence on the other end, and I took a breath and blew it out slowly. This was a bad idea. "Listen, I'm about to go…"

"You ever watch someone you love die?" Leslie blurts. Her voice hitches from the weight of that statement. "It makes you think about the past. All the wasted time and lost opportunities."

"I'm sorry about your father," I began, but Leslie cuts me off.

"Thank you. He was lucky. It was a minor heart attack. And I have help taking care of him. But I really wanted to tell you how I hated the way things ended between us. And I know it was my fault."

This was a surprising statement. "Umm, thanks for that." Leslie finally taking responsibility for the collapse of our relationship, should have sparked a reaction or emotion from me. I feel nothing but boredom.

"And I was hoping we could talk again. Maybe rekindle what we had. Or at least explore, if it's possible."

I thought it was clear rekindling wasn't an option. Leslie was definitely in my past. It was time to stop dwelling there and focus on making my future.

"We can be friends. So, how about I give you call next week?" I said to end the awkward conversation.

People rising at once signal the meeting is over. My legs are happy to stand from the cramped position wedged against the seat in front.

"He said HR will notify any employee that's getting relocated. Maybe your boy Devon can give us a heads up." Kayla reaches for my hand to help her teeter on the black heels she's wearing despite a wrapped ankle. Fashion over comfort always for this lady.

I automatically search for Carmen, but with so many moving people, it's impossible to get a bead on her. "If Devon knows anything, you know he can't hold it."

We walk back to our cubicles together. Kayla chats nonstop about the pending sale of the company, but my mind is running down my Plan B. I pull out my phone and send a quick text to Omar. We can talk tonight about my marketing proposal for his business. P&K is the springboard for me to learn and eventually branch out on my own. You can't build wealth by working for someone else.

"You ever think about starting your own business?"

Kayla is back in her favorite spot. Ass on my desk with her legs crossed.

"Not really." She takes lip gloss from her purse and applies it with a stroke. "You thinking about leaving?"

I swivel in my chair and tap the keyboard to wake up the screen. "My Pops always said a man should have a plan."

"Well, you can't leave," she pouts.

From the corner of my eye, I spot Carmen, who glides past, heading to her office. I don't realize I'm staring until Kayla taps me with her foot.

"Damn, you looking hard at boss lady."

Adjusting my shirt sleeves, I focus on tapping in my login. An email notification pops up that requires intense attention.

"What's up, B?" Kayla tries to get my attention.

"Nothing." I shrug and pick up the phone. "I need to return some calls, so I'll catch you later."

Kayla doesn't move right away, and I chance a glance. Her head is cocked to the side while she studies my profile. "You're acting real weird, right now."

Before I can respond, she leaves in a huff.

That was smooth.

We may be cool, but the last thing I need is for Kayla to figure out the full extent of my relationship with our "boss lady".

Chapter Twenty-Six

Carmen

 oug leans back in the mahogany leather chair and spreads his arms wide. "That's the jest of it. All I know. The sale is a done deal, and a percentage of our Marketing Team will be transferred to the new company."

Bisous is the name of the new company. The France-based company's name means beauty. They are a major player in the Beauty and Health Care field. Along the lines of L'Oreal and Estee' Lauder.

I flip through the packet spread over the small wooden table in Doug's office. Susan has already left for the day, claiming she has a doctor's appointment. Our working relationship has developed into me attending meetings and giving her a debrief later. "What made P&K decide to sell the beauty division?"

Doug's leg bounces under the table. A nervous tic I've noticed seems to appear whenever he's not being truthful. Ever since the ambush during my presentation, his leg has been getting a good workout whenever I'm around. What I once thought was a good working relationship has been soured by his not giving me a heads up about Susan. "Not sure," he says.

"And how long has this been in the works? Most corporate takeovers take months or years to become final." I close my portfolio. "Never mind that. Will there be an opportunity for advancement if you're transferred?"

The leg is doing double time now. My gut is telling me I won't get all the relevant details from my supervisor, and I make a mental note to schedule a meeting with Gary.

"Always planning to get ahead. That's what I like about you, Miller." Doug takes a swig from a sweating can of soda. "But if I were you and Susan, I would make sure all accounts are up to date. We can't afford to have any loose ends. The Bisous people will go over everything. We can't give them a reason to get rid of our people."

The rest of the afternoon is spent sequestered in my office, analyzing our accounts and researching Bisous. It helps distract me from my personal problems. And I don't want to risk seeing Braxton. The thought of him moving on with Kayla causes my jaw to clench, and I massage the back of my neck to ease the tension of losing him.

Ruth interrupts me by knocking on the closed office door. She hands me a jump drive. "Here are all the spreadsheets you requested."

"Thanks," I say without looking up. Clicking the mouse brings new emails on the screen. Some of our clients are getting word of the impending sale and have questions.

"Is there anything else?" Ruth wrings her hands. "It's getting late. Most of the staff has already left."

Time has swept by without me realizing its 6:00 p.m.

I shoot off the chair and collapse when dizziness makes me lightheaded. Melvin is working a double (again) and there's only thirty minutes to get Olivia before the late fees kick in.

Waving off Ruth's concerned look, I stuff my laptop and files in the computer bag. "Sure, Ruth. Have a good weekend."

Staving off a mini panic attack when I can't find my car, Melvin's truck is the lone vehicle in the parking lot. He finally took my car after it did the non-starting thing again. At this time yesterday, I was with Olivia after her dance class and we were stranded.

It's déjà vu when I rush into the school twenty-nine minutes later and Olivia isn't there.

I'm informed Melvin picked her up, but he neglected to let me know. Back in the truck, I check my phone for text messages or missed calls. I've gotten two calls from Maggie, but nothing else. Ignoring the sense of unease that curls into a ball in my stomach, I head home.

My car isn't in the garage when I arrive at the house. The ball in my belly churns as I screen negative thoughts through my mind. *Where are they?*

I rush through the door and see Melvin is sitting in his chair. Papers are crumbled in his hands.

"Hey. What's going on? Did something happen to the car?" My heart rate slows as I take several deep breaths.

Melvin doesn't answer at first and before I can register how odd it is that the television isn't on, he blows up my world with a question.

"Why was your car parked at the Courtyard Marriott on Ventura?"

I freeze. "What?"

"Why was your car parked behind that hotel?"

I drop my purse on the sofa and turn to face him. My mind goes into rewind trying to piece together what Melvin is saying. *How could he know?*

"What are you talking about? Is that where my car is right now?" My attempt at deflection falls flat.

Melvin leans forward. His entire body is clutched like the fist he rubs on his leg. "Now it makes sense. You kick me out the bed the other day. Serving me with divorce papers at my damn job. Why was your car at a fucking hotel near your office?"

My heart drums in my chest and I look around for a way out. I wipe my sweaty palms on my pants. "Where's Olivia?"

"Not here. Now answer the question."

"Where is she?"

Melvin's voice drops lower. "I always knew you thought you were smarter than me. But you must think I'm an idiot."

"I don't think that…"

He cuts me off with a shake of his head. "All those late-night meetings."

"Were just that. Meetings."

"And then I drive your car to work. And the one guy I can't stand, Jay, of all people, starts talking slick. Says he'll squash my debt with my wife's car. Tells me

'I bet you I've seen that car before'. He keeps picking like he knows something I don't. Like, how does he even know your car?"

Time stops.

I see myself standing in the middle of the living room, as my plans are imploding. The family photo on the mantel mocks the scene taking place right now. This isn't the way I wanted Melvin to learn about Braxton, but in a way, it's a relief.

Melvin stands in front of me with red-rimmed eyes. "So, I beat it out of him. How he helped you with your car. At a hotel. I know it was you. Checked your trunk. Saw your bag full of toiletry stuff. Why were you there, Carmen?"

I open my mouth, but the words I want to say evaporate in the desert of lies I've stored there. Only the truth can emerge.

"I...I had...an affair." I step back and wait for the blow. My chest constricts and I close my eyes. Wait to feel regret or remove the pain on Melvin's face.

I hear a thud and open my eyes. Melvin collapses on the couch and puts his head in his hands. "Why?"

"What do you mean? Our marriage hasn't been good for a long time and..." My body deflates as I fold on the couch beside him. The pain radiates from him in a wave, leading me to massage my chest. A part of me will always be remorseful for having created his heartache. He is the father of my child.

"I know I may not be the best husband sometimes. But we're married, and you cheat on me?"

Now is not the time to remind him how we ended up in this situation. The silence screams with all the things I don't say.

It's too quiet. I'm about to ask about our daughter when I notice the bruises on his knuckles. "You really hit him?"

"Jay wouldn't shut up. So, I had to close his big mouth."

"Good." The weasel got what he deserved.

We share a laugh. Our history includes a mutual love of action movies where the bad guy gets what's coming to him.

Melvin leans into me, but then jumps to his feet. "Who is it?"

The sudden change makes me dizzy and my sense of balance shifts as I'm bouncing on the couch.

He glares down at me. "Who is it? Some suit and tie from your office?"

"It doesn't matter." My arms fold over my stomach and I swallow the ache in the back of my throat. There is no way I'm saying Braxton's name in this moment.

"It matters that my wife is fucking another man." Melvin screws up his face and balls up the papers in his hands, throwing them at me. "You know what? I'm out of here. I can't stand to look at you."

My muscles quiver as I stand and unfold the papers. *Petition for Dissolution of Marriage*. Now I know why Maggie was calling. The process server was successful.

A quick survey of Olivia's bedroom reveals its empty. Our daughter's room is exactly as it was left this morning. The book she was reading is tossed on the checkered pink twin size comforter. A drawer on the white wooden dresser is left ajar, spilling socks like a secret. The scent of olive oil hair lotion lingers in the air. The absence of my baby causes my entire core to vibrate with rage and without another thought, I go to confront Melvin.

"Where is Olivia?"

"She's away from you." Melvin shoves clothes into a duffel bag. "Did you think about her when you were screwing around?"

My shoulders tighten and my stomach clenches from the low blow.

"What happened to the money?" The words come out low and slow.

Now Melvin freezes. A pair of socks drop to the floor. "Money?"

"How long have you been gambling?"

"What are you talking about?" Melvin recovers and flings a pair of sneakers into the case, turning his back to me.

That act, one he's done several times before, giving me his back, enrages me more. "Your buddy's just running around spilling everybody's secrets. He told me all about the bet you lost. Five hundred dollars on some football game. Who do you think paid him?"

"You did what?" Melvin's face contorts into something I haven't seen before. Shame.

My finger is shoved in his face. "Paid your debt, like always. That's right, Jay showed up on my doorstep looking for you. Told me you owed him the money and wouldn't pay."

Melvin's eyes go cold. "Don't try to turn this on me. I don't have a gambling problem."

"Where's my car then? Did you just lose my car in a bet? But you don't have a problem." My laugh has no merriment in it.

We stare at each other for several moments. This back and forth isn't accomplishing anything, and I take a deep breath and drop my hands. "Listen, let's take a beat. Our lines are getting crossed here. Now where's Olivia?"

"Don't try to use your 'corporate speak' on me." Melvin zips his bag and pushes past me. "Here's something you'll understand. You're a fucking terrible wife and you don't deserve a family."

The rage builds anew and spews fiery venom unleashes on Melvin's back. I pound him over and over. "Where is my baby? Where did you take my baby?"

Melvin tries to grab my hands, but I am a cyclone. I may lose a husband, but no one is taking my child.

"Would you stop? Calm down, Carmen." He twists away from my fury and runs to the other side of the room. Melvin could easily subdue me with one blow, but all restraint is gone. If I have to fight him, we'll be on the news tonight, but he's going to answer me.

I look around for something to hit him with. My eyes are slits as adrenaline rushes through my causing my chest to heave with each breath.

Melvin raises his hands. "Are you crazy?"

"Don't make me ask you again." I kick off a high heel shoe and raise it like a knife.

"Okay, okay. She's at Momma's. But she's not going with you."

I don't hear the rest of Melvin's rant. I snatch the keys to his truck and fly out the door to go get my child.

The forty-minute drive to Barbara's in West Compton is a blur. When my senses return, I'm standing on the porch pressing the doorbell and yelling Olivia's name.

Barbara answers the door, wiping her hands on a dish towel. The smell of freshly baked chocolate cookies greets me as I push past her into the house.

"Olivia," I call and find my daughter standing in the kitchen. Flour is spotted on her school uniform and the huge smile on her face reveals the missing tooth she lost a few days ago.

"Mommy, we're making cookies. Grandma said I can have one before dinner for being a big help." Olivia points to a batch of cookies cooling on the counter.

"That's nice, baby. Let's go. Where's your bag?" I turn to the living room looking for Olivia's bookbag.

Barbara rushes into the room. "You know she's welcome to stay." Melvin's mother shares the same pecan coloring of her son. Her small, chubby frame is draped in a purple flowered house dress. A Christmas present from Olivia and me. We've always gotten along, but I'm not sure what she knows and how she will react.

"It's time for her to come home," I say and grab the bookbag from the couch.

"But I'm making cookies with Grandma," Olivia whines. Tears are on the verge of spilling.

Barbara wraps me in a hug and I'm cocooned in a cloud of vanilla mixed with Estee Lander White Linen perfume. "Let the baby stay," she whispers. "You and Mel need some time to work through things."

The scent helps to douse the simmering flames of anger, but embarrassment causes heat to flush my face. "I'm sorry to barge in here like this. But Melvin..."

Barbara hushes me and leads me to a chair at the kitchen table. She sets Olivia up with a plate of cookies and a cup of milk in the family room and pops in a Disney DVD.

"Now we can chat for a bit away from listening ears." Barbara crosses to the stove and puts on a kettle. "Some tea will help."

My hands fidget with the bright yellow vinyl placemat. "I don't know what Melvin has told you about what happened today."

Barbara removes two mugs from the cabinet and places a tea bag in both. "Oh, he was in a state," she says, pouring hot water from the whistling kettle. "He went on awful."

Her knees creak when she settles in the seat beside me. I take the bottle of honey she offers and squeeze some into my cup. "It wasn't right what I did, and I ended things but..." I swirl the spoon in my cup. "Our marriage hasn't been good for a while now."

"Melvin Senior wasn't an easy man to love." Barbara takes a sip of tea before continuing. "Now he was a good man. Worked hard. Took care of his family. But he was set in his ways. Believed women should make the home and men should make the money."

Not wanting to interrupt Barbara, I lean forward and nod. We've had our share of conversations over the years, but getting in-depth knowledge about Melvin's father wasn't discussed. The man had been dead for years before I came into the family.

"Oh, I may have had dreams once. But then I was married and put them aside to focus on my family. Shoot, I don't even remember wanting to be anything other than a wife and mother. And now grandmother."

We both turn to check on Olivia, who is content munching on cookies. She is oblivious to us as she shimmies in her seat to the activity of the cartoon characters on the television.

Barbara taps her fingers against her cup. "Nowadays, you young ladies can have it all. I don't begrudge you that one bit."

My mouth falls open in surprise. "Really. Melvin would always tell me how I should be more like you. I thought you agreed with him."

"Melvin is spoiled," Barbara says and waves away my comment. "And no doubt about it, it's all my fault. When Senior died, I took all the love I had for that man and poured it into my son. Treated him like he was the star 'cause he was all I had left."

Her hands shake at the memory of her late husband, and I clasp her fingers with mine. "You did the best you could. No one can blame you for loving your son."

The telephone rings reciting the name and number of the caller.

"It's daddy," Olivia announces and springs to pick up the cordless phone on the end table.

Barbara pats my hands before releasing them. "What I'm trying to say is, don't let Melvin hold you back. If he can't love you the way you need, then it's best to move on."

I study her face but only see empathy in her eyes and a sincere smile on her lips.

"You know he has a gambling problem." I wince saying the words unsure how she will receive the realization. I'm sure she's seen the signs but I tell her about my missing car and why I'm in Melvin's truck.

Barbara nods and then Olivia bounces into the kitchen. "Daddy wants to talk to you."

She kisses Olivia on the forehead and takes the phone. Covering the receiver, she says, "Don't worry about Livvy. She'll be here when you're ready. I'll get Melvin the help he needs."

Chapter Twenty-Seven

Braxton

"Hey, have you seen Carmen this week?"

The dimly lit restaurant has enough light for me to see Kayla cut her eyes. "No, it's been nice to have Boss Lady missing."

I shrug and try to appear indifferent. "She hasn't signed off on my project yet. Holding me up." The management program finished up today and The Three insisted on celebrating with dinner at Major Domo's the hottest new restaurant in LA. Reservations are typically thirty days out but once again, Savannah has connections and we're seated on the patio of the restaurant at a large table for eight.

"Word has it that she's taking personal time." Kayla spears a sugar snap pea. "I'm surprised she would miss out on an opportunity to show off for the new buyers."

It is odd. Carmen would be working overtime to ensure our team has everything in place.

I turn to Devon. "Anything new with this buyout?"

He slices into his serving of smoked short ribs and talks with his mouth full. "Man, it's about to get real. The bigwigs are meeting again next week."

Before I can ask a follow up, Elena interjects. "Enough talk about work from you three. Show some manners in front of my girl."

Conversation turns to Sloan, a petite redhead with freckles sprinkled across her nose. She and Elena complete each other sentences which is annoying and cute at the same time. They seem happy.

Savannah and the moody Brent are a direct contrast. They sit at opposite ends of the table and ignore each other. Brent is buried in his phone and doesn't engage with anyone else at the table. Savannah goes around taking selfies and posting on Instagram. A few diners recognize her, and she poses for pictures.

Devon is ecstatic to be included in my new social group and can't shut up. I'm seated between him and Kayla, and listening to their exchange is giving me a headache.

When the check comes and everyone pays, I beg off and leave them for the rest of the planned night of club hopping.

"It's Friday night," Devon calls to my retreating back. "What you got going on?"

"Omar called earlier. He may come through." I return to the restaurant entrance to hug the ladies. "I'll catch you later."

And Omar did call. But I spend the night wondering if I should reach out to Carmen.

By the next morning, I can't keep from dialing her number. My fingers tap out her digits while I'm out walking Maxx and my heart beats in time to the ringtone. Something in her voice catches when she answers.

"Are you okay?"

We listen to each other breathe and she says two words I've been longing to hear. And dreading at the same time.

"He knows."

Maxx yelps when my abrupt stop yanks on his leash. Without planning it, our route leads us back to the Grove.

I sit and pull Maxx on my lap. Massaging his furry head is an apology for the pulled leash and helps to calm my racing thoughts. "What happened?"

Carmen tells me about the argument. Her daughter has been staying with her grandmother while she confers with her attorney and changes the locks and security codes on her home.

"Right now, it's best for Olivia to have some semblance of order. She's used to me being gone for travel. I talk to her every day and she's fine."

"And you? How are you?" Maxx jumps down and I allow his leash enough slack for him to sniff a potted plant. "You haven't been at work."

There's movement on her end and muffled words from someone in the background. Her voice echoes when she returns to the line.

"Sorry," she says. "Gayle's here. I had to go into the bathroom to get some privacy. She doesn't think I need to be alone."

"What do you need, baby?"

Her response takes an eternity, but when it comes, everything in my world is good.

"You," she says. "I need you."

I pace around the Grove, waiting on Carmen. She wouldn't let me come to her place for obvious reasons and agreed to meet me out here. Maxx and I wander through the Farmers Market and end up near the Fountain when she texts that she's at valet. I find a table outside of Barnes & Noble near the movie theater and wait for her to appear.

When she comes around the corner, it's like a slow-motion movie scene. Carmen is the picture of sophistication as she strolls past some admiring onlookers. She has on a pair of skinny jeans with a t-shirt bearing the word feminist. Her hair is pulled into a messy bun and her face is makeup free. But there are traces of fatigue in her eyes.

"Hey," she says when she is in front of me.

I want to grab her but take my cues from Carmen. "Hey."

We stare at each other until Maxx barks for attention. He puts both front paws on her leg and wags his tail.

"Hello to you too." Carmen bends to scratch behind Maxx's ears.

"He really does like you," I say.

"Surprised he remembers me. It's been a while, and we met through a car window."

I gesture for her to sit and Maxx follows the sign as well. "He's a smart dog."

Carmen looks around. A movie has ended, and the area fills with people. "Gayle told me I shouldn't come." She lowers her head and smooths a wayward curl behind her ear. "She doesn't think this is a good idea."

"Glad you did." Lifting her chin to make eye contact, I say, "You can tell me anything."

She gives me a further rundown of things that have taken place and an update on the divorce status. When she shares Melvin's gambling problem and losing the car, I'm enraged on her behalf. "My mom is disappointed in me. But my sister is supporting the decision. We've talked more in the past week than we have all year. So, something good came out of all this. But I've missed...work."

Carmen bites her lip and averts her gaze. I study her profile as a breeze blows a strand of hair against her neck. That soft spot where the shoulder blades meet calls to me, causing my mouth to water. It's been weeks without being in her presence, but the energy between us is still strong. I wonder if she feels it too. Pops once told me to never ask a woman a question you don't want to know the answer to. So, I don't. Instead, I say, "Are you hungry?"

Carmen swallows and gifts me with a smile. "I could eat."

"I live nearby. We can walk to my place and come back for your car."

"Are you sure? I don't want to interrupt anything." Carmen thinks she's being subtle, but with the tilt of her head, I know what she's really asking.

Taking take her hands in mine, I bring them to my lips. "I've been waiting for you."

She links her fingers through mine and closes her eyes, then takes a deep breath and nods. "Let's go."

We stand and I pull her into a hug. Everything is right in my world. Until I open my eyes and see Kayla standing less than three feet away with a box of popcorn in her hand and a frown on her face.

Chapter Twenty-Eight

Carmen

I was expecting a bachelor/frat boy pad punctuated with sports paraphernalia and littered with pizza boxes. Braxton's place is the definition of a young urban professional with classic pieces of leather furniture and highlighted by a 70-inch television. The only thing out of place is the large man taking up most of the oversized lounge chair.

He tosses the game controller aside and stands. "Damn, homie. You went out for a run and came back with a honey."

Braxton stumbles over a sneaker and grabs a chair to steady himself. "Carmen, please forgive my trifling friend." He motions to the pile of clothes spilling out of a duffel bag beside the guy's feet.

"I'm Omar," he approaches with hand extended and turns to Braxton. "Now I see why you were tripping."

"Excuse me," my eyebrows rise and I look in Braxton's direction. "You were talking about me?"

If Braxton could turn a shade of red, he would be purple. It's adorable.

Omar dramatically rolls his eyes. "I've known this dude since high school and he's on some other level behind you."

Braxton takes my hand and leads me to a bedroom. "Would you please give me a moment? My friend was just leaving."

I allow him to escort me into what I assume is his room. Before he shuts the door, Omar tries to whisper, "You didn't tell me she was fine as hell."

Alone in Braxton's room, I survey his space. The gray walls are accented by the navy-blue comforter set on the queen size bed. His nightstand displays a copy of Ta-Nehisi Coates' latest book, along with a Walter Mosley novel. Family photos litter the dresser.

I rest in a recliner in the corner. Maxx the Dog takes it as an invitation to hop on my lap. He lays his head on my chest and gazes up at me, causing me to smile. Olivia would definitely love this little dog.

Thoughts of my daughter make me reflect on the events of the past few weeks. After leaving Olivia at Barbara's that day, I didn't make it past the living room at my house without collapsing on the floor wrecked with guilt for destroying my daughter's idyllic life and losing leverage with Melvin. Thankfully, he was gone, and I took an Uber, leaving Melvin's truck at Barbara's. Gayle found me curled on the couch later that night. She helped me make a plan to get my car back.

Maggie was calling to warn me about Melvin being served. She also informed me about the intel on the fake judge. Seems as if there are ties to Melvin's family–the judge was his father's frat brother. Plus, he has a gambling problem, and it was discovered that he was susceptible to bribery.

But when Braxton called, I had to answer. I needed to see if what we had was real. Could it survive in reality or was it best preserved as a fantasy?

"Sorry about that." Braxton leans in the doorway with his hands in his pockets.

"No problem. Where was that picture taken?" Maxx the Dog wags his tail and shifts his position.

"You mean this one?" Braxton crosses the room and picks up a silver framed portrait.

I nod.

"Our last family get together years ago. Debra was leaving for London." The admiration he has for his sister is palpable. "She just got engaged."

"That's nice," I say, stifling a yawn and running a hand over Maxx the Dog's fur. He nuzzles my neck and tries to lick my face.

Braxton kneels in front of me. "You seem tired."

"It's been a rough few days." I don't elaborate on the insomnia which started when Melvin left. Worry has been a constant companion since I've been forced to truly deal with my sham of a marriage, Olivia needs, and what I really want.

"Well, I *have* been trying to get you into my bed." Braxton wiggles his eyebrows and nods toward the bed.

A familiar heat radiates from my core. I've longed to feel his arms around me once again.

Braxton moves the dog and takes both of my hands in his. He guides me to the bed and pulls back the covers. I snuggle underneath sheets that envelop me in the scent of lavender.

"Fresh sheets?"

"You came on laundry day." Braxton shrugs. "Mom raised me to change the bed every week. You never know when some sleep deprived woman will show up."

I wriggle a little more to make myself even more comfortable. "Lucky me."

Braxton kisses me on the forehead. "No, lucky me."

Clanging pots and the scent of garlic mixed with chili spices awaken my senses. For a second, I panic, looking around an unfamiliar room in the fading sunlight. Then Maxx the Dog enters the room and puts his paws on the edge of the mattress and pants dog breath in my face.

"Hey, buddy." Giving him a rub, I swing my legs off the bed and stand to stretch before going to find Braxton.

Stopping short, my sock covered feet slide and I brace myself against the wall to the kitchen. The sight of Braxton bent over closing the oven door warms me in several places. There's something sexy about a man cooking. He removes a pair of mitts and opens a wine cooler I didn't notice under the counter.

My mouth waters at the sight of the bottle. "That wouldn't be Chablis chardonnay, would it?"

"Perfect timing." Braxton turns and fills one of the wineglasses sitting on the bar with a place setting for two. "Food's almost done."

Taking a sip, I slide onto a barstool and watch Braxton across the space. "Smells good. What are you making?"

"Jamaican Jerk Chicken with Rice and Peas." He studies me with a grin. "It might not be as good as your mom's, but we can give it a try."

"Impressive. You remembered."

His gaze intensifies. "I remember everything you tell me."

The temperature of the room rises and it's not because of the oven. He stares over the rim of his wineglass and after taking a drink, licks his full lips.

My mouth parts in anticipation of his touch, and I run my moist hands down a pant leg.

Braxton puts down his glass and walks around the counter. Maxx the Dog picks that moment to bound toward the door and dance in a circle.

"Someone needs to go out," Braxton says. "While you were asleep, I retrieved your car." He points to a bowl on the edge of the counter which houses keys and his charging cell phone. "Do you need to leave soon?"

Olivia is with Melvin through the weekend. We've worked out an informal/formal arrangement blessed by Maggie where Livvy is with me during the week. Melvin comes every school morning to drop her off as per the usual routine. And on the weekends, I take her to Barbara's, where Melvin has been staying. Every time I leave her, I'm worried about getting her back, but so far Barbara is a fair middle person in the exchange.

"No rush," I say.

"You can stay?" Braxton lifts a leash from a hook by the door. The little dog spins around in a circle again.

Swirling the liquid in the glass, I take another drink before answering. "Only if you want me to."

"I want you to." Braxton opens the door. "Be right back."

When the door closes behind him, I call and check on Olivia. Barbara has been good at letting me speak to her without having to go through Melvin. Our talk that day has opened a mutual respect between us and she hasn't let Melvin's name calling affect her actions.

After telling Olivia good night, the phone is placed on the counter. I take my wine glass and browse Braxton's place further. Gayle doesn't think I should entertain this relationship, but being here feels right. My life is messy, but Braxton has a way of making me forget.

A buzzing sound grabs my attention from the view out the balcony window and back to the counter. Braxton's phone lights up with a call. A call from someone identified as 'Les'.

The ringtone ends and immediately plays again. Whoever this Les person is, they are persistent.

I hover over the phone and listen for it to sound again when the jingle of keys in the lock causes me to jump back. When Braxton and Maxx the Dog bound through the door, I'm perched on the bar stool again. Glass of wine in a shaking hand.

"That was fast," my voice raises and the cheerfulness lands false to my ears.

Braxton doesn't seem to notice. "Maxx knows how to handle business." He unsnaps the leash, hangs it back on the hook, and crosses to the kitchen. Running water in the sink, he scrubs his hands. "Ready to eat?"

I can only nod. While Braxton dishes up servings of food and places the plates on the bar, my interest is on the phone.

When it begins to ring again, I jump.

Braxton walks around the bar, glances at the phone, and shuts it off with a swipe. "Now you let me know if it needs some extra chilies or lime."

He takes a forkful of food and blows on it without breaking eye contact with me. My taste buds explode from the mixture of soy sauce, thyme and other spices. The chicken is so tender it practically melts and then the infamous jerk kicks in. All thoughts of the phone call are overtaken by the satisfaction of the meal made by this man.

Braxton watches me chew with his eyebrows raised in a question.

"This is really good." I tell him and scoop up a serving from my plate. "Almost as good as my mother's."

"Must be alright. You're putting a hurting on that plate," Braxton laughs. "And I was worried you wouldn't like it."

"Me too," I tease.

We eat in silence for a few minutes and then Braxton punches a button on a remote and soft music fills the air. The lights are dimmed, and he stands. "Dance with me."

With my hand in his, we sway to the rhythm of a popular jazz artist.

"You're full of surprises." I can't remember the last time a man cooked for me, let alone danced with me.

"All I needed was a chance to show you," he whispers and pulls me closer.

The heat from our bodies sends an electrical jolt to my core. His hands caress my back and move lower. I stroke his neck and inhale his familiar clean scent with the hints of cinnamon.

When the song ends, he doesn't release his hold. "I'm still hungry," he says.

"You barely ate anything." I start for the bar, but Braxton pulls me tighter.

He licks his lips, and the meaning is clear. He's hungry for me.

Braxton's hooded eyes seek mine and my knees get weak. His muscular arms help me remain upright as he tilts my chin toward him. Our lips meet and the sensation causes my breath to hitch. Braxton's tongue pursues mine.

Without breaking our connection, Braxton slowly walks us to the couch. He sits and pulls me on top. I straddle his lap and take his face between both hands. We kiss again. His lips tasting like wine aren't the only reason I'm intoxicated.

"Can't believe you're here." Braxton takes one finger to move a strand of hair and nibbles my neck.

There's no place I'd rather be than in this exact spot with this man. My body is a taut nerve stimulated by every touch. Especially when Braxton removes my shirt and slips off my bra. My breasts, the girls, are free from restraint and Braxton takes one in his mouth while caressing the other.

My moans must call to Maxx because the little dog leaps on the couch and tries to nuzzle in between us.

"No way, man," Braxton addresses the dog. "You're not going to mess this up. Maxx, bed."

At his command, the dog hurries to a furry pillow in the room's corner. He circles a few times and then settles down.

"Impressive." I grind on Braxton's lap and the sensation causing his mouth to fall open. "Now do me."

Chapter Twenty-Nine

Braxton

It feels like the first time. The adrenaline rush. The nervous anticipation. Leading Carmen into the bedroom, my thoughts are all over the place. This is what I wanted. She's here with me. Now I'm going to show her this is where she belongs.

"Stand here." I twirl her around until she's beside the bed. "Let me look at you."

The lights are off but the blinds are open, so her skin is reflected by moonlight. Her breathing is uneven as I approach to remove her pants.

I begin at her breasts, kissing, licking, and sucking them until she squirms. Then I unbutton her jeans, push them over that ample apple bottom ass. I follow the path to the floor. Sliding those red thongs down between toned legs. From this position, I am face to face with the prize. Her feminine scent luring me to taste her essence.

"Lay down," I command.

She looks at me with lustful eyes and bites her bottom lip. "Are you going to join me?"

I nod. "Most definitely. But I'm going to take my time."

Carmen's breath quickens when I remove my shirt. She relaxes as I massage one foot and then the other. Working my way up her body, I spend a copious amount of time on those legs. Tickle the sensitive area behind her left knee. Then kiss my way up to the promised land. The area men kill for.

I take her with my mouth. Savor her juices. Write my name with my tongue.

Carmen takes my head in both hands and grinds against my mouth. She's calling on me and God. I circle her pearl, the most delicate area, and tease it by gently stroking the nub.

"You like it, baby?" Coming up for air, Carmen is a vision laid bare before me. Her curly hair is wild, and the sheets are tangled from her thrashing. A light sheen of sweat glistens on her skin. She tries to make words but can only nod. "Tell me you like it."

"Yes," she pants. "Yes, Braxton. Oh my God. Braxton."

She chants my name when I dive back in. My only mission is to take her there. Her legs are around my neck now. I have a handful of ass in one hand, a breast in the other.

When I sense she's about to cum, I ease back. Play the game of hide and seek until her legs tremble against my face. Carmen rolls her hips and begs for release.

Taking a deep breath, I relish driving her to ecstasy. Making her cum on my tongue. Licking her until the quake erupts and the juices flow. I enjoy every drop.

"Damn, B," Carmen says when her eyes can focus again. "You were hungry."

"That was only the first course." I wipe my mouth and lick her juices from my fingers. "I'm still starving, baby."

Chapter Thirty

Carmen

The man is gifted. I already knew the man had some moves. Hell, those moves made me risk everything to be with him. But he's on another level tonight.

I lean up on my elbows and take a finger to beckon him closer. "Let me please you."

Reaching for his pants, I stroke him through the fabric, and his eyes close. His member strains to be free. Before I can go for the zipper, Braxton takes my hand and kisses it.

"Tonight is about you. Do you remember what I told you back in Monaco?"

I remember. The memory of the first time we made love is forever etched in my brain. The ocean breeze was at my back, Braxton's cologne of sandalwood blended with the scent of salt and sand. Braxton quoted Rumi before we kissed.

"No," I whisper while nodding. "Tell me again."

Braxton sheds his clothes and pauses. Now it's my turn to inspect every inch of his god like physique. From his size thirteen feet, up his muscular legs, the full-size penis standing at attention to the slow sensual smile with the dimple etched in his right cheek; the man is perfection. My desire for him rushes to my center, causing my legs to open wide.

"I once had a thousand desires." Braxton climbs on the bed and hovers over me, balancing on his knees and elbows. "But in my desire to know you, all else melted away."

The last words of the Rumi quote are swallowed when his lips meet mine and the familiar jolt that hits whenever we touch returns.

My body is an electric current of desire. Braxton awakens every nerve ending as his hands explore every part of me. When he strokes the delicate lips of my vagina and rubbing my clit, I squirm in delight and smile.

Braxton's eyes never leave my face. He returns my smile as the tip of his penis massages my opening. A gasp escapes and I pull him closer. Feeling the weight of this man and the delicious, wicked things he's doing to me heightens the experience. We're not having sex. We're making love.

"Tell me you want me," he commands.

The statement is repeated when I reach for his penis and caress him. His breath eases between his teeth and he grows even harder.

"Say it." Braxton eases inside my wetness and pulls away.

Torture is the best kind of pleasure.

He does it again. Gives me what my body craves and then withdraws. Clamping my legs around his butt keeps him in place for two blissful minutes, and then he stops moving again.

"Let me hear it."

Taking his face in my hands, I lick my lips. "I want you, Braxton. I want you."

The last words are caught in my throat when Braxton enters to the hilt and starts the rhythm of my favorite dance. His strokes are slow and sensual at first. We kiss in time to each thrust. Nothing else matters but us two. All the time apart has led to this perfect moment.

I'm almost at the crescendo of our lovemaking when Braxton slows it down again.

"Please don't stop." My pelvis swirls to keep him in place.

With one swift move, Braxton flips us around and I'm on top.

"Give it to me," he says.

My hands are on his chest while I grind on top. He knows this is my favorite position and has no problem with me taking control. Soon, I'm riding him like a tornado laying waste to a town. It's my turn to watch the faces he makes as he gets closer to orgasm.

He grips my ass as he matches me, stroke for stroke.

We fit together.

My head is thrown back and I'm panting when the pleasure builds in my pelvis, and I continue grinding. Braxton moans his sounds of pleasure, which lets me know he's almost to the edge.

Then we reach the peak together. The happy place where, for a blissful moment, we are suspended in space, our bodies erupting in tune with each other.

I collapse on Braxton's chest, and he wraps both arms around me. We're still connected, and his penis pulse as it loses its firmness.

Worries threaten to dominate my thoughts, rushing in like a river. Will Olivia be okay when her parents separate? Will Melvin get a handle on his gambling problem? Can I truly make a life with Braxton after keeping him a secret?

"This feels like the beginning," Braxton whispers while pulling a sheet over our cooling bodies. Being cocooned in this moment makes me feel safe. "No matter what, we can do this. I got you, babe."

How does he know exactly what to say?

I hold on tight, and Braxton's heartbeat lulls me to sleep.

Chapter Thirty-One

Braxton

I like to watch her sleep. Sitting in the striped club chair in the corner of the room gives me the best view. Her full lips part and my mouth waters. Last night feels like a dream. Finally, having the woman of my desires in my bed.

Carmen's hair fans across the pillows. She takes a deep breath, and those breasts speak to me. We got reacquainted with each other for hours. My muscles ache and my eyes are heavy from lack of sleep. It was worth it. Every agonizing month without her was worth it. Dwelling in the warmth of her felt like returning home after a long absence.

The jingling from Maxx's collar announces his arrival in the room. He looks from the bed to me as if assessing the unfamiliar presence in our space.

"Looks good, right?"

Maxx wags his tail in agreement.

The buzzing cell phone in my pocket pulls me away from the most beautiful woman in the world.

Devon is calling. Not the person I'm waiting to hear from, so his call is ignored. Pulling up the message app shows Kayla has read my text but still no response.

"Good morning." Carmen leans on her side with her head propped up by one hand. Her hair is a tangled mess and hangs down, hiding one eye.

"Morning, sleepyhead," I say, pocketing the phone. Maxx jumps on the bed to give Carmen his own greeting.

Her laughter is a lyrical balm to soothe my nerves. When I went to get Carmen's car yesterday, I called Kayla. Of course, she didn't answer. Then I ignored the call from Leslie last night by turning off the phone. Carmen didn't mention it, but I'm sure she noticed. Two women that need to be handled with minimal drama. Carmen is my sole focus, and I can't abide any more obstacles.

"What's the plan for the day?" Carmen snuggles with Maxx. His tail beats a staccato rhythm against the sheets.

Crossing to the bed, I sit on the edge. "Depends. I had planned to spend the day in bed with you, but Monroe called to remind me I promised to help him at the gym."

"Your Uncle, right? The one with the boxing club with no name?"

"That's the one." I run a hand down her legs under the cover. "But it shouldn't take long. When do you have to get Olivia?"

Carmen lays back on the pillow. "She normally stays through Sunday night. I'll pick her up from school tomorrow. I do need to go home and get a change of clothes, though."

"So, we have all day." My hand slowly moves up her body. "And all night."

She squirms as the sheet slides down and her nakedness is exposed. "Don't you have somewhere to go?" Carmen teases, her eyes deep pools of desire.

Maxx doesn't appreciate being dislodged from beside Carmen and starts to whine.

"First things first." My lips find hers and relish the sweet nectar. Monroe can wait. Omar can meet me there. The drama outside can wait. "Maxx, down."

The metal door bangs against the wall announcing my hour late arrival at the gym.

Monroe points at his wrist where a nonexistent watch would rest.

"I know. I know." My palms rise to the ceiling in surrender, and I hope to avoid the lecture. Judging by the grimace on Monroe's face, it's coming anyway.

"Your Pops taught you better than that. What was more important than honoring your commitment to this project? Which was your idea, by the way." Monroe shoots me a look that has scared many an airman straight. The one thing he hates more than tardiness is spending money. It's taken years to convince him to invest in new equipment.

Before I can respond, Omar turns off the treadmill and huffs out, "Told you he was into something. Man kicked me out when his lady walked in."

Monroe and Omar share a glance and then burst out laughing.

Tension leaves my shoulders. "I see somebody been telling my business."

Omar hands me the screwdriver he was using on the LED display for the treadmill. "What you expect when you put your boy out on the streets?"

"On the streets? Didn't you go to Devon's?"

Monroe walks by me and shakes his head in mock disapproval. A pat on the back assures me he is playing along as he's already heard Omar's spill.

"He's as bad as you. Well, not quite. I crashed at his spot, but he got a call and left. Haven't seen him since."

Pulling out my phone, I scroll through the call log. "He's been ringing me this morning. I've been meaning to call him back."

"Naw, youngblood." Monroe points to the various pieces of a weight bench strewn across the floor. "You got some work to do."

Accessing the mess of screws, bolts, and metal pieces, I can only ask one question. "Did you at least save the instructions?"

After tightening the last bolt on the weight bench, I stand and toss the wrench into the metal toolbox on the floor. "Alright, old man, I'm out."

"Not until it's tested." Monroe crosses the room in two strides and collapses all three hundred pounds on the leather bench. "Got to check your work. You've been moving at warp speed since you got here."

I shrug. "Told you. Had some business to handle." Thoughts of the morning romp with Carmen make me pat my pockets for the keys. I'm ready to get back to her.

Monroe's deep baritone laugh echoes in the gym. "She decided to come back, huh? Noticed your whole mood done changed. The other day you were a sad sack. Now you're the bionic man."

"Bionic man? Braxton?" Omar points at me and laughs.

"I know my nephew," Monroe continues. "He got his lady to come back, didn't he?"

Omar raises both palms to the sky. "Alright, maybe he got something going on to make a woman leave her husband."

I grimace. Monroe didn't need to hear that part. Omar caught on too late and mouths "Sorry".

Monroe raises an eyebrow. "You said your girl was with someone else. You left out the married part."

"It's complicated." An insufficient response to shattering my uncle's expectation of me, but it'll have to do.

Omar disappears to the back. Monroe grunts and crosses his arms. "Messing with a married woman is all kinds of complicated. Does her husband know?"

I nod. "Not sure how much he knows, but he wanted the divorce, then did something shady to keep her. She filed for divorce to officially end things."

Monroe contemplates this piece of information. "Well, if she told dude she was leaving for you, I guess you're good."

"She's fine as hell too, Unc." Omar returns with a trash bag to pick up the cardboard, plastic and other remnants from our work.

"You best be careful." Monroe gets serious. "Some men don't let their women go so easy. Especially they wives."

Omar waves away the concern. "B will be alright. Besides, he already won. Carmen chose him."

I turn to help gather the tools, but Omar's statement nags at me. *Did Carmen really choose me?* The story from Carmen is her husband found out and left. It's not like she told him she was coming to be with me. When she ended our thing, she was contemplating making the marriage work.

Monroe rises with a grunt and picks up the toolbox once all the items are returned. "Good job, guys."

Following Monroe's nod to the equipment we've installed around the room, I must agree with the compliment. Two new treadmills along with the four new weight benches makes the space feel more like a complete gym. The canvas floor on the boxing ring will be replaced next week. It's my vision to help Monroe attract a new clientele.

"I'll work on your social media next. Bring you into the 21st century. Although it would help if you gave this place a proper name. The Boxing Gym is too generic."

Monroe heads to the tiny office tucked in the warehouse's corner. "I like the name. That's what it is. And don't go putting me on that Book of Faces. That's how the gov'ment get you."

My phone buzzes again with another call from Devon. Then it's followed by a text to call him. *What has he gotten into now? And why does he keep blowing up my phone?*

Omar flexes in the mirror. "You're giving me a ride back? I took an Uber here since someone was knee deep in..."

Glancing back at Monroe in the office, I cut him off. "Did you tell Devon about me and Carmen?"

"Naw, man. I know that situation is delicate. Don't want to mess up your money." Omar rubs his fingers together to mimic cash in hand.

"He's been calling and texting me all morning. Wonder what he wants?"

"You can ask him when we get there. What you got planned for the rest of the day?"

Before I can answer, my buzzing phone lights up with a text from Carmen.

On the way back. Maxx the Dog and I will be waiting.

Omar snatches the phone. "I knew it. That big ass smile on your face broadcasted who this message was from. Guess I'm still bunking at Devon's tonight. If I didn't have a meeting with Ryan tomorrow, I'd be taking my ass back to Oakland."

"Sorry, but if it's a choice between you and my lady, you lose every time."

He tosses my phone to me. "That's the way it should be. Can't be mad at it."

We say our goodbyes to Monroe and head out. Cruising down the I-10 toward Culver City, Omar complains about staying with Devon.

"There's only one full bathroom in the house. Devon is a slob, man."

Devon's parents own a real estate company and let him rent a two-bedroom duplex. Rent being loosely defined. The place usually rents for four thousand dollars, but Devon pays a small portion.

We find parking on the tree-lined street right in front of the lavender colored stucco house. The garage is in the rear, but Devon's red Audi sits in the driveway.

"Looks like he's home." My car chirps when the keyless remote locks the vehicle. A figure approaching from the other end of the street looks familiar. "There he is. Wonder where he's coming from?"

Omar stops in mid stride toward the porch. "Is that fool skipping?"

A double take confirms Devon is indeed skipping.

When he sees us, his stride morphs into a jog.

"Man, I've been trying to call you," Devon pants while bending over with his hands on his knees.

Taking a step back, I hold up my phone. "Calling and texting. What's up?"

Before he can continue, Omar pushes him. "Dude, what's got you out here prancing down the street? And you out of breath from running five feet? Are you okay?"

"You'd be out of breath, too." Devon stands upright and gulps for air. "I had a long night."

A motorcycle backfires as it rides past, leaving a plume of exhaust fumes. A gang of kids on bikes makes us move from the sidewalk to the patch of concrete leading to the front door.

"Well, you going to spill or what? You know you can't hold water," Omar leans against a column.

I post up on the opposite side. "Look at you, about to bust right now."

Devon is practically bouncing on his toes. "You'll never guess where I spent the night. I can barely believe it myself."

We wait, but Devon just looks at me with a goofy grin on his face.

Omar loses patience first. "It's obvious you finally got some. Just tell us who was desperate enough to sleep with you."

Puffing out his t-shirt clad chest, Devon points at Omar. "Your jealousy can't steal my high, man. I just bagged the girl of my fantasy."

Omar swats Devon's hand away. "Ain't nobody jealous of you, shorty. It's about time you busted a nut in something besides your hand."

They go back and forth, taking digs at each other, but an uneasy feeling causes me to stand up straight. The girl of Devon's fantasy can only mean one thing.

I break up their exchange. "Don't tell me you slept with..."

Devon nods so fast his head mimics a bobble-head doll. "I'm living single with Regine. That shit was good, too. Girl's a straight freak. I tried to stay for breakfast, but she had some hair appointment or something. But man, a brother was all over it. Told you I would Form 54A her ass. First thing, Monday, I'm filling out the form 'cause I got to get some more of that." He pauses to take a breath. "Don't trip, B. Remember you said you wasn't interested, so when the opportunity presented itself, I didn't hesitate."

Omar's mouth falls open while listening to Devon's fast-talking recount of his night. "I'm confused. You slept with a 90s sitcom star? She made you fill out a form?"

"No, man. We work together. You know the three women B's been hanging with?" Devon pats his jean pockets for his keys. "Come on in. I'm thirsty."

We follow him in, but Omar pulls me to hang back. "Not ol' girl that tried to get with you."

I nod. "Yeah, sounds like Devon slept with Kayla."

Chapter Thirty-Two

Carmen

The music fades when the ignition is cut off, but the lyrics of the Alexander O'Neal/Cherrelle song sings in my head. My heels step in time to the chorus of "Never Knew Love Like This". The past month with Braxton has been the fulfillment of those words.

"Someone's in a good mood for a Monday." Ruth waits at the bank of elevators balancing a cup of coffee in one hand, a purse, a book, and her heels in the other.

Pressing the Up button with an elbow and offering Ruth a hand, my smile widens. "Had a wonderful weekend."

Ruth says something about taking her cat to the vet, but my mind drifts to the activities in the past two days. Braxton has made it his mission to "take me out" and he doesn't disappoint. Every weekend is spent together since my weekdays are devoted to Olivia. We've gone out to dinner with Omar and his girlfriend, Keisha. We've gone to a comedy show at the Laugh Factory, followed by an intimate walk on the beach at Marina del Ray. Sundays are spent lounging in bed, reading or catching up on work. Bouncing ideas off a like-minded partner is liberating. And just this past Saturday we went hiking in Griffith Park. The breathtaking views had Braxton taking selfies of us in front of the Hollywood sign.

"I can't believe you've lived in LA for years and never been here." Braxton stood behind me and wrapped his arms around my waist.

"Me either." The warmth from his body took away the slight chill in the air. People wandered around us. Some taking pictures, a family setting up for a picnic and others checking the trail location with paper maps or cell phones, but we might as well have been alone. We were no longer concerned about being seen.

A sigh of contentment escaped me, and I snuggled against Braxton. He kissed my neck and lingered there with a promise of more adventures to come.

"Are you okay?" Ruth stands outside the elevator, her face twisted with concern.

I shake off the memory and step out before the door closes. "It's all good."

Following Ruth down the hall, I glance at Braxton's empty cubicle. He left for New York this morning with the management training group. The project was complete, but the pending acquisition has added an extra layer to the program. Bisous' management group loved the concept of grooming employees for upper management positions and took over by expanding the curriculum to include their aspect of the company as well.

Movement from the right catches my attention. Kayla Pearson swivels around in her chair and looks me up and down. If looks were a weapon, I would be bloodied and bruised. Knowing the source of her angst, Braxton told me about their brief friendship and Kayla wanting more. I pause to give her the full view. My professional attire is on point, from the dark gray Theory flared pants with matching belted blazer to the black suede slingback pumps on my feet.

"Good morning, Kayla." My perky greeting doesn't match the glare in my eyes. She may have requested to be removed from my team, the best email I've ever received, but I'm still in management. She does not want to trifle with me.

She appears to get the hint and mumbles, "Morning" before pushing up from her chair and twisting by in a pair of black slacks a size too small.

The rest of my morning is filled with meetings with Doug and the representative from Bisous' transition team about integrating staff. Susan listens in on the conference call as she is working from home today.

"And that concludes all the employees from your unit to be offered transfers to our New York Office. Making room for some of our Paris counterparts here is a priority." Ethan closes his tablet and twirls the stylus in his left hand.

Ethan Smith has been here for over two weeks and his New York accent mixed with French still requires concentration to keep up. The man is the picture of a corporate insider. He only wears designer three-piece suits in various shades of black and blue and sports monogrammed cuff links. Every strand of blond hair is gelled into place. A gold band on his ring finger is the single piece of jewelry.

"There's one more name I'd like to add," Doug swivels in the conference chair to grab his ever present can of soda off the desk. He takes a drink, glances at me, and then says, "Kayla Pearson."

When Kayla requested a move from my tutelage, Doug jumped in. He insinuated I didn't like the competition from a younger woman. Kayla soon proved her bias to action. He had to agree with my assessment of the girl being lazy and unimaginative.

"Okay." Ethan scratches the cleft in his chin and reopens the tablet. "What is her role in the marketing department?"

Under the table, Doug's leg is vibrating like a helicopter blade about to lift off. "She's an asset we would hate to see move on, but I feel she's up for a new challenge in New York. Don't you agree Carmen?"

Hell, I want to give the man a high five. Instead, I agree. "Sure. We don't want to stimy her professional growth."

Ethan nods as he adds Kayla's name to his electronic list without further question. The meeting ends by scheduling the next one.

Alone in my office during lunch, I text Braxton an update. He should be out of his training classes with the three-hour time difference. His response comes quickly.

Good news. Now I don't have to worry about you fighting over me.

Me: You have jokes. How is the Biscous company treating you in headquarters?

B: Everything's top notch. Learning a lot. Only thing missing is you.

Me: Miss you too.

B: We still on for our 'date' tonight. I'll be waiting up for your call.

Me: As soon as Livvy is asleep, I'm all yours.

B: Yes, you are. Talk tonight.

The smile on my face from a simple text message exchange amplifies how deeply I've fallen for this man. And it's something I've never known before.

The clock on the wall shows I'm right on schedule. After dinner and a bath, Olivia gets to pick one activity before bedtime. She can choose between watching a television show for thirty minutes, reading a book or playing a game. Tonight, she chooses a card game. We sit on the living room floor with an empty bowl of applesauce between us propped on pillows from the couch.

"It's your turn." Olivia pulls my attention back to the game.

Uno is Olivia's favorite card game. It's played with a specially printed deck of four colored cards (red, yellow, green and blue). Each color is numbered zero through nine and includes special cards like 'Skip', 'Draw Two', 'Draw Four' and 'Reverse'. It also includes a Wild Card to change the color.

In order to win, you have to be the first player to get rid of all your cards. Everyone starts with seven cards.

"Uno," Olivia slaps down a Red 2 card and laughs. "I'm going to win."

She's mastered the card requirement of announcing she has one card left. A wayward barrette threatens to abandon its hold on her ponytail when Olivia wiggles in the seat.

I look at her happy, innocent face, and my lungs swell with pride.

"Not yet, baby girl." The Draw Two card slaps down into the space between us.

Olivia's face crumbles and I almost feel bad about playing to win. Almost.

"No fair." Her lips twist into a pout.

My voice is firm as I hand her two cards from the deck. "Remember the rules."

She crosses her arms. "You cheated. But you're a cheater, anyway."

My back stiffens. "Is dis mi child talking? What did you call me, little girl?" The cards are dropped back on the deck and my mother's Jamaican voice comes out.

Olivia puts her head down. "Daddy says you're a cheater."

The sudden heat of anger flushes through my body, but is quickly snuffed by the cloak of guilt.

Sighing, I get off the floor and sit on the couch. "Come here, Livvy."

Olivia glances up with watery eyes and unfolds her crisscrossed legs. My voice is calm when she stands in front of me. "Tell me, what makes a person a cheater?"

Her voice is whisper soft. "Somebody that breaks the rules to win."

Taking her hands in one of mine, I left her chin until we make eye contact. "That's right. And did I break the rules?"

She shakes her head.

"Of course not. Remember when I had one card left, and you put the 'Draw Four' card? I didn't get mad and accuse you of cheating. Because that's the rule of the game."

Olivia nods. "But I wanted to win, Momma."

"And you may have still won. You only had three cards. I had six. But maybe we shouldn't play anymore if you're going to act out when things don't go your way."

Olivia cocks her head to the side. "I'm sorry, Mommie."

Pulling her close, I kiss her forehead. "Mommie loves you. Now let's get you into bed."

Taking several deep breaths, I tidy up the living room, then go into the kitchen for a glass of wine. Braxton gave me a bottle of Chablis chardonnay before he left. Maybe my favorite drink will quench the urge to dial Melvin's number.

Our conversations of late solely center on Olivia. Any other subject is a land mine of accusations and hostilities. He insults and accuses me while I'm naturally defensive. We haven't spoken about our pending divorce for weeks, but he's about to bear the full brunt of my pent-up anger. Melvin broke the rules of co-parenting by bashing me in front of our child.

The wine didn't work. There's no answer when I punch Melvin's name on the phone. What needs to be said can't be condensed on a voice mail, so I end the call.

Rinsing the wineglass in the sink helps me resist the urge to have another glass. The microwave clock shows there's about twenty minutes until the agreed time to call Braxton. Thinking about getting under the covers and having his voice in my ear soothes my nerves.

I'm cutting off lights and walking to my room when the doorbell rings. Melvin is on the other side of the door. His cologne assaults me when I answer. "What are you doing here?"

He shuffles his feet. "Um, yeah. I need to get some more clothes."

The starched pressed khakis and navy polo shirt look brand new. "And you decided to just drop by? Not cool."

"Why? You got someone in there while my daughter's here?" Melvin puffs out his chest and tries to peer over me to see inside.

"Don't be ridiculous."

His lips turn up in a sneer. "You already cheated. Wouldn't put it past you."

I absorb the verbal jab but won't let the usual guilt sway me. "Just like I'd expect you to tell Livvy I'm a cheater."

Melvin's brows knit in confusion, so I share the conversation I had with our daughter. He shrugs when I finish.

"Since you're involving our daughter in grown people's business, maybe I need to tell her about your gambling problem." The effort of getting my car back from Jay still irritates me.

Melvin throws up his hands. "Hold up, now. I was just messing with you. Baby Girl probably heard me talking to Momma when I was venting. I wouldn't bad mouth you to Olivia. Even I have to admit you're a good mother."

The halved ass apology gives me pause. Melvin was always reluctant to admit fault. "Well, I would appreciate you being more mindful of little ears overhearing."

"Point taken. Now may I come in and get some things."

I step aside and wave him in. This is the first time he's returned to the home we used to share. He surveys the rearranged furniture but doesn't comment.

He disappears into the bedroom, and I busy myself in the kitchen. Another glass of wine is an urgent need now.

"Peeped in on Baby Girl. She's knocked out."

Melvin has my favorite Gucci carryall thrown over his shoulder. Typical of him not to bring anything to carry his things.

Swallowing the annoyance along with a sip of wine, I lean against the counter. "Soon as she hits the pillow, she's out. She was always a good sleeper."

"Even as a baby," Melvin adds.

"We were lucky with that."

"Best thing to come out of us was her, right?" Melvin rubs his hands together.

If there is one good thing about this marriage, it was having Olivia. The memories from those early days make me smile. Lack of sleep, washing multiple bottles and trading off diaper changes were rites of parenting we attacked together. "True."

An awkward silence stands between us. To break the tension, I move toward the door. "Well, see you in the morning."

Melvin follows me but pauses at the threshold. "Gamblers Anonymous."

"What?" My eyebrows knit while trying to comprehend what he's saying

He runs a hand over his bald head, a habit which clues me in to his discomfort. "Wanted you to know. I'm thinking about going. There's a chapter at Momma's church."

"You should go." I'm happy he's getting some help. When I checked his account last week, the balance was in the negative. I had to cover Olivia's tuition again.

"Don't like the idea of sitting in a circle discussing things that can be handled myself. It helps to focus on something else when I get the urge. Mostly I think about Olivia." Melvin lowers his head before adding, "And how I messed up things with you."

Discomfort tingles down my legs, causing me to grip the door handle to steady myself. "It's too late in the evening to argue, Melvin."

"I'm trying to erase the picture of you with another man out of my mind." Melvin takes a deep breath. "And it's my own fault. Maybe I shouldn't have tried to change you 'cause I felt bad."

My eyebrows knit together. "Why are you telling me this now? You filed for divorce to scare me straight because I was making you feel bad?"

Melvin shifts the bag to his other hand. "You made so much more money than me. I moved into your house." He gestures around the room.

"I never asked you for money," I say and lean against the door, crossing my arms. "Don't blame me for making you feel a way."

"See, that's what I mean. You didn't ask me for money, but I wanted you to." He sits the carryall at his feet. "The first time I won big, it felt good to take you and Livvy out."

The phone buzzes in my pocket, but I ignore it for the moment. "Again, why are you telling me this now?" Melvin can try to rewrite our relationship but his inadequacies don't excuse the way he treated me during our marriage.

His mouth opens to say something, but he composes himself and walks out the door. "Okay. I'll be here at 6:30 in the morning for Olivia. Good night."

Chapter Thirty-Three

Braxton

Hanging up the phone, I rear back in the chair and smile. Things are falling into place for me. The management program has ended, and the culmination is a hefty bump in salary and the offer of a new position. The position is Digital & Social Media Manager for the Bisous Corporation Men's Grooming Line. Fortunately for me, the bulk of the Men's Line is manufactured here in LA, so there is no option of relocating to New York. Plus, the position falls under Carmen's wheelhouse, so I'm stationed in LA for the foreseeable future.

The new title comes with a small office on the third floor. No window, but I have the most up-to-date computer equipment the company can buy. Any gadget imagined is ordered with a simple request. Plus, I get to spend most of the day monitoring the company's various social media accounts.

Things with Carmen are good. Being on a different floor from her helps keep our work obligations from being compromised. We both thought it best to keep things on the low at work, at least until she works out her marriage situation. The weekends are our time for adventures both indoors and out. It's refreshing to love her out loud.

The only thing that can throw a wrench into my life is the one person who's latched herself into my social circle. Kayla.

My time hanging with the Three was over the day Kayla saw me with Carmen at The Grove. Elena and Savannah texted asking what happened, but if Kayla didn't tell them, it wasn't my place to spill. Besides, once she slept with Devon, I didn't know what to expect. She's been avoiding me around the office ever since.

That's why I almost turn around when I drop into the cafeteria to pick up a sandwich and spy Devon at a table near the front glass doors.

"Hey, man." Devon waves me over. "Join us."

Kayla makes a face Devon doesn't notice, but I sit anyway. Whatever needs to be said between us must be addressed. She's not coming between me and my friend.

Placing my sandwich on the table, I reach for a napkin from the dispenser near her. "Kayla."

She doesn't respond. Devon fills in the silence by going into some spiel about the latest HR gossip. He makes a production of putting his arm around her.

Kayla shrugs him off. "Not at work."

"Wouldn't be a problem if you'll sign the form. Management doesn't care. It's not like I supervise you or anything," Devon says.

Kayla perks up. "So, if two people are dating and one supervises the other, that would present a problem, right?"

"Oh, yeah." Devon takes a chip from my bag and chews loudly. "It could get sticky. We had a situation like that last year. Guy got transferred."

My appetite disappears as a smile spreads across Kayla's face.

Devon's order is announced over the speaker, and he bounces up and goes to the grille.

As soon as he is out of earshot, my focus shifts. "What game are you playing?"

Kayla crosses her arms. "I don't know what you're talking about?"

The stern expression on my face broadcasts I'm not buying the lie she's selling.

Kayla asks through clenched teeth, "Does Devon know you're sleeping with Boss Lady?"

"Does Devon know you tried to sleep with me?" My jaw tightens and I lean into her space.

Kayla blinks in rapid succession. The shocked expression let me know she hasn't shared our past encounter.

"If you care about Devon at all, seems as if it's best we both move on. Truce?" My voice is a whisper as Devon is working his way back to the table.

She nods, but the uneasy feeling doesn't settle.

Chapter Thirty-Four

Carmen

Friday has become my favorite day of the week. It may not be ideal, but Braxton and I make the most of it. Until things are settled with Melvin, it's best not to flaunt our relationship. And then there is Olivia to consider. My concerns about her adjustment weren't warranted. She has gotten used to the new normal and already has her overnight bag packed for a weekend at Grandma's. But it's not time to introduce a new man to her.

I drop Olivia off and return home to get ready for the weekend. My phone buzzes with a text from Braxton.

B: Are you on the way?

Me: About to walk out now.

B: Been thinking about you all day. Dinner out or in?

Twirling in front of the mirror, the black lace lingerie screams for an intimate night where the only thing on the menu is me and him. I reply with a selfie of my outfit.

He replies with the bugged eye emoji and three words: Get. Here. Now.

Laughing, I respond that I'm on the way and slip on skinny jeans paired with a color stripped fitted t-shirt and a blazer. The high heels complete the look.

I can't remember the last time I relished getting ready for a date. Being with Braxton brings out a better side of me. A playful side. A sexy side. Gayle has even remarked that I've mellowed.

"Maybe you'll get your happily ever after," she says during our meet up at lunch earlier today. "But I still need to meet this young man."

We made plans to get together for Sunday brunch. Being a single parent during the week and crashing at Braxton's all weekend doesn't leave much free time for my friend. I can't wait for her to meet my man.

I'm backing out of the driveway when my phone rings. Melvin's number. When I answer, Olivia's voice quivers over the line.

"What's wrong, baby?" My heart rate increases.

"I forgot my Maisy doll."

Braking at the edge of the yard, I try to calm my daughter before a full-blown meltdown occurs. There is no way Olivia will sleep without her favorite doll. There's something about the heart-shaped face of the little doll baby that soothes her. Melvin bought her the toy as a gift after the first weekend he spent at his mother's. Now she takes the doll with her each weekend.

"Didn't you put it in your bag?" I ask. Olivia insists on packing her own overnight bag like a "big girl". I could have sworn she put it in there while I watched to make sure she included enough underwear.

"Yeah," she sniffs. "But I can't find it. Will you bring it to me please, Mommie, please?"

I can't let my girl down. Mommie to the rescue.

After sending a quick text to Braxton, I search Olivia's room for the doll, to no avail. The hunt expands to other areas of the house. My room, the family room, kitchen. Even the bathroom. No doll.

Finally, I grab a teddy bear from her bed and head back to Barbara's.

I ring the doorbell, expecting to be greeted by a distraught child. Instead, Olivia bounces on her toes. "It's a surprise!"

Melvin laughs at the confusion I'm sure is evident on my face. "You know Luv Bug can't keep a secret."

"But," I reach out with the teddy bear. "Livvy called about her missing Maisy doll."

Something isn't adding up here. Melvin avoids making direct eye contact but motions me to step inside the foyer.

"Dad found it." Olivia runs back into the house and returns clutching the doll. "Now come see your surprise."

"What surprise?" The question is directed at Melvin, but he smiles without saying a word.

Olivia grabs my hand and leads me to the kitchen.

The scent of Barbara's signature rosemary baked chicken steams from the dish on the center of the table. A pan of macaroni and cheese bubbles alongside a dish of string beans. The table has a place setting for three.

"We made dinner," Olivia announces. "I get to be the waitress."

"Alright, what's going on? I only came to drop off a toy. A toy that miraculously reappeared."

Melvin pulls out a chair and ignores the implication. "Well, Mom helped Luv Bug fix dinner in her restaurant. We're her first guests."

I hesitate and start to make an excuse to leave. This feels like a setup, but then I look at the wide grin on Olivia's face. She puts on a little apron and grabs a pad. "Mommie, what do you want to drink?"

"What's on the menu?" Resigned to letting this scenario play out, I settle in the chair. Melvin takes the seat next to mine.

"I'll have sweet tea," he announces and tucks the napkin into the collar of his shirt. "This is going to be good."

Olivia is distracted pouring drinks into glasses. I watch to see if she needs assistance handling the pitcher but whisper so Melvin can hear me. "Really low blow, hiding a doll from your child."

He feigns innocence. "She must have misplaced it when she got here. I'm glad we found it or no one in this house would have gotten any sleep."

"And when did she find the time to plan an entire meal with your mother?"

Melvin shrugs. "The girl can multitask."

It seems as if Melvin was the one multitasking. He not only got his mother to cook an entire meal, but she is nowhere to be found.

"Mother is at the Pastor's appreciation tonight. Her friend will bring her back around 9:30," Melvin says when I inquire about her whereabouts.

"So, what's the end goal here?" I sneak a glance at my watch.

Melvin notices. "You got somewhere to be?"

There's no way I'm telling him the truth. He doesn't know I'm seeing the man I "cheated" with and now is not the time for that conversation. "This isn't what I had planned for the evening."

"You need to loosen up," Melvin says and leans back in the chair.

A heavy sigh escapes me. "What game are you playing here, Melvin?"

"I play to win, remember." The dual meaning in the phrase conjures up the first time we met and his obsessive need to best me at everything. And mold me into some version of a wife that doesn't fit.

Before I can voice an objection, Olivia proudly serves the drinks and climbs up onto her seat. "Now we can eat. Family time."

Melvin immediately starts spooning food on his plate, but Olivia's pronouncement gives me pause. The simple act of eating dinner together in the evening as a family was an important ritual our family observed. Melvin and I established the dinnertime routine once Olivia was old enough to feed herself. Before he fell back into betting on games, Melvin preached to Olivia and to me he looked forward to family time at the dinner table. Seeing the happiness on my daughter's face boxes me in. Melvin watches me as he cuts into a chicken breast. He knows I won't disappoint my daughter.

My phone buzzes and I know it's Braxton, but there's no way to respond without being obvious.

"Mommie, guess what? Daddy said it's Fun Day tomorrow. We're going to see Mickey Mouse." Olivia talks with a mouth full of food.

"Swallow your food first." I pass her a napkin. "What's this about Disneyland?" I turn to Melvin. We had talked about taking Olivia for her birthday since last year. Actually, I talked about taking Livvy. Melvin grumbled about the cost of tickets. Now he seems as if he'll be the one to take her without me.

Melvin spears the remaining string beans on his plate and pauses with his fork in midair. "Mom's church is taking the Youth Group. I was volunteered to chaperone. Luv Bug and me can get in for free."

"Sounds fun." My growling stomach nudges me to at least fix a plate. Might as well eat. The sooner we finish this meal, the sooner I can get to Braxton's.

Two and half hours later, the meal is done; the kitchen is clean, and we've watched an episode of Olivia's favorite Nickelodeon show. I excuse myself to the bathroom and text Braxton that I'm finally on the way. He doesn't respond.

I kiss Olivia good night and make a beeline for the door. Melvin insists on walking me out, but my mind is on Braxton. That's probably why I don't hear him until he grabs my hand and repeats the statement. "I've been thinking I need to move back home."

Taking a step back, the dueling emotions leave me momentarily confused. "Really? You've been thinking?"

"Yeah, I know we have some things to work out." He shoves his hands in the pockets of his jeans. "After our conversation the other night, I figure if I can get past you cheating, you can get past the gambling."

"You've got it all figured out." I unlock the car door and toss my bag inside. "Have you gone to one meeting yet?"

Melvin gestures toward the house and ignores my question. "Olivia deserves to have her family intact. We can't keep up this back and forth. I mean, Mom and I were talking, and we agreed…"

"Do you hear yourself? You and your mom agree."

"What's wrong with that? I'm staying in her house. And it's time you stop your foolishness and be a good mother and wife. I saw you checking your phone. You always have something more important than this family. It used to be work. What is it this time?" Melvin's hand balls into a fist.

I only have enough in me for one conversation with an angry man. Melvin is not the one I'm concerned about now. "Thanks for dinner," is tossed over my shoulder as I get into the car.

Maxx the Dog greets me when I open the door to Braxton's place. "Hey, boy." I kneel to scratch behind his ears.

Locking the door behind me, the silence speaks volumes. Remnants from a candlelight dinner are evident on the table, although whatever was prepared has been put away. The vague scent of tomato pasta sauce lingers in the air.

Braxton is perched on the bed. His bare chest of washboard abs ripple as he turns a page in the book. It's clear he isn't reading, but he doesn't look up when I enter the room.

"Sorry I'm late," I say and toss my overnight bag on the chair. Maxx places two paws on my leg for attention.

"Didn't think you were coming at all." Braxton closes the book but still doesn't make eye contact. He points and orders Maxx out of the room. "You just left me hanging over here."

"It was a surprise to me, too. I was dropping off Olivia's toy, and they had this whole dinner prepared."

Now he turns the full blast of his gaze on me. "And you couldn't call or text what was going on?"

"I tried. It was awkward with Melvin right there."

"So what? Are you ashamed of us? Of me?"

That's the furthest thing from the truth, but I'm not sure how to explain the situation to Braxton. We started this relationship before I made a clean break.

Thinking it may take his mind off the reason for my tardiness, I slip off my clothes and sit on the side of the bed. "That's not it."

"Then what is it?" He pauses when he sees the lingerie, but shakes his head. "'Cause what happened tonight wasn't cool."

"Agreed. But if you saw Olivia's face, you would know why I couldn't leave. It's hard enough on her adjusting to everything."

His cell phone rings and is quickly silenced. The name Les pops up. Now it's my turn to ask a question. "Who was that?"

"Nobody important." He turns the phone off. "Don't try to change the subject. We're talking about your lack of communication tonight. And how that made me feel."

"I get it." Something nags at me about the missed call. "But is there something you need to tell me?"

Braxton huffs out a frustrated breath. "You know what, good night, Carmen." He punches the pillow and turns his back to me.

The familiar feeling of unworthiness settles over me like a cold mist and I hug myself, rubbing my arms. Swinging my legs over the edge of the bed and reach for my pants.

"What are you doing?" Braxton rolls over.

"Leaving. You're obviously done with me."

He sits up, curiosity written all over his face. "What makes you say that?"

I stand and fasten the zipper. "You. You turned your back. I know what that means."

Braxton bounces off the mattress and stands in front of me. He takes my hand. "Babe, talk to me. What does that mean?"

Seeing the concern in his dark brown eyes makes the words I'm hesitant to share spill from my lips. "Melvin would turn his back and give me the silent treatment for days after an argument."

"I'm not Melvin."

"And my Dad," I continue. "The last time I saw him, he turned his back and walked away. Haven't heard from him since."

The memory of that day in the mall and my fifteen-year-old self, standing in the food court processing the pain hits out of nowhere. My knees quiver and Braxton pulls me onto his lap on the side of the bed.

"I'm sorry, okay. I didn't know that would trigger you."

Laying my head on his chest, I take deep breaths to stem the tears that threaten to fall. "Me either."

"We're gonna argue. Every couple does. But I can promise you, you'll always be my first choice."

Braxton cups my chin until my eyes connect with his. "And I know your daughter is the highest priority. No disputing that. But I need to know Melvin isn't an issue."

"He's not." In that moment, I wish Braxton was Olivia's father. By settling for a husband, I didn't wait for the opportunity to have a true partner.

"Alright, then. Let's get those clothes back off."

Chapter Thirty-Five

Braxton

When Carmen sent me the sexy picture earlier, I was beyond excited. Having our relationship sidelined to the weekend was almost unbearable. But I understand the situation. Her daughter takes precedence. I get it.

Dinner consisted of a quick meal of baked spaghetti and a salad. Pulled out the candles. Set the mood.

And waited.

The text about dropping something off wasn't any actual concern. Kids forget things. That's before an hour went by. Then another.

I'm on the verge of losing it when the phone rings.

"Guess where I am?" she said when I answered.

"Home." No mood for playing a guessing game.

Leslie laughed. "No silly. I'm on a movie set at our old stomping grounds. El Segundo High is being used as the prop for this television show. I have a small part playing the gym teacher. Which reminded me of your unfortunate incident."

I groaned. "History proved that wasn't my fault."

"Anyway, remember that little side room no one knew about?"

Of course, I remembered 'the make out spot' as the kids called it. The place was an abandoned utility closet, but someone broke the lock, and it was a teenage boy's dream to get a girl in there.

"Is that still there?"

"No, looks like some renovations were done. It's gone. But the wall is still there. Your artwork survived the repairs."

My one and only attempt at graffiti. 'Braxton loves Leslie'. "Can't believe it wasn't painted over."

Leslie was quiet on the other end. Voices were muffled in the background. The sound of a beeping truck faded away.

"You sure you never think of me? About us trying again?" Leslie's question is whispered and not asked for the first time.

She knows my situation. I've been open to communication as friends, but Leslie hasn't been exactly shy about her intentions. "I think there is no us."

"Damn, B."

"Sorry. I'm sorry. Just a little stressed here." No need to take my angst out on Leslie.

The line was quiet for another beat before Leslie offered a respite. "Tell me about it."

There was no way I was discussing Carmen with Leslie. I made up some excuse and ended the call. But talking to her clarified one thing for me. The issue with my past relationship could be boiled down to a simple fact. Leslie didn't choose me.

Lying in the bed next to the woman I love, it doesn't feel like she'll choose me either. When I asked her if she was ashamed of us, I was hoping for something a little more definitive.

And Leslie called my phone again.

Maxx whines at the door and I roll over to see the time. Carmen is still asleep when I take Maxx out and come back.

The revelation about her father was surprising. I spent the night holding her, sensing it's what she needed. Crawling back under the covers, I caress her face. She's a mystery and intriguing as hell.

"You okay, babe?" Carmen reaches for me without opening her eyes.

"I'm good," I reply and wrap her in my arms. *But why does it feel like it may be the last time?*

Chapter Thirty-Six

Carmen

Who do you choose?

The question plays in my head on a loop. Melvin or Braxton. Braxton or Melvin. I never thought Melvin could get past my supposed cheating. Although the charade of a family dinner he put on would indicate otherwise. The divorce proceedings are still pending. Maggie is preparing for us to go to court. Melvin left me a voicemail last night pleading for us to talk.

But Braxton makes my soul sing. I didn't mean to break down and share the incident with my father. When Braxton turned his back, something snapped. I couldn't stand the thought of him rejecting me. It felt good to share with someone who understands me and helped me heal a small part of myself I didn't realize was still hurting.

An incessant buzzing breaks into my thoughts. It stops for a minute and then starts up again. Braxton's phone hums on the nightstand. He mumbles something and fumbles for the phone to quiet it.

He squints at the phone and sits straight up. "Shit."

"What? Who is it?" He never said who the mysterious phone call was from last night.

"My parents. I forgot they were coming today." He dashes into the bathroom.

I scan the floor for my pants, with my heart racing double time. "Your parents?"

Braxton emerges in a pair of sweatpants while tugging on a t-shirt. "Totally forgot."

"Wow," I say. "I don't think I should be meeting your parents."

"Too late now." Braxton hands me a pair of shorts and kisses my forehead. "They'll love you."

He takes my hand, and we go to answer the door.

I've seen pictures of Braxton's parents and the couple standing on the threshold are carbon copies. Bernard Frazier smiles and raises one eyebrow in a move reminiscent of Braxton's and exudes warmth. Hannah Frazier is a beautiful woman. She has on a gray velour sweat suit with a pair of white Keds on her feet. Her salt and pepper shoulder length hair is permed in a stylish bob. And by the stern look on her face, she isn't happy to see her son with a woman who clearly spent the night.

But that's no comparison to the other person, standing there with her mouth open.

"Leslie," Braxton says. "What are you doing here?"

Leslie as in Les. The name I saw on Braxton's phone. The name that popped up on the screen last night. *This should be interesting.*

"Son, seems like we caught you at a bad time." Mr. Frazier fiddles with his baseball cap then kneels to greet Maxx the Dog, who rolls over to get his stomach rubbed.

Braxton looks down and then straightens. "Um, no, sir. We were just..."

"Are you going to invite us in?" Mrs. Frazier stares at her son until he moves aside and ushers the crew into the apartment.

"Mom, Dad, I want you to meet Carmen," Braxton makes introductions after his mother takes a seat on the couch. Leslie hovers near the door.

Mr. Frazier offers his hand. "Nice to meet you, Carmen."

"Nice to meet you too," I manage to croak out.

Braxton's Mom looks away.

"Carmen, this is Leslie." Braxton clears his throat. "She's an old family friend."

Leslie mouths the word 'Wow' and shuffles her feet. "Well, alright then," she says out loud.

Braxton doesn't acknowledge the outburst, and she pouts. Her face looks familiar but before I can explore the thought further, Maxx the Dog barks and goes to the door, signaling the need to go out.

"Um, want to go with me?" Braxton looks toward the door.

The question is directed at me, but his mom answers. "You go ahead. We can get to know your lady friend a bit better."

Braxton hesitates and looks at me.

I raise my chin and then nod. If his mother wants to try to intimidate me, I'll show her that's a lost cause.

"I'll walk down with you, son." Mr. Frazier shoots a pointed look at his wife. She stares back. Their nonverbal communication tells me there has already been a disagreement about something.

The guys leave and to alleviate the awkward silence which descends in the room like a weighted blanket; I turn into a hostess.

"Would you both like something to drink?" I walk into the kitchen. "There's water, tea, or I could put on a pot of coffee."

Neither one of them responds, so I continue my monologue. "Nothing like a cup of joe to get you going in the mornings. Braxton usually has it programmed for first thing, but he must have forgotten last night."

Braxton has a Keurig coffee maker with the pods. Water has already been added, so I place my mug on the drip tray and insert my favorite brand of Peet's coffee. Because of the open floor plan, it's easy to watch the ladies. Leslie browses the decorations and then sits beside Mrs. Frazier. They lean in close and whisper to each other.

"Are you sure I can't interest you in a cup? Braxton introduced me to this new brand of coffee and it's really good." Blowing on the mug, I take a sip and step back into view.

Silence.

They both continue talking to each other as if I don't exist. As if, I'm not good enough for a cordial conversation. Biting back a more cutting remark, my eyes narrow from the effort. "It was really a pleasure meeting you both."

"What are you doing with my son?"

The question from Braxton's mother halts my escape to the bedroom. I stall for more time to gauge her intentions. "Excuse me?"

"Now I trust my son's judgement." She flicks lint from her pant leg. "Your judgement, however, gives me pause."

"I'm not sure how to respond to that." Glancing at the door, I will it to open. What is taking the guys so long to return? Would it be rude to cold dash and run around the block? I think better of it and stand there waiting.

Hannah settles back on the couch, gives Leslie a conspiratorial look and then gestures for me to join them. Taking a deep breath, I perch on the love seat which is the furthest away from her. She smiles at my futile attempt at safety. Clasping her hands in her lap, she levels me with a gaze that makes my stomach clench.

"Braxton told us he was dating someone new. He didn't mention you were older, but that's not surprising. He always gravitated toward mature women after his break from Leslie, that is. They never last long." Hannah waves a hand. "And although you wear it well, I would guess you are in your late thirties."

"Thirty-six."

She nods. "Any children?"

"A daughter." Thinking of Olivia causes me to smile.

Hannah tilts her head. "And where is this daughter?"

The implication of being a bad mother trumpets through her tone. I lift my chin. "With her father."

"And where is the child's father?"

I tug at the hem of the shorts, feeling unbalanced and hoping Hannah doesn't recognize they belong to her son. "I'm not sure how much Braxton has shared with you."

"About you? Nothing." Hannah fiddles with the cross pendant on her necklace. "But Leslie has been a part of our family for years. They reconnected when she moved back home a few months ago."

Leslie interjects. "You never get over your first love, you know."

The look leveled by me causes her to squirm. Heat flushes through my body, the anger I've held at bay threatens to erupt.

Hannah puts up a hand. "Braxton and Leslie are destined to be together. She's a God-fearing woman and an accomplished actress."

So, that's it. Olivia loves the catchphrase 'I couldn't eat the whole thing' from some fast-food commercial. Thought I recognized her.

Shaking my head and blowing out a frustrated breath. I turn to Braxton's mother. "What are you trying to say?"

"I'm saying you're wasting your time. God spoke to me, and Leslie and Braxton are meant to be." She sits back on the couch with a smug smile, like she just proclaimed the eleventh commandment. But what I heard was a familiar refrain. *You aren't good enough.*

"Excuse me, I need to get dressed."

Maxx the Dog bounds into the bathroom a few minutes later, followed closely by his owner.

"Sorry, that took a while. Pops wanted to talk." Braxton washes his hands in the sink and then grabs the hair sponge to define the curls in his faux mohawk.

I kneel and scratch behind Maxx's ear. He reciprocates with a wagging tail.

Braxton leans against the counter. "I know this may be a bit weird. And it's not exactly the way I wanted you to meet my parents..."

Maxx rolls over and gives me his belly to rub. "Not exactly," I repeat.

"But this may be good. We're going to The Grove. Mom loves that place."

"That's nice, but I'm going home." I stand and start gathering my toiletries.

Braxton's eyebrow wings up. "Why? What happened?"

A buffet of emotions churns through my mind. The anger has been doused by a side dish of shame topped with doubt about this relationship.

"Your Mother," I begin, but stop and shake my head. "Never mind. It's probably best if I let you be with your family."

Braxton takes my hands when I try to slide past him and settles me between his legs. "Look at me, baby."

He tilts his forehead against mine, and his deep brown eyes convey care for me. I rest against his chest and recount the conversation. "According to your mother and Leslie, God says you don't belong with me."

"What?" Those same eyes narrow, and Braxton flexes his shoulders. He threads his fingers through mine and kisses me on the forehead. "Come with me."

When we walk back into the living room, we find Leslie and Hannah still huddled on the couch. Their conversation ceases when they notice us standing there holding hands. Maxx the Dogg trots behind us and sits at Braxton's feet. We're a united front.

Mr. Frazier leans against the bar, a bottle of water in one hand. "What's going on, son?"

Braxton clears his throat. "First, Leslie, I need to apologize if I led you to believe we were rekindling a relationship. What we had is in the past. You made your choice back then. And a lot of time has gone by. You can't force something based on history."

Leslie starts to say something, but Braxton raises our locked hands and cuts her off. "We can be friends. That's all I can offer." He turns and looks at me. "As long as my lady is comfortable with it."

Gazing up at him, I'm filled with the warmth of the passion I feel for this man. He kisses my hand, then straightens.

"Mother, I know you only want the best for me, right?"

Hannah purses her lips and nods.

"Then I need you to understand no one, not even you, can tell me who to love."

"But I prayed about it and the Lord God told me it's Leslie. She's the one for you." Hannah taps Leslie's leg.

"You heard wrong. Carmen is the one for me. Not even Jesus could tell me different."

Hannah clutches at imaginary pearls, and her eyes widen. "Bernard, do you hear what your son is saying to me?"

Mr. Frazier takes a drink of water. "I hear him. Do you?"

She looks back at her husband. "But…"

"I told you this wasn't a good idea before we got in the car. You insisted on bringing Leslie along to surprise the boy. Looks like you the one got a surprise." Mr. Frazier winks at Braxton. "Proud of you, son."

The fluttering in my stomach matches my racing heartbeat, which swells along with the warmth evading my body. I've never felt more secure before. I marvel at this man standing beside me and standing up for me.

Braxton leans close and whispers, "I'll always choose you."

My lips part, and the urge to kiss him is unbearable. An arm snakes around his waist, and he twists so we are face to face. Fighting the attraction is torture, but his mother is upset enough.

Hannah lunges from the couch and Maxx barks in surprise. She stomps toward the door. "I'm ready to go."

Mr. Frazier twirls a set of keys around one finger. "Thought this would be a quick visit. Nice meeting you, young lady. Talk to you later, son."

He follows his wife out. Leslie takes her time gathering her things and pauses at the door. "Braxton, I…"

"Bye, Leslie." I say and my hand cups Braxton's face. His breath hitches and then his mouth covers mine. Our tongues intertwine and dance together as the heat rises around us.

The door slams, but the sound barely registers as I'm lost in the essence of Braxton. I nibble his neck and inhale the fresh masculine scent that heightens my longing. He groans and presses the bulge of his erection against my core. My panties are drenched and the throbbing between my legs intensifies when Braxton's hands trail from my back to my ass. Groping and clutching my behind, he walks us to the couch without breaking the kiss.

"Come here, baby." Braxton sits and glides my hips to straddle him.

Maxx the Dog takes it as an invitation to join us on the couch. He jumps up and tries to snuggle between us.

Braxton points. "Maxx, bed," he commands. The dog hangs his head but complies with his tail tucked.

"Aw, look at him. You made him sad." I watch Maxx slowly maneuver onto his pad and sit.

"He'll be alright." Braxton raises my shirt. "He's always trying to block my action."

My response is inaudible as Braxton flicks his tongue to tease a nipple while one hand squeezes the other breast. I close my eyes and my body hums as Braxton feasts on my chest, neck and back to my lips. His hips grind into me, and I press against him, feeling the roughness of his sweatpants through the shorts.

"Braxton," I moan.

He traces more fiery kisses down my body, and I respond in kind, ripping his shirt off in one movement, desperate to feel his skin against my own. Braxton wrangles his pants down and the shorts are removed with both hands shoved down my ass. The space of cool air is quickly replaced when Braxton plunges inside, filling me completely.

Our hands are everywhere. Rubbing, touching, exploring and sucking when the heat builds and drives me mad with desire. My back arches as I match him thrust for thrust. I throw my head back and dig my knees into the cushion.

Braxton grabs both butt cheeks and I close my eyes as my body surrenders to an awakening as the pleasure builds.

"Look at me," Braxton says. He stills until I pry my eyelids open. "Let me see you," he repeats.

We stare into each other's eyes while he begins to stroke, driving into me, swiveling my hips as I ride him. The blissful electric current of an orgasm churns again and intensifies with each thrust.

"I love you, Carmen," Braxton pants out as the explosion grips us both.

The words I want to say are trapped in my throat as the current takes my breath and flushes throughout my body. The tingling runs from my head to my toes.

I collapse with my head on Braxton's shoulder, arms wrapped around his neck. He doesn't stop moving until every convulsion has passed and breathing returns to normal.

We stay coupled together even though our sweat coated bodies begin to cool.

"I meant what I said." Braxton's breath warms my ear. "I love you."

Sitting up, I can see his eyes share the same message. The love is written in every heartbeat I feel through his chest. He uses one finger and pushes a wayward curl behind my ear. I study the face of this man who makes me feel seen and supported. Foreign sentiments to me.

Before I can bite back the emotion, it makes its own confession.

"I love you, too."

Chapter Thirty-Seven

Braxton

"You broke, Mom." Bernie's statement is drowned out by cheering in the background.

"What? What are you talking about, and where are you?" Tapping a button on the remote lowers the volume. Maxx and I are lounging on the couch this lazy Sunday afternoon when a surprise call from big brother rings through.

"I could say Mom is already broken, but it's late here and I don't want to take that negativity to bed." Debra is on the line, too.

It must be serious if Bernie did the three-way call.

"I'm at Brianna's soccer game. Jeanine wanted her to be on the AAU team, which is good. Baby girl can play. But they have games all the darn time." The surrounding noise fades, and I envision Bernie moving away from the field.

"What did Mom tell you?" I'm certain the reported exchange has been embellished to elicit this response from him.

"Just that you were rude and put her and Leslie out of your house behind some old woman. What's going on? When did Leslie get back in the picture?"

Debra's laughter is a mocking sound. "She's being extra dramatic, isn't she? Bernie, you should know B would never be rude to Mom."

Bernie takes a deep, audible breath, and I can hear him cracking his knuckles. A move he does whenever he's frustrated. "All I know is our mother is upset and Braxton needs to fix it. Mom needs a win. Debra is doing her own thing. She thinks you and Leslie are meant to be."

Debra chimes in. "You always take up for her. And I'm not doing my own thing. I'm engaged to be married. If Mom won't acknowledge it, that's her problem."

They go back and forth. I might as well pull on the well wore zebra-striped shirt and referee. A role held since childhood when it comes to these two. "I know she means well, but she can't decide who I end up with."

Debra goes on a rant about Mother's tendency to overstep boundaries. My mind wanders back to the evening with Carmen.

We made love on the couch. Made love again in the shower. Once we were spent, the rest of the day we just hung out. I read a book while she laid her head in my lap. Took Maxx for a walk. Picked up food and then rocked each other to sleep.

I was looking forward to more time, but Carmen left this morning. She said she had to pick up Olivia earlier than usual. I got the sense she was overwhelmed. My girl was spooked by her confession.

"This is ridiculous. It's after 8 p.m. here and I'm going to bed. Braxton, I'll talk to you later." Debra barely gives me a chance to say goodbye before the call is disconnected.

Bernie starts on another tangent, but it's gone on long enough. "Listen, bruh. I know you mean well, but you need to let this go."

"But Mom..."

"I said let it go." Maxx perks up at the abrupt movement of me, lowering my legs to the floor. Rubbing him behind his furry ears calms us both down.

A whistle chirps in the background, then the faint roar of cheers. "I'm missing the game for this. Fine. Do whatever you want."

"Hey, you called me." Bernie doesn't mean any harm, but he's not here to see Mom's manipulative ways. "I was relaxing this Sunday afternoon."

Bernie is silent for a beat. "Well, tell me about this new woman that got Mom in an uproar."

I can give a dissertation on my girl, Carmen. I'm getting warmed up when we are interrupted.

"Oh, Jeez Louise, there you are." Bernie's wife, Jeanine, has a booming voice that carries me across the country and lands me directly in an episode of *Fargo*. "You're missing all the action."

Bernie mumbles something, and then Jeanine is on the phone. "My favorite brother-in-law."

"My favorite sister-in-law," I return our usual greeting. "How's Brianna doing? She kicking ass on the field?"

"She's doing it, dontcha know." Jeanine laughs. "Wanna be the next Megan Rapinoe."

We chat for a few minutes about the game and Brody's upcoming track season. "Can't believe Brody's graduating next year. We talked last week about colleges. You know, USC is on his list."

"Only if I come with," Jeanine says. Her little midwestern way of saying she's not letting her only son go far away to school.

Then Bernie is back on the phone. "Take care, little brother. And call Mom."

Giving it a few more days before talking talk to Mom seems like a better plan. Maybe then she'll respect my choices. Carmen is the only one for me.

"It's about to go down, bruh," Devon says after getting his cup of coffee. "Who did you piss off?"

"What are you talking about?" I hear my name called and go to the counter to retrieve my Monday morning order of bacon, gouda and egg sandwich. The brioche bun is toasty just the way I like it. "You're the one who called me insisting on an early link up, remember?"

He adds more cream to his cup and takes a sip. "Couldn't chance someone seeing us at the office."

I raise an eyebrow. "Why's that?"

"Alright," he leans across the table. "You ain't heard this from me but...someone filed a sexual harassment complaint."

A piece of egg lodges in my throat. "A complaint? What's going on?"

"Overheard my boss talking on the phone." Devon leans back and throws an arm over the chair next to him. "Did a little digging and your name came up."

The sandwich loses all flavor and is pushed away. "How could my name be linked to sexual harassment?"

Devon's eyes narrow. "Something you need to tell me."

His body language switches from the goofy guy I know so well to this shifty pose like he has me dead to rights on some foul shit.

"Something *you* need to tell *me*." I give him the same energy back. "You acting like it's a problem between us. What's up, D?"

He can't sustain the mean mug for long and relaxes. "Naw, man. Kayla got me tripping. Cause it's your name on the complaint, but I know you wouldn't harass my girl. Tell me what's the deal with you and Kayla. You tried to push up on her and got shot down or something?"

"What did Kayla say?" I don't want to reveal any anecdotes if Kayla hasn't shared how she tried to sleep with me that day in her apartment. Although, it's unclear to me why I'm even thinking of protecting her.

Devon removes the top off his cup and drains the last of his drink. "She doesn't know I've seen it and I'm not asking her. I'm asking you."

There is no way I'm telling my boy that Kayla tried it with me before she settled for him on a possible "get back at me" situation. Not sure his ego could take it. He seems to really be into his fantasy.

I stall for time by gathering my trash and taking it to the nearby receptacle. The place is filling up with patrons, stopping in before continuing their morning commute. I maneuver around an overworked assistant, balancing multiple orders teetering on three cardboard carriers. The smell of various coffee blends with the toast of breakfast sandwiches. A line has formed at the counter and the harried baristas move in choreographed motion. The low hum of conversations and clanging pots aren't offering any inspiration to my dilemma. And then the slamming of a microwave door jolts me with the answer.

"Kayla's trying to get back at Carmen."

Devon looks up from his phone as I drop that nugget on him and retake the wooden chair across from him. He tilts his head.

I fill him in on the fallout from the merger. Some members of the Marketing staff are being reassigned to New York with Kayla's name on the list. She thinks Carmen is trying to get rid of her, but it was actually Doug, Carmen's boss, who made the decision. "Kayla must be using this made-up case against me as a way to get back at Carmen."

"You mean Cruella," Devon says and laughs.

Now I'm confused. "Who's Cruella?"

"That's what Kayla calls your boss lady. Cruella. She complains about her all the time. It's crazy how she goes on about the woman." He shrugs and shakes his head. "Claims Crue..."

"Her name is Carmen," I cut him off. It may be mildly amusing, but I can't let him or Kayla disrespect my lady.

Devon stops shredding a napkin and gives me his full attention. His eyebrows furrow and he leans back in the chair. Maybe I was too sharp in my correction.

"But why would Kayla file a case against you to get back at Carmen?" His fingers drum on the arm of the seat as he looks around. I can practically see the moment the truth snaps into place.

"Yoooo," Devon's mouth falls open before he remembers how to close it. "You and your boss lady. Are you hitting that?"

Without hesitation, I say, "Yes."

Devon rears back in the chair so far, he starts to fall and has to catch himself by grabbing onto the table. "Damn, man. What? How? When? And why didn't you tell me? Bet Omar knows, huh?"

"First things first, are you alright? Almost busted your ass there." I'm laughing, but Devon keeps a straight face.

Checking my watch, I motion for him to follow me, and we walk back to the office. The city block is enough time to share the condensed version of the story of Carmen and me. "Kayla saw us together at The Grove a few weeks ago. She knows we're dating. And she knows it could compromise Carmen's standing in the company."

"You know the HR policy states that any consensual work relationships should be disclosed to Human Resources. I filled my paperwork out as soon as Kayla let me sample the goods." Devon points a finger to emphasize his point.

Nodding in agreement, we pause outside the building. "We know the policy. But figured it's best to keep things on the low. Besides, things were over between us...until it wasn't."

"Still can't believe you didn't tell me." Devon holds the door open for a woman balancing a briefcase, her purse, and a stained fast-food bag. "Wait? How long has this been going on?"

"Long enough for Kayla to use it against me." Noticing Devon's confused look, I clarify. "To get back at Carmen. You need to talk to your girl."

Devon turns to walk away. "You're on your own, man. I put you on notice, but that's as far as it's going. I got to support my lady."

Bad timing for Devon to champion for Kayla. He thinks he's supporting his girlfriend, so I can't hold it against him. Sure hope Kayla doesn't break his heart. Although it's only a matter of time before Kayla dumps him when she thinks she has gotten her revenge on me.

Chapter Thirty-Eight

Carmen

I love him.

"I hope we can work on us when you get back," Melvin says.

And he loves me. He chose me.

It's been a couple of weeks, and the glow of this new revelation still warms me from within. Braxton makes me believe we can work out.

Melvin waves a hand in front of my face. "Are you listening to me?"

"What?" I pause from placing the folded blouse into the open suitcase and focus on the man standing on the opposite side of the bed. He wasn't supposed to be here until after I left. The arrangements for my business trip to New York included Melvin staying at the house with Olivia. We both figured it would be easier for our daughter to maintain her routine. A decision I already regret, and I make a mental note to change the locks again when I return. Silly me for thinking he wouldn't arrive until later when he picked up Olivia from school.

"I was saying we need to work on getting back together." Melvin makes eye contact but looks away when my mouth falls open.

"Are you bringing this up again now? Or better question, why?" All good feelings dissipate as I regain control and the ability to speak returns. Leave it to Melvin to kill a vibe.

He sits on the bed, but then moves to the chaise in the corner when I raise an eyebrow. "I told you at dinner the other night. But we have one big reason. Olivia."

A big reason indeed. "Olivia is adjusting to the arrangement you initiated, remember?"

"Yeah, I remember." He crosses both arms over this chest. "I also know it didn't take you long to have an affair."

I knew he would pull on that string and it has the desired effect of making me curl around the familiar band of defense. A pair of high heel shoes to punctuate my next point. "You can't keep throwing that out every time I disagree with you. If you really wanted to repair our relationship, you would know that."

Melvin crosses one leg over the other and waves away my statement. "And we're still not officially divorced."

I shrug and zip the case close. "So?"

"It's a sign we really shouldn't end things." Melvin takes a breath. "I messed up but we can still be together."

Raising an eyebrow, I shoot him an incredulous look. "What's your angle? You spent years telling me I'm an unfit wife and now what? It was an alternate reality we're supposed to pretend didn't happen?"

"I'm just saying." He plants both legs on the floor and rubs a hand over his head. "It's expensive. We spending all this money on lawyers and stuff. I can't afford to get a place and I'm tired of staying with my mom."

Mental note to thank Maggie for the financial advice of separating funds from Melvin. "So, it's really about money, then?"

"No..no," he stutters. "Not the money. I mean, like I said, it's expensive is all. We need to get this family back together for Olivia."

I shake my head and sigh. "It's the money. Why didn't you pay Olivia's tuition for the last few months? Gambled away the little money you had left, didn't you? Now you want me to bail you out again with your promise of a "family"?"

He doesn't respond, so I turn and retreat into the closet. Grabbing my favorite black blazer, my purse, and the last of my patience, I return to the room. Melvin is no longer lounging on the chaise. Relieved to end the conversation, I relax and wheel my suitcase into the front room.

"You must think dude you're sleeping with really wants you, huh? Probably didn't expect me to know that."

Melvin rears back in the recliner. He gives me a tight-lipped smile and lobs more angry words my way.

I stand up straight. "He does."

It doesn't matter what Melvin thinks he knows. The thought of Braxton gives me the strength to withstand Melvin's mind games.

"Why would he want you? A cheating, lying woman." Melvin cracks open a beer I didn't notice he had and takes a deep swallow. "Does he know you have to prove you're better than your man? Does he know you'll drive him crazy trying to prove you're better than everybody?"

My phone buzzes, announcing my ride is outside. The car I ordered earlier will take me to the airport.

"My ride's here." I turn to walk out the door and away from Melvin. This is a situation to be dealt with when I return.

"Hell, you should be happy I still want your ass. Every other man left you, right? I'm the only one who stuck around."

My hand freezes on the knob. "What did you say?"

Melvin stands and points a thick finger at me. "You heard me. The man you thinking can replace me. He's going to leave just like your first fiancé. And we can't forget about your dear old dad. He left cause he knew the truth. You ain't good enough. He was definitely right about that 'cause you ain't good enough to be a wife."

My shoulders slump, causing the purse to slide down my arm. I feel exposed. Melvin knows the sensitive places of my heart and he punctures each one. Cosigning on the hidden truths of my soul. *You're not good enough.*

The phone buzzes again. The driver sends a text warning that he will leave in five minutes.

I adjust my purse and straighten my back. Melvin watches with a smug look on his face. He feels he's beaten me. And I can't let him win.

"You're right, Melvin. I'm not a good wife."

His smile falters, but he crosses his arms.

A tilt of my head causes him to gesture for me to continue. "Why do you want us to *work* things out? It's been established that I'm no good, and no one wants me. Why do you?"

Melvin runs a hand over his balding head. "You're my wife."

"Not a good one, though, remember?" The driver sends a final warning, and I open the door to signal I'm on the way out.

"Still love you." Melvin moves closer. "I love you. You're the mother of my child and…"

I put up a hand to cut him off. Him repeating things is a clear sign Melvin is full of it. "What do you love about me?"

"Huh?" he asks.

"That's what I thought. Take care of my baby. My itinerary is on the fridge. I'll be back in five days."

Melvin follows me off the porch. "That's the problem, right here. Work always comes first for you. You don't want to fix our marriage, but I'm not going anywhere."

I whirl on him so fast he trips over his own feet, trying to backpedal. "You know what? You can't stay here."

He's off balance when I rush past him to close and lock the door, engaging the alarm. "I'll get Gayle to bring Livvy some clothes for the week."

"Wait, I didn't mean anything. It's just easier if we're together." Melvin gestures toward his truck. "I'm behind on my payments, alright?"

The driver blows the car horn, and Melvin shouts a curse word at the man to wait. He points at this wrist and shrugs.

I wheel my suitcase down the driveway. "Sounds like you need to better manage your money, Melvin. I'll call your mom on my way to tell her about the change of plans."

Melvin grabs the car door I'm about to shut. "You can forget about seeing Olivia. I'm not going anywhere. All this back and forth has got to stop. I'll get custody of her and make you pay me child support."

"Don't threaten me, Melvin. You try to take my daughter, and your secrets will come out in court too. Bet on any games lately? And I'm sure your ol' friend Jay will make an excellent witness for me. Now back up."

He stands on the concrete and shoves his hands in the pockets of his khakis. Finally mute, although the threat of his words follows me long after the car turns the corner, and he is out of sight.

Chapter Thirty-Nine

Braxton

People surround me, but I'm only focused on one person. I watch her get out of the car at the Delta terminal and engage with the skycap. He takes her bag and the tip she offers before smiling in appreciation as she walks away. I know that look. Carmen receives appreciative stares of longing in most men.

My baby is gorgeous. Even in skinny jeans hugging every curve, a vintage t-shirt and her favorite blazer, she stands out in a crowd. Her hair is gathered in a messy bun, and she rocks a pair of oversized shades to complete the travel look.

She doesn't see me at first. I'm leaning against the far wall across from the check-in kiosks and her back is to me as she scans her boarding pass. An elderly woman approaches and appears to ask for assistance. Carmen takes the time to help the lady and walks her to a ticketing agent.

When she returns to head toward security, I'm standing in her path. "Hey, babe."

Her mouth falls open, and she takes a step back. "Braxton. What are you doing here?"

We embrace and I inhale the scent of her perfume. Being near her makes me high in the best way.

"I had to see you." I make a flourish of taking an arm from behind my back and presenting the gift-wrapped box. "And give you this."

"You're full of surprises," she says.

She makes no move to reach for the box, so I take her carryon and put it inside a zippered pocket. Carmen fidgets and glances at the board listing arrivals and departures.

"What's wrong?" I stroke her hand and with the other remove the glasses, hiding her eyes. "What happened?"

Carmen looks up at me and says one word. "Melvin."

My body tenses. Her soon-to-be ex-husband still has the power to upset her, and I feel incapable of protecting her. She rubs my clenched fist and leads me to a bench out of the walkway from a team of teenagers racing through the terminal.

"He's being difficult," she elaborates and gives me the rundown of their earlier confrontation.

"Are you going to be okay?" I ask studying her closely.

She nods, and a soft smile claims her lips. "Seeing you helps."

I want to tell her. *Need* to tell her about the storm brewing at work and the harassment case from Kayla. Last night, I received an email requesting a conference with the HR Director this week. But I can't burden her with this when she already has her child to worry about. So instead, I simply say, "I love you."

She surprises me with her response. "Why?"

"Why do I love you? That's easy. You're smart, generous, ambitious, loyal, and an excellent cook of Jamaican cuisine."

That elicits a full smile. So, I continue, "You've opened my life to new possibilities. We can talk about anything for hours. You're the first person I think about in the morning and the last one I pray for at night. Plus, you're fine as hell."

Carmen pulls me close. "Thank you."

"I left out the best part," I tease. "You got that good stuff and put it on me. Blew my mind with just one touch."

We laugh and share a kiss. Then she turns serious. "You shouldn't have to put up with my baggage. You deserve better."

"You're worth it."

A loud message blares over the PA system, reminding passengers to keep their luggage close and report any suspicious bags. The crackle of a security officer's radio competes with the small talk from a family of four who stop in front of our seats and debate whether to use the bathroom before or after getting in line.

Carmen's breath tickles my ear when she leans in close. "Maybe we should take a break."

I shake my head, certain I didn't hear her right. "Take a break? Again?"

"My life is a mess right now. I need to figure out what's best for my daughter, and I don't want to drag you through the drama." Carmen stares past me as if she can see a future where I'm not in it.

She stands, releasing a sigh. "I need to go. My flight boards soon."

"Wait." Now I'm standing and it feels as if this is the end of something that is only just beginning.

Carmen gazes up at me with sad, wide eyes. When her lips find mine, all background noise fades and it's just me and her. Two lovers saying goodbye. But it doesn't have to end this way.

I press fully into her. She needs to feel my heartbeat. The way I've given myself totally to her and only to her. None of the other stuff matters. I don't care how messy her life gets, as long as I'm there to help clean up the pieces.

"Bye, Braxton." Carmen gathers her things and turns to walk away.

I grab her hand. "I choose you. But I need you to choose me back."

She nods and then is swept in the current of bodies winding their way through the maze, taking her away from me.

The conference room is as cold as the woman sitting across from me at the large wooden table.

Kayla drums a stylus on a dormant tablet and avoids direct eye contact.

"What's going on? I thought I was only meeting with an HR rep." My question is directed at Robert Engelman, HR Director and Devon's supervisor. But my eyes never leave Kayla.

She squirms under my stare. Small consolation for this manufactured situation she put me in.

Engelman clears his throat. "Some information has been brought to light and we need you two together."

New information? That gets my attention, and I swivel in the leather chair. Engelman takes off wired rimmed glasses, then pushes them back on his thin nose.

The email didn't directly state the agenda for this meeting, but thanks to Devon; I know what Kayla claims happened. She is trying to use text messages I sent to her months ago to claim a pattern of harassment. I pulled up everything said between us during the time we were hanging out until she saw me with Carmen. The only one that can be misconstrued is the message sent on that Saturday. It read, *"We need to talk about what happened yesterday. You're probably feeling uncomfortable with things. Please call me."*

"Let me go make sure Doug knows we're waiting." The chair is left spinning when he springs up.

I lean forward. "You want to tell me what that's about?"

Kayla ignores me and pretends to be concentrating on her phone.

"You know what, I'm out of here. This whole thing is bogus, anyway." I push away from the table and stand.

"Wait," Kayla looks up. "You can't leave."

Her eyes dart from me to the glass door. She stands, then returns to her seat. I can't help but notice Kayla put extra effort into her makeup and attire today. She toned down the club dress and looks more the part of an executive. Time slows down as a sense of unease prickles the back of my scalp.

"What did you do?"

Kayla screws up her face and then relaxes back into a sly smile. "Guess?"

Carmen.

This woman has found an angle to implicate Carmen in this fiasco. Before I can call her on it, the door opens and Doug enters, trailed by his assistant, Ruth.

"Good. We're all here." Engelman returns with a coffee mug and takes his seat at the head of the table. Doug sits beside Kayla with Ruth occupying the seat to his right. Leaving me on the opposite side of the table alone.

Since Doug is Carmen's boss, I study the man to get a gauge of where his loyalties are in this moment. The man gives me a wry smile. "Thanks for agreeing to meet with us."

"I didn't agree to whatever this is." I stare at each of them in turn. "Will someone please clue me in on what's happening right now?"

Engelman nods at Doug, who motions for Ruth to take notes. "Okay, you're aware of Ms. Pearson's allegations."

I look at Kayla and nod. "Untrue allegations. Whatever's been claimed, I'm sure it's untrue."

"Well, Kayla has amended her complaint. We need to ask you some questions about Carmen Miller."

The temperature in the room has gone from arctic to hell. At least it has on my side of the table. "What about Mrs. Miller?"

"You two work together. She was assigned as your mentor in our department."

Doug is stating facts everyone knows, so I don't respond. He glances at Kayla, and she shoots him a look. Some unspoken communication passes between them. Ruth is typing on her tablet and Engelman seems oblivious to the body language.

"It's okay, Braxton." Kayla pipes up. "I told them how she manipulated you. No one blames you for her behavior. But you need to tell them the truth."

My body tenses and I'm rigid on the edge of the chair. "The truth? This entire meeting is based on a lie. A lie you told."

Kayla places a hand on her chest. "I'm not the enemy here. Cru...Carmen is a menace and has to be stopped. You don't need to cover for her anymore."

I address Doug through clenched teeth. "Carmen works for you. You know she didn't do whatever Kayla is fabricating for your entertainment."

Doug's leg vibrates under the table, causing his chair to bounce. "Now, hold on. Company policy dictates that we investigate all complaints of this nature. Kayla has presented evidence that Carmen abused her authority. First by pursuing you and then having Kayla transferred when she found out about the forced relationship."

The bomb is dropped. Kayla's evidence is me, and Carmen's career implodes before my eyes.

"Let me state for the record," I begin after massaging the tension from the back of my neck. "Carmen did nothing wrong. Kayla has a personal grudge against her for some reason. The truth is Kayla wanted a relationship with me and felt rejected when she discovered I was seeing someone else. Any text message she showed wasn't about harassing her and she knows it."

Engelman nods, Ruth looks back and forth, taking in the show, and Kayla shakes her head.

"But you know she had me transferred. She tells you everything." Kayla points a finger to make her argument.

"You're right about that. She told me Doug was the one who put you on the transfer list," I say.

Kayla twirls in her chair to confront him. "Is that true?"

Doug mumbles. "Um, well. The list was prepared by the Bisous rep."

They engage in a back and forth with Engelman, watching with an amused look on his face.

Kayla does her usual spoiled girl/pouting routine. I finally see the petty, insecure woman she really is. Maybe Devon will see through her before he gets hurt.

Pushing back from the table, I rise. "You all wait to accuse an employee when she is out of town representing *this* company and can't defend herself."

Engelman scowls and finally speaks. "Seems as if Doug dragged me in here for nothing. This added information tells me the Company needs to conduct an investigation into the entire Marketing Department." His posture is rigid when he stands. "Doug, I'll meet you in my office."

"I won't be a part of any effort to scapegoat a loyal employee. If my relationship with Carmen is a problem, it can be solved right now."

Gathering my things, I stomp to the door. "I quit."

Chapter Forty

Carmen

This entire trip has been a disaster.

The sparse applause mocks me as I hurry from the podium and wind my way out of the ballroom. Avoiding any colleagues seeking to engage in shop talk, I dash into the waiting elevator and ascend twenty-three floors to the safety of my hotel room.

I toss my purse and laptop on the desk and sink into the chaise lounge in front of the window. Turning away from the scenic view of Central Park, I dial Doug's office. Figure I would report my disastrous performance before word leaked back to LA.

Getting no answer on the other end, I double check the time. Four o'clock here means it's one in the afternoon back home. I've been doing the time conversion in my head since landing here. It's important to know what time to call Olivia.

She's accustomed to my travels for work and we have a routine when I'm away. I call when it's her bedtime and we share the events of our day. We end each call with a countdown of the remaining 'sleeps' or nights until I return.

It's no wonder I'm off my game today. Melvin is being an ass. He not only threatens to take Olivia when I was leaving, but he's being a stickler about my call time. Last night, I was ten minutes late, and he claimed Olivia was already asleep.

"Let me talk to my daughter," I said.

There was a dinner for all attendees, followed by a mixer and night cap at a club in Times Square. I left early, but navigating through traffic got me back to the hotel at 11:10. Olivia goes to bed at 8:00 p.m. on the dot.

Melvin repeated his denial. "You know Livvy's bedtime. One day you'll focus on being a good mother instead of your precious career."

"You know she's waiting on my call," I pleaded, hating the desperation in my voice. "I'll be quick. I just need to tell her good night."

Melvin would not be persuaded. I could hear the pleasure in his voice as he asserted his control over the situation.

It's no wonder I couldn't focus and stumbled through my PowerPoint presentation like a new hire and not a professional with fourteen years of experience. Maybe I can find a way to redeem myself and impress the higher ups.

I'm changing into something more comfortable- off goes the black power pantsuit, and I slip on a pair of leggings and an oversized t-shirt, when my phone rings.

"Hey, Baby C," I greet my sister.

Whenever my travels bring me to the East Coast, I send my itinerary to Mom and Cassie. It's easier to touch base when we're all in the same time zone.

"Thanks for the hookup with the job," Cassie gushes about her new customer service position. I contacted an old classmate and asked her to look out for my sister.

"No thanks necessary," I say as I rummage through my toiletry bag for make-up remover wipes. The gift from Braxton teases me. The square box wrapped in light blue paper doesn't give a clue about its contents.

I've avoided opening it. After seeing Braxton at the airport, it seemed clear to me that the best path forward was one where I freed him from my drama. He didn't agree. When I landed, there was a text from him.

I'm going to give you space to figure out next steps. You know I love you. –Braxton

Cassie's voice blares over the speakerphone. "Are you still there? Hello?"

"Sorry about that." Running water in the sink, I pause to rinse my face. "It's been a long day, and it's hard to focus right now."

"You missing your boo thang," Cassie teases.

I towel the water from my face and fold the towel over the rack. "Don't say that too loud. Mom will start preaching about the need to stay married." I study my reflection in the mirror. "Although it would be easier if I did."

Filling Cassie in on Melvin's latest antics causes a headache to tingle at the base of my skull.

"You've always been a bad ass. Why are you giving in to Melvin?" Cassie asks. "Besides, you divorce him, and Mom won't think you're the perfect child anymore. Give me a chance."

She says it as a joke, but I hear the pain underneath. "Sorry about that, Baby C. But no worries, Mom still isn't speaking to since I filed."

"She'll come around." Cassie changes the subject. "Why don't you send me a picture of this guy, anyway? I'll let you know if it's worth it or not."

My silly sister can always bring light into any situation. I wish she recognized her talents in all areas of her life. Strolling through my phone, I walk back into the main room and sit at the desk. The perfect picture, a shot of us on a hike with the postcard worthy view of the coast, is sent.

"Damn, sis. He's fine," Cassie screams over the phone. "No way you turn that down and stay married to old man Melvin. I never thought he was your type, anyway."

We end our call with an update on our kids and a promise to talk later.

Now I'm left with only my thoughts inside this empty room. Turning on the television only serves as a temporary distraction from the one man I've been trying to forget. I've ignored the box for three days. Maybe what's inside can soothe my fears of the future and alleviate the stress of the present.

I settle in the middle of the king-sized bed with the box in hand. The wrapping paper is removed to reveal a hard-bound leather edition of The Love Poems of Rumi. Another box is tucked among the tissue paper along with a note.

This charm bracelet represents all the things you love. Wear this as a reminder that you're loved in return, exactly as you are. –Braxton

The charms include a dog paw print with diamonds, which makes me think of Maxx the Dog. Olivia's birth stone on a charm engraved with the word

'Daughter'. And a smooth sterling silver heart with an infinity style love knot. It's beautiful. And the most thoughtful gift anyone has ever given me.

My heart swells as I lay back to read all the ways Braxton loves me.

The alarm from my phone jerks me awake. Night has fallen through the open curtain, and I panic, thinking I've slept through the time to call Olivia. Only 9 p.m. And it's Gayle ringing my phone.

"Hey," I say, shaking the remnants of sleep from my eyes.

"Alright, listen," Gayle has never been the type to prep you for news, and her tone has an edge that makes my stomach tighten.

Now I'm alert and sit on the side of the bed. "What happened? Are you okay? Is it Wayne or the twins?"

"No, um, I have Olivia."

"Okay." I run a hand over my head. "What's going on?"

"Hey, Mom," Olivia calls out. "Auntie said we're going to McDonald's."

This must be serious if Gayle is gracing the fast-food chain. She prefers to visit restaurants with cloth napkins.

"Hey baby, have fun." I can picture the excitement on my daughter's face. This is a rare treat for her. "Now you really need to tell me what's up, Gayle."

"Hold on." I hear the dinging of the car door being opened and Gayle instructing the twins to take Olivia and order some food. "Go ahead and get a table. I'm going to be right here where I can see you."

I'm up closing the curtains, turning on lights and strengthening the sheets. Anything to keep busy while I wait on the bomb to land.

"Melvin didn't pick up Olivia from school. They called me."

The information causes me to sink to the floor. "Where could he be? Did he call you?"

"No answer. All I know is he didn't pick up Olivia, and the school contacted me because Olivia told them you were out of town."

I lurch from the floor and start throwing items in the suitcase. Placing Gayle on hold, I try Melvin's number myself. It goes straight to voicemail. Reconnecting with Gayle, my decision is made. "I'm coming home tonight. Keep Olivia with you and I'll pick her up from your place."

"Girl, you know I have your baby, but how are you going to get a flight at the last minute? And don't you have a conference to attend?" Gayle says.

One sweep of an arm knocks toiletries into a bag. "I'm not worried about any more sessions. I'll get on the first thing available."

After assuring Gayle she'll get a text with my itinerary, I do one last survey to ensure nothing is left behind. The bracelet from Braxton is secured on my wrist.

The call to the airline is conducted on the ride to the airport. I'm in luck. A flight to LA is leaving in two hours. I book it despite the high price and race through the terminal to make it to the gate on time. It's only when I'm on the plane that my heart slows down, and I can try to relax. In four hours, I'll be home. Melvin's whereabouts are still unknown, and I can only imagine he must be on a gambling binge or dead to forget to pick up our daughter. If it's the first situation, he's going to wish he was dead.

When I touch down, I call Gayle and let her know I'll take a car service to her house. It's late and the kids are asleep. I'll spend the night at Gayle's and figure out Melvin in the morning.

"Traffic is nuts, but I'll get you there." The young, scruffy driver assures me overhearing my conversation with Gayle. "Sounds like you're eager to see your little one."

I nod, staring out the window as we leave the lights of the airport and merge onto the highway. "You have no idea how crazy this day has been."

The driver, Sean, looks at me in the rearview mirror. "Hope you have someone waiting on you beside the kid. After I've had a rough day, my lady makes it all better."

Sean lays on the horn as a black sedan races past the car and swerves to cut in front.

Typical LA road traffic.

Wanting Sean to focus on the road, I settle back in the plush leather seat of the SUV and look down at my phone. But his last comment brings me back to the missing piece. No matter how many times I try to push it away or pretend it doesn't exist.

The infinity love knot seems to glow in the dimly lit car as overhead lights and the errant headlight reflect off the stones when I twist my wrist. The signs are clear.

The vehicle lurches and Sean yells an expletive before righting the SUV. I can't wait any longer.

My phone dials the number and as soon as his voice fills my ear, there's no denying my feelings any longer. "Braxton, I ..."

Chapter Forty-One

Braxton

"You might want to ease up on those reps, man." Omar stands at my head, spotting while I do chest presses. "You liable to pull something."

I ignore him and grunt through seven more pushes before clanging the weighted bar back on the rack. Sweat is pouring from my body when I sit up and grab a towel. "I'm good, bro."

Omar looks doubtful but has the sense not to question it. Instead, he goes to the cooler sitting in the corner and grabs two bottles of water. He passes one to me and leans against the mirrored wall. Silence fills the space. Monroe's gym is not busy around this time of day.

Since quitting my job, I've spent mornings hanging around the gym. Monroe seems to appreciate the help and takes full advantage. Today he's out running errands after a business meeting with the bank.

"You ready to say what's been on your mind all day?" Omar crushes the empty water bottle and tosses it in the metal trash can.

He already got the full rundown of what happened at Parker & Kramer. No need to rehash the situation. Besides, we both know my actual concern.

"Had to give her space, man."

Omar completes reps with a pair of dumbbells. "Don't worry. She'll call."

"It's been three days," I say and wrap the towel around my neck.

"She'll call," he repeats. "In the meantime, you can focus on your future. How's the new company coming along? Heard you already locked up one client."

Frasier Digital Marketing Solutions is less than a month old, but Omar and his partner hired the firm. We discussed social media campaigns, and I've designed a new website for Practice Squad Bar & Grill. I've floated the resume out to a few top marketing firms in the area and my savings should cover me for a few months. Pops says a man should always have a plan and I've put his words to good use.

"Appreciate the business," I tell Omar. "I'll have a new proposal for you guys to look at next week."

Omar stretches, and something over his shoulder gets his attention. "I got you, bro. We both do."

"We?" I follow Omar's stare and see Devon standing in the door.

I haven't spoken to Devon since our clandestine meeting at the coffee spot when he chose to believe Kayla's version of events.

"How did you know where to find me?"

Devon motions with his head. "Omar."

Omar throws up his hands. "You guys need to talk." He turns and goes into Monroe's office, leaving us in an uncomfortable silence.

After a beat, I ask, "What's up?"

Devon is unusually quiet and takes a deep breath. "Heard you quit. You're the talk of HR. Old man Engelman made it seem like you were some hero."

"Don't know about all that, but I'm going to do my own thing. Plans been in motion for a minute." I remember discussing going into business with Devon a while back, but he was more concerned with getting a guaranteed paycheck.

He nods and looks around the building. "Monroe updated some equipment since the last time I was here. Remember when he tried to get me in the ring? Man, I did my best Ali impersonation, dancing around to avoid getting hit."

I grab a broom and start sweeping up. The evening crowd will file in soon. Monroe took my advice and started offering boxing sessions for people to learn the fundamentals of the sport. The two classes filled up fast.

Devon watches for a while and then blurts, "About Kayla. Sorry, man. I didn't know she was so foul."

No words are warranted, so I shrug and brush the gathered debris into the trash.

"We're done. Kayla and me," Devon says.

This warrants a reaction. "Oh, yeah."

"Yeah, we got into it, and she basically admitted she was using me to make you jealous." He runs a hand down his face.

Placing the broom on a hook by the supply closet, I process this piece of news. "I'm sorry to hear that. I was never interested in her like that. And you know I wouldn't play you."

Devon makes eye contact for the first time since he came in. "I know."

"We cool then." When I offer my hand, he pounds my fist.

"Bout time, ya'll squash that." Omar must have been watching the entire thing. He bounds out of the office. "Now let's go get something to eat."

We hang around the gym until Monroe returns and then head to a burger joint. Over burgers and beer, Devon catches me up with the events at J & K.

"Kayla ended up recanting her claim. She admitted to misunderstanding your text. And in order to keep her job, she agreed to relocate to New York." Devon talks with a mouth full of fries.

According to him, the company wants her out of the building before Carmen returns. Doug received only an oral reprimand for his inadequate investigation of a personnel claim. And since I quit, they can't do anything to Carmen for having a relationship with a former employee. Devon says she'll probably be questioned about the situation and warned about workplace relationships.

Later, I'm in bed for the night when my cell phone lights up with Carmen's face.

"Hey," she says.

And all is right in my world. Until I hear a male voice curse in the background. "Where are you?"

She tells me she's back in LA. Her daughter needs her.

"Thank you for the gift. I love it." Her voice is soft and husky. "Braxton, I..." she begins and then shrieks, "Watch out!"

I call her name, but all I hear is the squeal of tires braking, the sound of glass breaking and Carmen's scream.

Chapter Forty-Two

Carmen

My eyes open to fluorescent lights and the beeping of a machine. The scent of sanitizer and the over bleached sheet draped over my body cause my stomach to churn. I try to sit up, but am restrained by the tug of an IV piercing my hand.

Why am I in a hospital? Bits and pieces flood my brain like a computer program downloading.

Sean, my driver. The reckless car. The phone call with Braxton.

"Someone's up." A mousy haired nurse hovers into view and punches buttons on a machine. A band tightens around my arm.

I try to speak, but my throat feels raw. The nurse, sensing my discomfort, offers a sip of water from a cup on the nearby stand. "You'll feel that for a while. We had to intubate you when they brought you in. I'm Tracy, one of the nurses taking care of you."

"Olivia," I croak out.

"Your daughter, right? Cute little thing. I saw her yesterday." Tracy pulls her pad closer and taps the screen.

Yesterday? "How long have I been here?"

Tracy pats my hand. "Two days. It was a nasty accident. But the doctor will be in shortly to discuss treatment."

Before any more questions can form, I succumb to the blackness again.

I dream of Braxton.

He strokes my face and whispers that things will be alright. I can feel his lips on my forehead and the essence of his cologne snakes through my senses.

"Braxton," I call out.

A sinister chuckle causes my eyes to fly open.

Melvin stands beside the bed. "Figures you would ask for him. That chump had the nerve to try to come up in here. Like he had a right. I had his ass banned."

I shift in the bed and swallow. Melvin looks disheveled. There is bruising around his mouth and one eye looks swollen. "What happened to you?"

"Had to handle your friend," Melvin says.

The thing I feared, getting Braxton entangled in my drama, has been realized with a fight I'm sure was started by Melvin. From the look of his face though, Braxton put a hurt on him. A sense of contentment warms my chest, but it's soon replaced by the need for answers.

"No, why didn't you get Olivia?" My voice is raspy and sore. It hurts to speak, but I remember his absence leading me to rush home. "How could you leave her at school like that?"

Melvin shuffles his feet. "A situation came up."

"You were too busy gambling to pick up your child, you mean." One of the machines makes a beeping noise.

Melvin tugs at his shirt collar and looks away. "No, I wouldn't do that too, baby girl. I was on a roll. Only needed a few more minutes to make my truck payment. Gayle was able to get her, so she was fine. You weren't here, so you don't know. I was on the way."

He continues to spew lies and the pace of the beeps increase. My head is pounding and the nausea feeling returns. "Water."

Melvin looks at the pitcher on the table right beside him and turns away. "Get young boy you calling for to give you some water. I'm done with this, Carmen."

Tracy rushes in and checks the monitor. "You need to leave, sir. The patient has to rest."

A security guard crosses his arms outside the door. Melvin sees him and touches the bruise on his face. He probably doesn't want another whipping after the fight with Braxton.

"I'm leaving." Melvin shows his palms to the guard. When he turns to me, Tracy shields me with her body. He leaves without another word.

The tension in the room disperses when the negative energy exits. Tracy fusses with the wrap on my wrist and asks about the pain.

"Thanks for that," I say. After waiting a beat, I add. "Love is...complicated."

"Tell me about it. I'm on my third husband." Tracy laughs. "This is the one, though."

"From the looks of things, I'm down a husband myself."

Tracy's blue eyes twinkle when she leans close. "Well, you have a contender out there." She points down the hall. "There's a young man who's been asking about you. He hasn't left the waiting room far as I can tell despite that other man going on."

Braxton.

Before I can ask for him to come in, the doctor enters. He details the car accident, my concussion and broken wrist and discharge orders. "We'll get you out of here tomorrow. Vitals look good, although you'll probably have headaches for a while. We'll get you a prescription for painkillers and give you a follow-up appointment with an orthopedic doctor."

Tracy follows the doctor out of the room with a promise to check back before her shift ends.

I'm fiddling with the television when Gayle peeps her head around the doorjamb. "I brought someone to see you."

Olivia bounds into the room. "Mommie, I was worried."

I gather her in my arms, careful to not jar loose the IV. "I was worried too. Are you having fun with Auntie Gayle?"

Gayle catches me up on what happened. "When you didn't get to my house in time, I tried your cell. Then the phone rings. Good thing I'm your emergency contact. Your driver got into a back and forth with some idiot. The police called it road rage. The other vehicle rammed your car on purpose. He's been taken into custody. Your driver had a few scrapes, but he's fine. You took the brunt of it."

"When did Melvin show up?"

"That fool," she begins and catches herself when Olivia looks up. "He came around looking for Livvy late last night after being MIA for two days. But I told him she was fine to stay with me. Wayne convinced him it was best for everyone."

Wish I could have seen that go down. Olivia cuddles against me and I'm thankful to have my baby girl next to me. But there is someone else I need to see.

"Remember what you said about happily ever afters?" I ask Gayle.

Her face scrunches in a quizzical expression. "Vaguely. Why?"

"I need you to meet the one who makes me happy."

Chapter Forty-Three

Carmen

Four months later

Back at the Monte-Carlo Bay Hotel & Resort property. The irony is not lost on me that this is the place where Braxton and I began with a kiss.

This year, making the trip without Braxton feels empty. Not having him in the office every day took some getting used to. Although he's somewhat of a legend among some staff, who tell the story of him quitting to salvage my reputation. HR did an investigation, and I had to undergo management training with an emphasis on manager/employee relations. Plus, I haven't been assigned any more new employees to train. Seems as if I'll need to work even harder to get that elusive promotion.

I didn't win any awards this time around, but decided to spend an extra day. Olivia is in South Carolina with my mother. The drama with Melvin could wait.

The walk to the beach is a quick stroll down the breezeway. I'm on the way back up the stairs and across the terrace when a lone figure emerges from the hotel.

I freeze in my tracks.

Leaning against the rail leading into the hotel, he's a vision in beige linen pants and a white shirt, clothing to match the warm climate. I'm thinking my imagination is playing a trick because he is as still as a statue.

And then he taps his chest with two fingers. Our symbol.

"You came." My breath comes in a rush as I race to close the distance between us.

His eyes lock onto mine. "I did."

"And that means..." My stomach seesaws as I anticipate his answer.

Braxton reaches for my hand and a grin breaks over his face. "We make it work."

My entire body buzzes, and I squeeze his hand in return, ignoring the twinge in my wrist. A remnant from the accident.

At the hospital, after introductions were made to Gayle and Olivia, Braxton and I talked.

"You were right," he said. "It's a lot that you're dealing with. I met Melvin."

I caressed the bruise on his cheek, partially hidden by his overgrown beard. Evidence he hadn't shaved in a few days.

"I'm so sorry about. About everything. I want to tell you..."

Braxton cut me off with a kiss. "Now that I've seen you're going to be okay, I can say this. It was wrong for me to insist we be together before you could make a clean break from that man."

A coughing fit disrupts his speech, and he pours me a glass of water. Once I've sipped the liquid and reclined back against the pillow, Braxton sits in the chair next to the bed.

"Look." he ran a hand down his face and scratched his beard. "You need to focus on your daughter and handle this divorce. If that's what you really want to do."

I nodded while feeling my chest tighten. "Okay. But what does that mean for us?"

Braxton's gaze was full of longing and love when he said, "It means I wait for you. But I need you to be sure I'm the one you'll choose."

The weight of his words gave me some solace as he stood to leave the room. My vision blurred, but I could see he didn't turn his back to walk out. He kept his eyes on me, moving backwards until he was out of sight. In that moment, I felt secure in his gesture to not cause me any further mental anguish. At that moment, I knew what I had to do.

"The divorce is final. Melvin is threatening to contest because he wants more money. Things will get ugly." The court ordered he attend Gamblers Anonymous, and we both had to participate in parenting classes. Maggie earned her legal fees and secured joint custody without having to pay alimony.

"Do I look scared?" He takes a step closer to me and I breathe in his scent. My heart quickens.

"And your mom isn't a fan."

Now he leans in. "She'll get over it."

I take a deep breath and speak my truth. The words I was trying to say before the car accident. The feeling and emotions he gave me the time and space to be certain of. "You're the one I want. It's always been you. I should have never thought about settling."

The time apart hasn't dulled the fire, which ignites whenever we're together. My body aches for him and all doubt escapes my mind. He's so close to me now, our heartbeats in sync to the rhythm of our love.

When Braxton kisses me, it's with the promise of forever.

Acknowledgements

This story has been a long time coming. It seems as if the characters took over my life for a few years before I stopped procrastinating and put fingers to the keyboard. But it's a relief to finally reach the end and release a new cast of characters into the world. I hope you enjoy reading it.

Writing is a solo task, but it's not done in a vacuum. I would like to thank everyone who read chapters, suggested a situation or inspired an action. A special thank you to Rhonda McKnight, who helped me be bold and write the story I really wanted to write. To my favorite editor, J. L. Campbell of The Writer's Suite, thank you for your encouragement and insightful suggestions/critiques. A big thank you to Terri Ann Johnson, who helped me see and adjust a pivotal plot point in the novel. It made the story better. For the authors who provided inspiration, motivation, instruction and the model for me to emulate: Rhonda McKnight, Kennedy Ryan, Yasmin Angoe, Rachel Howzell Hall, Steven Barnes, Tananarive Due and Victoria Christopher Murray.

To my husband and my two daughters, thank you for the support and understanding as I pursue this dream. To my extended family and friends, I appreciate the encouragement to keep going at it.

And to you, the reader, thank you for taking the time to read, review and/or email. I hope you continue to enjoy my made up love stories and maybe see yourselves in the tales of hope and forgiveness.

Thanks for everything and stay tuned for the next adventure.

Click below to enjoy the *Settling Up Spotify Playlist:*

About the author

Her pen sharpens spine-tingling tales of betrayal, lies, consequences ... and their fallout when the truth comes out. Fitting for her brand of literary inspiration – shining the light in the darkness of deceit.

Michelle D. Rayford is a doting wife, rocking mother and the dynamic CEO of Barrington Drive Publishing. The seed for Michelle's gift of storytelling was planted well before she was old enough to drive ... now this talented scribe is driven to INSPIRE. Her red-hot keyboard has cranked out hits for several anthologies, as well as her soulful debut novel–*Moment of Truth* and the chilling *Not That Nice*.

Michelle's laptop is housed in the colorful south, where she lives with her husband, who she's spent half her life crushing on, and two daughters who push her to keep the dream going. When she's not reading, jamming to her 80's music playlist or playing NBA2K, Michelle is hard at work, hanging out with her vivid imagination, developing stories about the messy parts of relationships and the aftermath of declaring *I do*. She loves chatting with readers and book clubs; reach out to her at michelle@michelledrayford.com or through her website - www.michelledrayford.com.

Also by

Books by Michelle D. Rayford

Moment of Truth
Not That Nice-A Short Story
50 Days of Pleasure (cowritten with Anita L. Roseboro) -Days of Pleasure Series

Book Discussion Questions

1. As the story begins, Carmen is having an affair with Braxton. What are your thoughts on cheating in a marriage? Do you ever feel it's justified?

2. When you meet Melvin, do you understand Carmen's unhappiness in her marriage? Do you believe in traditional gender roles?

3. Carmen appears to be driven and decisive in all areas of her life. Why do you think she settled for marriage with Melvin?

4. Carmen is ten years older than Braxton. What are your thoughts on older women dating younger men?

5. Melvin has an issue with Carmen making more money than he does and tries to control her in other ways. Do you think it was fair to request a divorce and then change his mind?

6. Early on Braxton tells Carmen she should have waited for him. Do you think most people settle for a relationship or marriage based on society or family expectations instead of waiting for the right one to come into their life?

7. What are your thoughts on Carmen's relationship with her mother?

8. Carmen has childhood trauma stemming from her missing father. Do you think that affected her marriage to Melvin?

9. Melvin's mother didn't automatically side with her son and supported Carmen. Did this surprise you?

10. Do you think Braxton should have reconnected with Leslie? Was there a time you returned to a past relationship for closure?

11. Office relationships can be difficult to navigate, especially if things turn sour. Have you been involved with someone you work with? How did it end?

12. What are your thoughts on Braxton's relationship with the Big Three? Were you surprised that Braxton didn't sleep with Kayla?

13. Kayla had her sights set on Braxton from the beginning and when she saw Carmen and Braxton together, she felt betrayed. Do you think she was justified in her later actions? Why or why not?

14. Carmen considers staying with Melvin for the sake of an intent family for Olivia despite her own unhappiness. Do you think parents, especially mothers, should do this? Is it beneficial to the child to live with unhappy and unfulfilled parents?

15. Carmen and Braxton's story will continue in the series, No Ordinary Love. What questions or scenarios would you like to be answered for the couple?

www.ingramcontent.com/pod-product-compliance
Lightning Source LLC
Chambersburg PA
CBHW011053130726
47906CB00010B/1039